SLEUTH

PRAISE FOR CHARLOTTE LANGLEY

'This thriller is a read-in-one-gulp triumph'
Claire Frost on *The Blame*

'This absorbing mystery also takes a look at police misconduct'
Heat* on *The Blame

'I love a police procedural, and this debut ticked a lot of boxes. The tension kept me swiftly turning the pages'
Nina Pottell, *Prima* on *The Blame*

'Fun as well as thoughtful, this will be gobbled up by fans of Cara Hunter and the like'
Daily Telegraph* on *The Blame

ALSO BY CHARLOTTE LANGLEY

The Blame
The Intrusion

SLEUTH

CHARLOTTE LANGLEY

NO EXIT PRESS

First published in the UK in 2026 by No Exit Press,
an imprint of Bedford Square Publishers Ltd,
London, UK

noexit.co.uk
@noexitpress

A CIP catalogue record for this book is available from the British Library.

ISBN
978-1-83501-341-0 (Paperback)
978-1-83501-340-3 (eBook)

2 4 6 8 10 9 7 5 3 1

The manufacturer's authorised representative in the EU for product safety is Easy Access System Europe, Mustamäe tee 50, 10621 Tallinn, Estonia
gpsr.requests@easproject.com

Typeset in 11 on 14pt Garamond MT Pro
by Avocet Typeset, Bideford, Devon, EX39 2BP
Printed and bound in Great Britain by
CPI Group (UK) Ltd, Croydon CR0 4YY

FSC www.fsc.org
MIX
Paper | Supporting responsible forestry
FSC® C013604

The manufacturer's authorised representative in the EU for product safety is Easy Access System Europe, Mustamäe tee 50, 10621 Tallinn, Estonia
gpsr.requests@easproject.com

1

Ruth

3 June

I'VE ALWAYS THOUGHT THE mountain near Braeside looks like a slumbering guardian – lying on its side, sleeping with one eye open. All it takes is an event like this, and the mountain becomes something else entirely. Unfamiliar. Dangerous. A place where your luck can suddenly run out.

I've parked my patrol car on the edge of the forest track. Summer arrived a few days ago in full bloom. Insects hum in the air and the fields rolling out in front of me are all saturated colours, the stormy greys and ruddy tones of south-west Scotland replaced by verdant green. It's early but I unzip my light jacket. Already the heat is picking up.

They should be here soon.

Just then I hear the sound of tyres crunching over gravel. I turn around to see an emergency services vehicle ploughing down the forest lane towards me. I step out of the car and wait while the search and rescue team park their Isuzu nearby. Three volunteers climb out. Instantly I recognise Raymond. He has the wiry body of a greyhound and leathery skin thanks to years spent on the hills. He is 52 but as he comes over to greet me, I'm reminded he has the clear eyes of someone ten years younger – made more dramatic by his large, scruffy grey eyebrows.

'So we think she came this way?' he says.

'This would be the most obvious path for her to follow,' I reply.

The footpath ahead curves round the Devil's Hand, named after its five mountains. Tod Fell is the tallest. I look up at the jagged summit, where layers of rock are packed in tightly like books in a bookcase. Streams of water glitter between the dark folds of the mountain.

It looks deceptively close from here, as if you could reach the top in no time. But I know from years of experience that it's four hours there at a good pace. Not that it'll be me going up today.

Mountain Rescue is made up of highly experienced walkers like Raymond. The middle of the night or New Year's Day, if a call comes in, they have to answer it. None of them get paid. They answer a couple of dozen call-outs a year. Almost everyone is found safe and well.

A group of volunteers came out to search the area last night with a dog unit after Lily's family reported her missing. Finding nothing, they'd gone home this morning to rest. Now Raymond's team is stepping in.

'You say she left her family a note?' he asks.

'Yes.'

'But it didn't say what exact route she was taking?'

'Afraid not.'

Raymond lays his OS map flat on the bonnet of my car and marks 'X' at this point, then the local youth hostel, and begins silently tracing possible walking routes. Once he's done, he lifts his head and surveys the hills, squinting in the morning sun.

'It's a big area we're searching here, Ruth. About eight hundred square kilometres. We sent her a link but she still hasn't clicked it.'

Mountain Rescue uses the SARLOC system to text a link to a missing person's phone. If they click the link, Mountain Rescue receives the handset's location data.

'No one's heard from her. Phone must be dead,' I reply. Trying to reassure him, I add: 'She should know the area pretty well.

The family were up on holiday. But Lily had been staying here by herself for a few months before that.'

I know exactly what Raymond will say before he says it: 'Anyone can have a problem up here.'

And he's right. The Devil's Hand range is modest by mountaineering standards. But all it takes is one wrong turn, low cloud, an edge you didn't see, and the situation can turn fatal.

He says: 'Look, the conditions are as good as they could be. We've got clear skies. No rain. Other walkers out roaming around. Fingers crossed we can find her before nightfall. If she's run into trouble, let's hope she's got some shelter and water.'

As he's speaking, a pair of orange pinpricks emerge from the forest ahead.

'I'm worried about a different kind of trouble,' I mutter.

Two walkers with brightly coloured backpacks are beginning their long ascent up the mountain. Even from here I can tell they are men. Clearly they have only just started walking. They could not possibly be involved. But even so, I feel my throat tighten as I picture Lily setting off with her backpack on and her long red hair flowing out behind her, totally alone but for the odd stranger who passes by.

2

THE LOCAL YMCA IS tucked away at the bottom of a hill, surrounded by a cluster of trees. It is nine in the morning and the air is so fresh it stings my face as I climb up the steps towards the front door. A guest is lacing up their boots outside.

Once inside, I follow the sound of laughter and clinking cutlery through to the dining area, where about a dozen guests are eating breakfast on stainless steel tables. One side of the room is lined with vats where baked beans and greasy hash browns glow underneath heat lamps. Silence falls as one by one the guests notice me standing in the doorway.

The hostel manager who's welcomed us says: 'Sorry to interrupt your breakfast, everyone. If you could please just give a few minutes of your time to Inspector Lindsey, she has something she needs to talk to you about.'

I step forward. 'Good morning. You may already be aware, but a woman has gone missing in the area. At the moment we don't have reason to think it's suspicious. But I would still encourage you all to exercise caution when walking in the hills. Stick in small groups.'

The guests are mostly young apart from a group of men in their fifties. One woman who must be in her early twenties is watching me with wide eyes.

I circle the room handing out fliers. 'Lily is twenty-four with red hair. She was last seen yesterday. We think she was walking along the Devil's Hand.'

Each guest takes a moment to study the photo of Lily's face before passing it on.

I continue: 'If anyone's seen her, or someone acting suspiciously, please contact the number at the bottom of this page.'

I can study the faces of the guests for any flicker of recognition. All I get are blank stares. But then one girl starts whispering urgently to her friend, who takes the flier out of her hand and peers closely at it. They are nodding now. My heart races as the girl looks up and her eyes find mine.

'We saw her,' she says.

'Do you remember when?'

The women search each other's faces, trying to remember. 'Yesterday. Maybe half past eight in the morning? We went to Braeside to get snacks for our walk. We were heading to Spar and she went past us in the street, walking in the opposite direction. She looked like she was going hiking. She had her backpack on.'

'Was she with anyone?'

They shake their heads.

I drive back down into the valley. I still know the route to Braeside by a series of landmarks, embedded in my brain from years driving here to visit my parents. First there is a silvery glimpse of the sea, assuming the day is clear enough. Then the three hawthorn trees bent out of shape by the wind, frozen mid-dance. After that a small stone bridge. A field by the coast filled with weather-beaten sheep. For a moment the world looks completely open and green. And then the conifer forest begins. You plunge into the darkness, trees flying past, knowing that any moment you will emerge at the top of a hill. And then Braeside appears, rolling out beneath you, and towering in the distance, the mountain, Tod Fell.

I never thought I'd come back. Growing up here as a child, I would lie on the floor of my bedroom, looking up at the ingrained wallpaper on the ceiling, listening to the rooks squabble in the trees outside, and think Braeside was the most boring place on earth. I regularly fantasised about escaping. The land here stretches so far into the distance that I thought I could walk and just carry on walking until I stumbled across an undiscovered world. In my imagination, the neighbouring towns and villages were bustling cities waiting for me to arrive so I could start my real life.

I moved to Glasgow as soon as I could. For over a decade I worked there on the Major Investigations Team. I thought that would be my whole career. I could not have foreseen the chain of events that blew me back here, now aged 46. But I think the truth is that Braeside has always been in my blood – the hills, the wind, the sea.

History tells me that Lily will be found and safe and well in a matter of hours. And yet I can't get rid of the knot in my stomach. When did I last see her? Slowly, it comes to me. Saturday, two days ago. I'd been driving up the hill towards the town centre when she came striding up on my right. She'd been in Braeside for a couple of months at this point. But I still hadn't gotten used to the sight of this beautiful young thing strutting around town, her hair falling in an auburn wave down her back. She stood out like a sore thumb – all tatty East London elegance, long slip dresses with heavy boots and big earrings.

This is the kind of town where everyone knows everything about each other. I know the daughter of my neighbour two doors down recently got a promotion at an accountancy firm in Edinburgh. I know David who runs the corner shop never got over his wife shagging his friend in school even though it was years before they got together. You do anything here, and within 24 hours, everyone will know about it. But Lily – Lily is a blind spot. Her family turns up once or twice a year to stay in their holiday home. Despite owning a restaurant on the outskirts of town called The Lighthouse, they seem to have little role in actually running it. They've never integrated into the community. Lily at least tried.

As a youngster she made friends with a few locals but how many did she keep in touch with? Did she go out with anyone here? Piss anyone off? I have no clue. And that scares me.

The high street, abandoned in winter, comes alive in summer. It's quiet now but give it another hour and it will fill up with tourists. Families heading for the beach, young men looking unprepared for a day's hiking, seasoned elders up for the eight-hour loop around the Devil's Hand. Most of them finish their trek with a pint in the Nag's Head. Seeing my tattered outdoor wear, and guessing I'm a local, they'll tell me how lucky I am and how much they want to live in Braeside. Spend the winter here, I always tell them. If you can put up with the long nights, the bitter cold and the days of constant rain, then you're ready to call this place home.

I find Georgia Reid in the Nag's Head, wiping down tables. Her dad owns the place. The moment I come through the door, she straightens up, staring at me with her owlish eyes.

'Have you seen anything?' she says.

'Not yet. But Mountain Rescue is up there now. Do you want to chat outside?'

There is a narrow, concrete outdoor space behind the pub for the bins, where the kitchen staff come out for a smoke. Two upside-down metal buckets serve as makeshift seats. They look extremely uncomfortable so I opt for standing while Georgia sits herself down.

A shaft of sunlight finds its way down to us, making Georgia squint. 'I thought maybe she'd contact us this morning, but—' she holds out her phone with a look of despair '—still nothing.'

'When did you last hear from her?'

'She messaged me yesterday morning.'

She opens her phone and passes it over to me. The first thing I see are Georgia's most recent missed calls to Lily. I scroll up through the WhatsApp conversation. One message stands out, interrupting the otherwise pleasant dialogue between the two women.

For the first time in a long time, I feel free

What do you mean? You okay? Haha

Hey your mum says you aren't home, everything all right?

Missed call

Are you okay? Sorry, apparently you're not back when you said you'd be and me and your family are worried. Call me when you get this

Missed call

The text – 'I feel free' – had been sent at 11 o'clock in the morning, probably shortly after she began her walk. As far as I know it might be the last message Lily sent to anyone.

'Does she normally talk like that?' I ask.

'No. It's really out of character.'

'In what way?'

'She wouldn't send something like that that's just going to make me worry without explaining what she means. I honestly thought she'd sent it to the wrong person. Or someone else had sent it.'

'Someone else?'

'I don't know. I just mean it's not like her.'

'Who else does Lily hang out with when she's up here?'

'Only me and Harris. And he hasn't seen her either.'

'When did you last see her?'

'About two weeks ago. But we spoke on the phone more recently.'

'Did she tell you about this walk?'

'Not this one exactly. But she goes on walks by herself all the time. I sometimes offer to go with her but she says no because she knows I hate walking, she'd just be dragging me along.' She squeezes her eyes shut and wipes the side of her face in distress. 'So stupid. I should never have let her go by herself.'

'Don't be silly. She's probably gotten lost up there. In which case, Mountain Rescue know those hills like the back of their hand. They'll find her. How many times have you seen Lily since she came up here?'

'Pretty regularly over the last few months.'

'Did she seem okay to you?'

'She'd been struggling for a while. She told me she felt anxious. She wasn't sleeping well. She was sort of manic sometimes when she was talking to me.'

'How do you mean?'

'Fixating on things. Ranting about them.'

'What things?'

'The things that normally annoy her, like family stuff. Her parents being difficult.'

I nod. The Howards aren't the most harmonious bunch. In a rare sighting last week, I spotted Lily and her mum in the local café having a lunch that looked deeply unpleasant. Lily had rolled her eyes while Vanessa complained about the food. Then Lily had started rolling a cigarette, at which point Vanessa had retreated into an icy silence for the remainder of the meal.

I frown. 'Is that why she came to Braeside by herself for a couple of months before her parents joined? Because of family trouble?'

'Not necessarily. She just wanted a break. This is her sanctuary. She told me: "It doesn't make things better. But it's a way of pressing pause on everything else. It's a time out." The sea's always going to be here. The woods. The hills. Me. I'm always still here.' She shrugs awkwardly. 'Doing the same thing.'

I resist the urge to roll my eyes. Georgia is 24, like Lily, but her lack of confidence makes her seem younger. That's what living here in your twenties will do to you, if you ask me. A long bus and a train ride away from the nearest club, never far from the watchful gaze of your parents, with fuck all jobs, young people stay young for too long.

They'd met when they were teenagers, on a week-long sailing course. Lily was on the course; Georgia was working in the sailing centre's kitchen. They had always struck me as an unlikely pair. But I think they each had something the other wanted. Lily must have offered Georgia a window into a more glamorous world, whereas Georgia must have made this quiet town feel like home.

'It's a big house, did she not want someone staying with her?'

'Looking back, I don't know if it was the best idea. She said she was fine on her own but I'm not so sure she was.' She continues: 'I guess she came up and felt she could forget about everything else for a while. She wasn't content.' She sniffs. 'I feel like in your twenties this huge divide opens up between you and other people, you know? Suddenly some friends have everything sorted out. They're already living the lives they're going to be living for the next ten, fifteen, twenty years. And some of us are still scraping by, trying to work things out. That's how she felt. She travelled to Southeast Asia last year. Then she started teaching. It was a horrible school, really stressful. So she decided to take a break. Focus on her art. She was thinking about doing a masters. International relations. But I don't think she really wanted to do that. I think that's what she felt she should be doing. Something worthy. What her family wanted. I was trying to convince her to do her own thing. Maybe give teaching another go. Prioritise her art. She's really talented. I think she came up here for some peace and quiet. But I don't think it helped. I'm worried it made things worse, being up here alone.'

'Has she ever done anything like this before? Gone off on her own without contacting anyone?'

She shakes her head. 'Never. She's usually good at replying as well. Posts on social media a lot. But she hasn't been active since she sent me that message. Well, apart from this. Around the same time.'

She shows me her phone again. Lily had posted a story that morning, at around the same time she texted Georgia. The first video is of rolling fields, crayon-green in the June sunshine, with cows grazing in the distance. The only thing disturbing the tranquil scene is the distorted sound of the wind crackling through the speakers. The second clip shows the tops of the conifers sliding past on either side as she walks through forestry.

Watching these clips feels eerie. I think of the stars. How the light takes thousands of years to reach us – so long that by the time we're looking at them we're staring into the past.

'Georgia, do you think there's any chance Lily would hurt herself?'

Georgia flinches. 'I don't think so. I really don't think so. That message she sent… I don't know what it means.'

'Okay. Was she seeing anyone?'

Georgia shakes her head.

I place my hand on her shoulder. 'People get lost on those hills more often than you'd think. And she's smart. She'll know what to do.'

I try to sound reassuring. But inside my heart is pounding. As soon as Lily was reported missing, a unit tried to contact her. They hadn't got through so instead they'd sent her a text: Hello, it's the police. Please can you call us on the number below quoting incident number 48204. We have concerns for your welfare. Still nothing. We assumed her phone had died on the mountain. But now I've seen this text to Georgia – now I'm not so sure.

I check my phone once I'm back in the car. The day's running out and still nothing from Mountain Rescue. I open my car window and outside I can hear the gentle rattle of dried leaves blowing across the tarmac. I use my radio to contact the control room.

'Ruth,' says the sergeant on the other end. 'Please tell me you have good news for me.'

'No sign of her yet,' I reply. 'Listen, I think we need to review the level of risk. I've just heard from a friend of Lily's called Georgia Reid that she was struggling with anxiety. She also sent a strange text to Georgia yesterday morning. Something about being free. I want to escalate this and record her as a high-risk misper. I also want a telecoms search for her mobile phone and her call data.'

'Got it.'

'Any update on your end?'

'Officers are going door-to-door now, seeing if there've been any sightings and doing CCTV checks. Have you spoken to the family yet?'

'Going there now.'

3

THE SHOREHOUSE SITS RIGHT by the bay, at the end of a private road.

Rumour has it that Vanessa bought the place after taking an Ancestry DNA test and discovering she was ten per cent Scottish. Probably bullshit – but it has a ring of truth.

Martyn lets me in. Lily's father is a stocky man in his sixties, recently retired. He made his money as the financial director of a recruitment firm in London. Usually he has a healthy golden complexion, topped up by frequent holidays abroad, but today he looks grey in the face.

I've never been inside the house before. After the family moved in, it was featured in some interior design magazine, where Vanessa described her decorating style as 'Scandi-Scot'. When I read that, it made me throw up in my mouth a little bit. But now, standing in the five-bedroom property, I can see what she meant. If a Swedish filmmaker were searching for a lair for their Scottish villain, this is probably the setting they would pick. The main living space is sparsely decorated with a vaulted ceiling, resembling a church hall. Sheepskins lie over a huge cream sofa which faces a marble fireplace. I groan inwardly at the sight of a pair of brass stags sparring on the mantelpiece.

I can't deny, though, that they've chosen a good spot. Large windows overlook their small private beach. The sea is a sheet of brilliant silver against the reddish-brown hills on the other side of the bay.

'Is Vanessa back yet?' I ask.

'Still out looking, but she's on her way. Toby as well.'

Toby is Lily's older (much less agreeable) brother.

'So you haven't seen Lily since the night before last?' I ask.

'No. She didn't say anything about going on a walk. We woke up and she'd left a note. It said she'd be back by 5 o'clock yesterday evening.' He rubs his eyes. 'Then 5 o'clock came and went. She wasn't answering her phone. We must have called the police at about 10.'

'Have you noticed if anything's missing from the house?'

'She took her backpack and a water bottle. That's all I can work out. Her laptop's still here.'

'Mind if I see Lily's room?'

'Of course,' he says.

We climb up the stairs and into Lily's room. With a shallow ceiling and the walls painted crimson, it is a comforting, almost womb-like space. She must have stayed here only a few weeks at a time over the years but she has slowly made the room her own, covering the walls in photos, art prints, album covers. Paramore next to Talking Heads. A childhood drawing next to a painting of the sea. You can see the passing years, the different versions of her, like rings in the trunk of a tree.

Unlike the rest of the house, Lily's room is a tip. Clothes are heaped on a chair in the corner and the desk is strewn with artworks at varying stages of completion. I pull on a pair of disposable gloves before sifting through a pile of papers that are stiffened with watercolour paint. Mainly landscapes. Georgia isn't just being kind to her friend. She's definitely talented. I recognise the distinctive outline of Sunkhead Bay. No paintings of hell, no drawings of creepy stalkers. There's not much in here that gives away what her state of mind was like at the time. But there are diaries and notepads everywhere, which could prove helpful.

I start opening drawers, finding a packet of prescription medication. Melatonin, reads the label.

'Was Lily struggling with her sleep, do you know?' I ask Martyn.

He peers into the drawer. 'Maybe she mentioned sleeping badly once or twice. Is that…' He squints. 'Is that medication?'

'You don't by any chance know if there are any drugs missing here? If she could have taken any with her?'

'I had no idea she was taking that.'

It doesn't surprise me that Lily might have withheld this information from her parents. I can imagine Martyn and Vanessa telling her to keep a stiff upper lip rather than go to the doctor.

I shut the drawer and scan the rest of the room, feeling my frustration rise. Of all the ones to go missing, why did it have to be her? I should be bringing years of experience and gossip and instead I feel like I'm starting from scratch, feeling in the dark for a sense of who she is.

And that's when I hear the front door slam shut.

The sound echoes up the staircase, making Martyn and I immediately lock eyes. A second passes and Martyn shoots out, with me following him down the stairs, hoping, praying, that a red-haired woman might be standing in the doorway.

I re-enter the living room, and my heart tightens.

Lily's mother Vanessa is standing there with her eyes popping out of her face, looking like she's about to kill me.

4

EVEN IF THEY WERE both right in front of you, you wouldn't know Vanessa and Lily were mother and daughter. While Vanessa keeps her hair immaculately coloured and blow-dried, Lily lets hers grow long and tangled. While Vanessa wears gold jewellery and cashmere cardigans, Lily drapes herself in charity-shop finds.

But today Vanessa is dressed for searching the hills. She wears expensive-looking leggings and a cotton t-shirt, her hair tied back, forehead beaded with sweat. A pair of women's Hunter wellies sit on the porch outside.

'Have you seen her?' she demands. Her eyes are wide with desperation.

'Mountain Rescue's searching for her now.' I reply. 'They'll let us know as soon as they see or hear anything.'

'Mountain Rescue isn't enough. You need to look at criminals in the area. Sex offenders.'

I already know what's coming. No matter what I say, from Vanessa's perspective, this is completely my fault.

'We're looking at all possibilities, but the information we have so far suggests she may be lost or injured in the mountains.'

Without acknowledging her husband, Vanessa shrieks: 'She wouldn't just stop replying to messages and calls like this. I know my daughter. That isn't something she'd do.'

'I'm sure you need to rest. But I do want to get as much

information as I can from you about Lily and where she might be. Do you have any security cameras?'

Vanessa sits down on the cream sofa, holding her head in her hands. 'No,' she replies.

'She was here by herself for two months. And then you both came up last week, with your son, is that right?'

'That's right.'

'Did she seem okay? Was she struggling with any mental health problems that you were aware of?'

Martyn and Vanessa shake their heads with bemusement. I'm feeling more inclined to believe Georgia's account on this one.

'And you say she's never done anything like this before? Gone for a walk without answering her phone.'

I know some people who do that. Turn off their devices so they can immerse themselves more fully in nature.

'She's not an idiot,' snaps Vanessa.

'Had she experienced any threatening behaviour, anything like that?'

Vanessa looks at me with vicious hatred.

'I told you,' she says. 'The hares.'

Ah yes. I had almost forgotten. The fucking hares.

I still remember the first time Vanessa summoned me to the Shorehouse and took me to the edge of her sprawling garden where a stiff-legged hare lay stretched like a ribbon in the grass, its burst and flattened stomach writhing with maggots.

I hadn't taken it seriously. I told her it wasn't a police matter and she should dispose of the animal herself. The hare had been run over. So I thought maybe an animal had taken it here, got spooked, and left it behind. Or that someone had chucked it thoughtlessly over the wall to get it off the road.

But then the bodies kept coming. Always hares and rabbits. One after the other, every time the Howards stayed up for more than a few days.

And these ones hadn't been run over. These had been shot. Right through the lungs. By someone who knew what they were doing with a rifle. Hares are a protected species. So I'd left the case with the Wildlife Crime Liaison Officer. As far as I know, since then they've made fuck all progress.

'I don't think that has anything to do with Lily going missing.'

'How can you say that? It was a threat! A threat to my family. And you ignored it.'

'We didn't ignore—'

'Last week! Last week was the most recent one, wasn't it, Martyn? Someone's got her. I just know. In my gut. Oh God.' She clutches her stomach and looks at me. 'Your – your colleagues asked me to send a photo. Do you know what it's like having to look through photos of your child and – and choose one for a post saying, "Have you seen this person?" How do you choose a photo like that?'

I have never in my life felt sorry for Vanessa but my heart feels like it's swelling up in my chest. 'We're going to put absolutely everything into finding Lily.'

'You don't understand, that's your problem.'

'Vanessa, I do under—'

'How are you the best person to find her? When you couldn't even look after—'

She stops and her mouth falls open in shock at the thing she almost said, didn't quite say but might as well have done.

It's like I've missed a step going downstairs. A space opens up beneath me. I realise I can't control the next thing that comes out of my mouth so I grit my teeth and look at the floor.

Vanessa says tentatively: 'Ruth – I wasn't thinking—'

I start zipping up my jacket. My fingers are trembling and the zip keeps getting caught. I hope Vanessa can't see but I know she can. 'I'll give you a call as soon as I have an update,' I manage.

She's being a bitch because she's scared, I tell myself, as I head out, close the heavy door behind me and step out onto the flagstone porch. But then I think: no, she's always been like this. The sky is darkening and scrappy clouds are moving in, casting shadows on the cows in the distant fields. And I can't believe this is happening and I never do this and I can't believe I'm doing this – because of Vanessa, fucking *Vanessa* – but even though it's been years since I've cried the urge has hit me out of nowhere and I have to stop halfway down the path to breathe deeply and collect myself. The wind stirs the trees, blowing strands of hair into my face.

It's been a long time since I was this relieved to come home. My feet are heavy as I traipse up the road towards my place, a detached cottage on the edge of town, a ten-minute walk from the centre.

I call Raymond as I'm coming up the garden path. They haven't found anything. They'll keep searching into the night. I saw it coming but there's still an ache in my chest as I wish him good luck and turn my keys in the door.

My house looks like it belongs to someone a million years old, owing to the antique furniture I've inherited from my mother and the frilled green curtains left behind by the previous owners. But I can't be arsed to change anything. And I think it has its own charm, with its low ceilings and small doors and uneven flooring. Kirsty texts, asking if she can pick anything up. You still haven't eaten?! I reply.

All good, wanted to wait for you, she texts back.

I feel guilty about that. I have sausages and tinned tomatoes; I'll make something quick, pasta.

It was good of Kirsty to suggest coming over. Before she gets here I take a few moments lying flat on the sofa. I'm so exhausted I could fall asleep right now. Douglas slinks into the room and gives my hand an exploratory sniff before jumping up on top of me and curling up on my stomach.

After dinner Kirsty and I drink tea in the garden. The

temperature's dropped so we've taken the blankets off the sofa and laid them over our laps like a couple of old ladies.

'It's possible she wasn't as fast as she thought she'd be or got injured and camped somewhere for the night,' says Kirsty.

'There's no camping stuff missing from the Howards',' I reply.

'There are a couple of abandoned farm buildings around there though.'

The last of the daylight is disappearing behind the mountain. I watch it, sipping my tea. It will be cold up there at this time. And dark; pitch-black. The once-comforting mountain now feels like it's mocking me. *She's mine now. Come and find her.*

I think about what Georgia said. *This is her sanctuary. I guess she came up and felt she could forget about everything else for a while.* I get that. I've always felt like Braeside has its own time zone. It's easy to forget about the rest of the world while you're here. Had Lily come to this town to escape something? And found she couldn't get away from it, even here?

'When did she last go over to yours?' I ask.

Lily has been tutoring Kirsty's 14-year-old son Archie lately.

'The day before yesterday,' Kirsty replies. 'She seemed fine to me.'

'Did you get to know her much?'

Kirsty shakes her head. 'Never that well. She seems like a lovely girl, though. She's good with Archie, which is saying something. And she's always seemed very sweet with Georgia and Harris.'

In my head, they are still teenagers. I remember years ago seeing the three of them trying to start a barbecue on the beach when Kirsty and I were sunbathing. Swimsuit-clad, they had battled to get a light going in the sea breeze, attempting to shield the flame with their beach towels. They were that age when everything they did seemed ridiculous and nothing they said made any sense – lost in a world of their own, with a long summer ahead of them.

'Something changed between those three, though,' she says.

'I've seen them around a lot this summer, but something's different. They're less silly. I thought they were just growing up, growing apart. But now I'm not so sure.'

I take a sip of tea. 'Vanessa's house is something else.'

'I saw the photos from the magazine shoot.'

'I half-expected bagpipes to start playing as soon as I walked in. I feel like if you were going to sacrifice a local child, that's where you'd do it.'

To my disappointment Kirsty doesn't laugh. Or play along, like she usually would. She stares down the bottom of the garden with a grimace.

'What?' I say.

'Nothing, just… her daughter's missing, right? Maybe lay off.'

'Yeah, and I care about the daughter. I don't need to care about Vanessa.'

'Are you all right? You must be tired.'

I don't *have* to tell her. I could take the easy way out of this conversation. Agree that I'm shattered after a hard day.

But hiding things from Kirsty never has been an option for me.

I force the words out. 'She said something about Molly.'

'Who did?'

'Vanessa. Well, she almost did. She said, "Are you really the best person to look after…" and then she shut up. But it was obvious what she was going to say.'

I glance sideways at her. The horror in Kirsty's face is too much to bear and it makes me look back into the garden again.

'That bitch,' she says decisively.

'This was my thought exactly,' I mumble, and take another sip of tea.

I listen to the squeak of Kirsty shifting in her seat. 'Prick.'

'I know.'

'Does she even know the whole story? Does she know what she's talking about?'

'Probably not. Not even sure how she found out, given no one here speaks to her.'

'Don't listen to her. You're the absolute best person to find Lily. She's lucky you're here.' She picks up her tea cup and reaches for mine. 'I'll do some washing up.'

'No, don't.'

'No, you've had a big day and you've cooked for me. I insist.'

She disappears into the house, leaving me in the garden, watching the mountain.

When I met Connor for the first time, I knew it was him. I was only 19 but a part of my soul nodded in recognition – yes, this is what he looks like, this is always and only ever what he could have looked like. And when Molly was born, only four years on (early, much earlier than I'd planned, but I got pregnant by accident and couldn't bring myself to end it), my soul nodded again – yes, this is her, it was only ever her.

I keep a photo from that time in the drawer of my bedside table. We'd come up to visit my parents in Braeside. In the photo, we are mid-hike. Connor is wearing shorts and his strong legs are streaked with mud. Molly is strapped to his front, her tiny face mushed against his chest, fast asleep. There is so much lightness in my expression.

I keep this one physical photo in my bedside table because I worry one day I'll need to remember what they looked like. But I hardly ever take it out. I find seeing all that carefree joy very difficult now.

A cool wind enters the garden. It sweeps through the oak tree in slow motion, so the air is filled with the sound of rustling leaves and the earthy, broken smell of the nearby wood. Douglas creeps over to gently nudge my hand with his wet nose, and I stroke his soft head, reassuring us both.

Part of me thinks: *This is exactly what you came here to get away from.*

I shake myself and push the thought down.

5

Police Scotland

Missing Persons

Searches are continuing in South West Scotland for missing woman Lily Howard.

The 24-year-old was last seen at around 8:30 a.m. on 2 June in the town of Braeside. She had told her family she would be hiking in a group of hills called the Devil's Hand in the Southern Uplands.

A major search operation involving assistance from specialist support units including the Police Scotland helicopter, dog unit, dive unit and Mountain Rescue was subsequently launched.

Police are urging anyone with information or dashcam footage to come forward as officers continue work to identify her movements.

She is originally from London and is described as 5ft 6ins tall and of slim build with long red hair. When last seen, she was wearing a green top and black leggings.

6

Reddit

r/LilyHoward

Anyone know anything about this case?
Not much detail, I wonder if there were suspicious circumstances
I really hope she is found soon
Bring Lily home
The Devil's Hand, not looking good with a name like that lads
Her mum has posted on FB saying Lily's phone is off. Obviously it could have run out of battery but it seems unlikely an experienced hiker – as it seems she is based on her IG – would leave the house with a phone on low battery or without a battery pack. Doesn't feel right.
Her poor parents, my heart is with the family
Very small town. Population 500.
Popular with walkers though.

7
Mia

4 June

MY MAKE-UP FEELS LIKE it's melting underneath the light. The interviewer leans forward in his seat. 'Do you need me to repeat the question?'

For the past thirty minutes he's been trying to make me feel it's just us two. But it's impossible to ignore the cameraman looming in one corner of the room and his assistant adjusting the light in the other. Twice, a runner has had to jump in with a small brush and powder my perspiring forehead.

'Yes, please,' I reply.

This is not what I expected. I'd thought taking part in this documentary would be no different from filming in my room. But now that I'm here, in this obscure studio in Hackney, I realise this isn't true. I have no idea what I look like, and it makes me worry constantly what my face is doing, which makes talking even harder.

I'm used to having full control over my image. Normally, I have two purple lights in the far corners of the room and an LED ring light around the camera to even out any blemishes. My followers often comment that it's very slick and professional, so I'd asked the production team if they could recreate the aesthetic. But the producer had said it wouldn't match the look of the other interviews.

'Let me rephrase that one,' says the interviewer, also the director of the documentary. 'You obviously have a much bigger platform since the Hayley Pieterson case. Do you think it's a positive thing for the outcome of investigations that some internet sleuths like yourselves now command so much influence?'

Okay, that's an easy one.

'My follower count went up from about five thousand to fifty thousand after this case. I think it can only be a good thing if sleuths – if that's what you want to call us – have more visibility because it means the case gets more publicity. The more people engage, the more information you have to work with. So with this case, yes I narrowed down a list of suspects from social media, but it was only because followers sent in photos they'd taken or found online that I was able to show the killer had lied about their alibi.'

'But it's usually the residents of the town or the real people involved who pay the price for that publicity, isn't it? What are your thoughts on that?'

The light burns out of the corner of my eye. I glance briefly in its direction, where the camera assistant is watching from the darkness.

I swallow. 'If a lot of people arrive in your town to take photos, but the crime gets solved, I don't know, I'd say that's a fair price to pay.'

There is a long pause. What if *am* being set up? What if that response is all they show? What if they cut out all my well-researched answers?

'Do you think Hayley Pieterson's family would agree with you there?' he asks.

The lights seem to glow even brighter. I blink rapidly. It feels like something is caught in my eye.

'It was awful what happened to them,' I reply. 'But if that case hadn't gone viral, it would still be unsolved today. Hayley's family still wouldn't know who killed her.'

The director gives me a weak smile, signalling he's asked all he wanted to ask.

'So what's the next case?' he says.

I smile back. 'We'll see.'

I leave the Tube station and walk to my flat feeling overdressed. Londoners spill out of pubs and onto the pavement, drinking lager out of plastic cups, gaudily dressed for birthdays and budget weddings.

So what's the next case? I look down at my sandals on the scorching concrete. I wish I knew. I feel like I've been waiting months now for the right thing to come along.

The make-up artist did a great job. I'd hate to waste this look. Taking a shortcut through the park, I film myself strutting down the path and combing my hair with one hand. *Summer vibes*, I write. Then I post. For a few moments I stare at my screen, transfixed. No one is reacting. Why is no one reacting? But then the likes start to trickle in. My heart rate slows to a steady pace.

I head up to my shared flat. To my relief, it's silent and none of the lights are on. No one is home.

I live with two other girls. But really I live alone. We've become highly skilled in the art of avoiding each other. Even though their everyday rituals are the soundtrack to my day – the 28-year-old divorcee paces when she's stressed, the homesick graduate calls her mum every night – we lead separate lives, cooking at different times to dodge conversations over the limited kitchen space. It's possible to go a whole week without seeing each other, except for when someone has to venture into the main hallway and bundle their dirty clothes into the washing machine.

I learnt when I was younger that women don't understand me. At school I longed for the sisterly relationships others formed. I wanted one of the popular girls to take me under her wing. I wanted to dress up together before we went out, do each other's hair and make-up, watch movies until midnight, or whatever it was those girls were doing when they posted selfies together on

Facebook from their bedrooms. But I know now that's not for me. I think differently. I'm too little and too much all at once. Out-of-time. Out of sync with the seasons. Out of rhythm with the rest of the world.

As soon as I get inside I let my bag drop to the floor. Dry heat from the city presses in through the walls. The window of my third-floor flat only opens a few inches. I think it's a safety thing, in case the occupant tries to throw themselves out. Barely any air gets through. Just the noise of the traffic from the busy road below.

I wonder if I could ever afford to rent a place by myself. Income from the sleuthing is ticking along. I've recently started selling merchandise – *help solve cold cases; buy a t-shirt* – and it's bringing in some cash. But it's not enough. I need to find something. My next thing. But not just anything. It has to be right.

The interview and the walk back from the station has sent my anxiety through the roof so I lie down and scroll. I fall into the digital world and my mind purrs with relaxation.

The SHOCKING truth behind this '90s murder

One of the most CHILLING images in the Blue Boy case

Reddit sleuth cracks case after recognising view from window

REVEALED: the clue that proves Rachel Taylor WAS killed by her husband

I've set up news alerts on my phone and every day I look through forums, other sleuths' channels and crimes reported on in the local and national papers. This is how I spend my time when I'm not working in the salon. I only move when I need to eat, work or go to the gym. Nothing interrupts me apart from her texts.

The last one was on Monday. **Evil bitch how do you live with yourself?** I went for a long walk by the canal after that. Inside I felt completely empty. I took a photograph of the sun setting over the bridge and uploaded it to Instagram. The water looked like it was on fire. London town looking beaut, I captioned it. Over fifty likes, when I last checked.

You always know the right case when it comes along. Just from the first opening paragraphs of a news report or the photo of the victim, frozen in time. Your skin starts to prickle and your heart rate picks up and in that moment a bond forges between you and the person on screen. *It's like the case chooses you*, is how I once described it to my followers in a live Q&A. You don't know this person. But suddenly you want to know everything about them. Suddenly all you can think about is finding out what happened to them.

I want that feeling back again.

8
Ruth

4 June

I ARRIVE AT THE station early the next day. Braeside used to have its own police station but it was closed not long after I arrived in a big cost-cutting drive by Police Scotland. It's about a 40-minute drive to my division's headquarters.

Before the briefing, I check my emails. Tech have sent through the cell site analysis. Lily's phone last connected to a mast at around 11 o'clock on the day she went missing. Since then, nothing. I scroll through her call records, noting a few short calls with her mum and a few longer ones with Georgia in the preceding weeks.

Then I swipe through Lily's social media, looking at the snapshots from her first few days back in Braeside. The first shows her standing in the sea in a swimsuit, water up to her thighs, dolphin-smooth, arms joyfully outstretched. Then there's a selfie with Georgia, grinning cheek-to-cheek in what must be the garden of the Nag's Head. A photo of an ancient yew tree with multiple intertwining trunks. A mountain flower. A cup of tea beside an open sketchpad with a half-finished drawing. The sun setting over Tod Fell. I read one caption. *Inspiration comes from retreat.*

'Ruth?' calls Kieran Thompson, the superintendent, holding the door open to the briefing room, which is slowly filling up with officers. 'You coming?'

We gather around a long table. One of the officers has already stuck a map of the area on the whiteboard.

'So here's the timeline we have so far,' I say. 'Lily left the house without saying goodbye to her family members on the 2nd of June. She left a note on the kitchen table saying she'd be back at 5 o'clock that evening. We've found CCTV footage of her heading into Spar, the local convenience store, at 8.33 a.m. Mr Young says he remembers she bought a couple of energy bars. She sent a text to her friend Georgia at around 11 o'clock. Saying she felt "free" for the first time in a long time. She posted twice on social media while she was out walking, before and after the text to Georgia. But after that, no online activity.

'Looking at cell mast data, the phone hasn't pinged since around the time she sent that text. It's going straight to voicemail, so it must be either dead or turned off. Georgia says she posted every day and was quick to reply to texts so this length of time offline is unusual for her.

'Everything we have so far suggests she's around the Devil's Hand. We need to work out exactly where she was in those last two Instagram posts to help Mountain Rescue with their search. And we need to find out if other walkers have seen her over the last two days. There's a good chance we're going to find her injured on a mountain. But we can't rule anything out at this stage.

'I want a detailed search of the area covered by the phone mast. Let's pin down what she's been up to over the last week, who she's been speaking to, if anyone's noticed anything unusual.'

Thompson speaks up from the back of the room. 'The public appeal has been getting a lot of attention online. A reminder that all eyes are on us.'

As the officers file out one-by-one, he shuffles over, his eyes fixed on the image of Lily on the screen.

'You know the family. What do you think are the chances she'd do this deliberately? Go off grid for a week or two.'

'She's never done anything like it before. And she's not had much experience camping that the family and friends are aware of.'

He nods, lips set in a hard line. I'm sure he's thinking about his two daughters, currently in secondary school. He talks about them all the time, keeping me up to date with their latest accomplishments.

'Did you get anywhere with the—' he struggles for the words '—the hare thing?'

I resist the urge to put my face in my hands. 'I really don't think the hare thing is relevant to Lily going missing.'

'Still, we need to look into it. Take another look at the evidence.' He scratches the side of his nose. 'I've spoken to the chief superintendent. If we don't find her today, they want to deploy a detective from another MIT to help with this.'

'Of course.'

I knew this would happen. There's no way they'd expect one local detective to handle a case this big by themselves. But even though I saw it coming, I have to suppress a groan of disappointment. I've gotten used to working alone, treating my command area like it's my kingdom.

The DSU clearly senses my frustration.

'They're good, Ruth,' he reassures me.

'As long as they don't need much looking after.'

The tingle in my bones reminds me of midwinter swims. I feel like I'm wading into icy water, bracing myself for full bodily submersion.

The first twenty-four hours is vital in a missing persons case. And it's already been and gone, like that.

9

I BASH THE DOOR knocker, step back and wait.

The terraced houses on the high street are under the constant watch of the mountain. Tod Fell sits like an eternally half-risen sun – as if following the road would leave you straight to its peak. The properties here don't have porches or front gardens and standing out on the pavement like this makes me feel exposed. The doily curtains on the neighbour's bedroom window shiver as 70-year-old Sue Bridges peers down to see what I'm up to.

The door opens, revealing a tall, thin man in his early twenties. Most men grow out of their teenage lankiness but Harris never did. He has large eyes and brown hair that falls in tight curls down to his brows, giving him a puppyish look.

I sense he was just about to head out – a pair of walking boots sit ready and waiting at the foot of the stairs behind him.

'Morning, Harris, all right if I come in?'

He looks nervous as I follow him through the narrow hallway into his parents' living room. Once we're alone, I realise why. Wafting from his clothes is the faint, earthy smell of weed.

I raise my eyebrows at him. 'Really?'

'Sorry,' he says.

I narrow my eyes at him. 'Your friend is missing.'

'Yeah, and I'm stressed as fuck,' he throws back. He runs his hands through his curls. 'Look, I'm sorry, Ruth. Honestly, I'm going to look for her now. I just needed to calm myself down first.'

I want to tell him that Lily probably doesn't need a stoned man stumbling around the hills looking for her. But now's not the time. I shake my head.

'Whatever, we have bigger things to deal with. Have you heard from her?'

He squeezes his hands and shakes his head. 'Nothing.'

'I know an officer checked in on you at work yesterday to see if she was staying with you. But do you mind just talking me through when you last saw her?'

'Georgia and I went round for dinner at the Shorehouse about two weeks ago. Before the rest of Lily's family arrived.'

'Did she seem okay to you?'

'Fine, yeah. Pretty normal.'

'Was she worried about anything?'

'Worried about what she's going to do next, I guess. She's in between jobs at the moment. But you know, no more worried than she usually is.'

If that's true then maybe Lily's mental health problems have nothing to do with this. But then Harris never has struck me as the most emotionally astute person. And maybe Lily confided more in Georgia than in him.

'Did she mention any desire to go hiking for days, anything like that?'

He screws up his face. 'No. She likes walking, but I can't see her deciding to do something like that. I don't know what happened but she must be in trouble up there.'

'How regularly did you see Lily?'

'The three of us hung out maybe once or twice a week.'

'Long gap since you last saw her then.'

Harris blushes. 'I don't know, I guess, with her family being up, she's been distracted.'

That's strange, because it sounds like she's been desperate to get away, I can't help thinking.

Harris speaks up, interrupting my thoughts. 'Sorry I'm not being very helpful.'

'No, it all helps. I'm sure she'll turn up. We've got Mountain Rescue searching the hills. But let me know if you hear anything, okay?'

'Sure thing.'

Before I leave, I shoot him a disapproving glance. 'If I smell that on you again, I'm telling your mum.'

10

As I drive along the glassy bay, I can see The Lighthouse glinting in the distance. If you ask me, the Howards' restaurant is an abomination – an ultra-modern glass box perched like a spaceship on the fern-covered hillside.

A sign on the door informs me the restaurant is closed today for 'essential maintenance'. Framed photos of Vanessa and Martyn cutting the ribbon are mounted on the wall above the receptionist's desk. I wonder when the Howards last came here – if they ever do these days.

I find Craig, Kirsty's husband, on his knees in the bar area, wrenching up broken tiles. He gets up for a quick hug. Craig is a very hairy person – hairy arms, hairy legs, and the kind of beard so thick it grows from his cheekbones. He steps back and wipes his hands on his t-shirt, surveying the tiles with a look of despair.

'I swear this will never end,' he groans.

'Shouldn't have done such a shit job to begin with, I guess?'

He shoots me an unamused look, then goes back to staring in frustration at the task at hand. 'I told them a million times, if you don't want things breaking in a couple of years, it's going to cost you. But no, they cut every corner they could.'

Craig is the only handyman for about twenty miles. If you need work doing here, he's your go-to. When he first started working at the restaurant, he complained about it non-stop for a year.

'Is this about Lily?' he asks.

I nod. 'Kirsty said she was at yours the day before she went missing, tutoring Archie.'

'She was. I saw her briefly before she left.'

'Did she seem okay to you?'

Craig shrugs. 'She seemed fine. Nothing out of the ordinary. Not that I've spoken to her much. It's just Martyn I deal with for work.'

'There's something else I was going to ask you about. The hare thing.'

'What?'

I'm so reluctant to bring it up that I've mumbled my words. I say, louder: 'These hares appearing on the Howards' land.'

Craig's eyes widen in surprise.

'I remember late last year you were joking about it in the Nag's Head,' I continue.

'Was I?'

I narrow my eyes at him. 'Come on.'

The image is clear in my mind. Midwinter. The Christmas pub quiz. Silver tinsel on the mantelpiece. Mulled wine coating my teeth and layering my tongue. Craig three or four pints in, his friends collapsing with laughter around him as he mimed Vanessa squeamishly picking up the corpse by its hind legs and flinging it in the bin.

Craig's face colours, as if he's just remembered this too.

He says: 'Well, obviously, I feel like an arsehole now, don't I? But it wasn't *me*, Ruth.'

'When did you first hear about it?'

'The first time she posted it on social media, I think. Someone shared the link with me. Why?'

'Whoever's done it isn't in serious trouble. I just need to know who it is so I can rule them out from the investigation.'

'What, they think whoever killed those hares has something to do with this?'

I shrug – even hearing someone else say it out loud reminds me how ridiculous this theory is.

'You never know. The family are saying they felt threatened. With a woman gone missing, we need to look at everything.'

'I honestly don't know who it is, Ruth.'

'Okay. I have to ask. Now, what did you do yesterday?'

'I was working here. Oh, and I went to the Nag's Head to see Declan.'

'What time was that?'

'Around midday. I was there for about two hours before coming back.' He pauses. 'If you could maybe not tell the Howards I was two pints in while retiling their floor, that would be grand.'

'Okay. Thanks. I'm going to check in on Kirsty and Archie now at the café. Get their accounts.'

'It's the Devil's Hand where you think she's lost, right?'

'It seems that way.'

He nods. 'I should be done here by the early afternoon and then I'll go up there and help look.'

'Bless you,' I say. In the chaos of the last twenty-four hours, this is what's comforted me the most: people's willingness to go out and look for her themselves. Giving up an hour here and then. A whole day if they can afford to. 'Just don't get an injury up there. We don't want to be looking for two people.'

Craig frowns. 'That's the weird thing. It's a challenging walk but it's hardly the most difficult terrain in the world, is it? Just makes you think… is she definitely lost?'

11

As soon as I step inside Kirsty's café, a wave of drowsiness hits me. She always keeps the place too warm. I'll never tell her this – the café is her pride and joy – but I can't spend more than two minutes here without feeling like I'm going to fall asleep.

Kirsty has done well to run a business so successful in Braeside. Plenty of others have tried and failed. It's usually due to the limited clientele during the winter period. The survivors on the high street are a bakery, Spar, a pharmacy and two pubs. Other former shops lie empty. The latest casualty is a gift shop that sold candles, local art and posh honey. It's been cleared out for months but the shopfront window is still emblazoned with an optimistic: 'Welcome!'

The room is filled with conversation and the gentle rattling of plates. Someone has pinned a poster up on the wall: *Have you seen Lily?*

Kirsty is serving eggs on toast to a young English couple. As soon as she sees me, she comes over for a hug. 'Is it Archie you want to see?'

'Yes please,' I say loudly, over the scream of the bean grinder. 'Your husband's working hard.'

Kirsty takes me behind the counter where a spotty youth is making coffee. 'He hates it in that place. We've still never eaten there. Never will at this rate.' She leads me into the kitchen. 'Archie? Ruth wants to talk to you.'

Working in Kirsty's café is practically a rite of passage for young people around here, and her son is no exception. Looking self-conscious in an apron and hairnet, he abandons the counter he was wiping down and heads over to us. Archie has been extremely short-sighted since he was young. He wears glasses with lenses so thick his eyes are magnified.

'This won't take long, Archie. I just wanted to talk to you because I understand Lily's been tutoring you once a week.'

He nods.

'When did you last see her?'

'The day before she went missing.'

'Did she seem okay to you?'

Archie blinks at me. 'Fine. I guess.'

I will never understand how someone as friendly and outgoing as Kirsty could have a child as introverted as Archie. I know he's struggled with bullying over the years, and I suspect this has made him retreat further into himself.

'Other than the lesson, did she talk to you about anything? Did she mention what she was up to?'

'No. But she was texting a lot. She apologised for it.'

'What about the times before that? Has she ever seemed… stressed, anything like that?'

Archie's round eyes flit around the kitchen. For a second I'm convinced he's going to tell me something.

But by the time he looks back at me, the strange expression is gone.

'No,' he says. 'She seemed fine.'

12
Mia

5 June

I TURN MY CLIENT's hand over in mine and begin gently pushing her cuticles with the pointed end of my metal file.

Today the salon is a refuge from the stifling heat outside. The windows are open, letting in the noise from the street in Soho. Electric fans are on full blast. Every ten seconds I feel the relief of cool air rushing over my shoulders before the fan closest to me slowly rotates back the other way.

Hands tell you a lot about a person. The twenty-something-year-old in front of me has hands as smooth as a pebble that's been turned over and over in the sea waves. Her nails are long, strong and pearly. No signs of picking or biting. Whatever she does, it's people-facing but relaxed. Looking good matters. An office job. Communications, maybe. Mid-level seniority; she still has enough spare time in her week to keep up a good nailcare routine. She owns a cat. A dotted arc of dried blood on her wrist is days from disappearing. She is too tidy and sensible to hide a secret cat from her landlord. It's her parents' cat; she lives with them.

We play out the conversation I've already had with three other women today.

'Is it busy for you at the moment?' she says, looking at the identical pairs of nail technicians and customers lined up on either side of us.

'Always is this time of year. Everyone's going on holiday or going to a wedding. Are you going anywhere?'

'I'm going to Greece tomorrow, with my boyfriend.'

'Ooh, exciting.'

'Yeah, I'm living with my parents at the moment—' knew it; I feel a glow of satisfaction as I switch between her fingers, still prodding her cuticles '—so it will be good to just have our own space for a week.'

'I'll bet.'

I move onto her right hand. My colleague has old school R&B playing and it sends me into an almost hypnotic rhythm as I work. Soon I'm thinking back to the interview. The documentary won't be out for another six months, they told me. So long. I need to put out some other content in the meantime. I want – need – another case.

My client's hand tenses in mine. Panic shoots through me as I realise I've poked the cuticle of her right thumb too hard and a tiny bead of blood has emerged in the corner of the nail.

'Sorry about that,' I say quickly, reaching across the table for a cloth.

'That's fine,' she says, but her eyes are wide as I dab away the blood.

I need to focus. For the remainder of the treatment I concentrate on making her manicure as neat as possible. Once the gels have dried, I take her to the counter for payment.

'So sorry to add to your injuries,' I say, once she's finished typing her pin into the card machine. 'My parents had a cat too, I always had scratches growing up.'

She stares at me blankly. 'Hmm?'

'Oh, I noticed your scratch,' I say, smiling and gesturing to her hands.

She looks down at her manicured fingers in surprise.

'Sorry, I'm always noticing little things like that,' I say.

'Oh that,' she says, spotting the mark. 'That was from gardening.'

I feel a jolt of confusion. Gardening? She doesn't look like she gardens. Not with those hands. Surely she would wear gloves? In which case, how did she get the scratch? Heat rises up my neck as my confusion turns to anger. How could I have got that so wrong?

I snap back into the room when I notice her awkwardly fluttering her eyelashes, waiting for me to finish the transaction.

'Oh! I see. Would you like a receipt?'

After the transaction, I watch her leave, biting the inside of my mouth in frustration. Gardening. Of course. Stupid. I should've thought of that.

I've got ten minutes until my next client so I sit at reception and check my phone. A notification pops up. And it's as if the news alert has grabbed me by the front of my top and pulled me inside my phone. Suddenly I can no longer hear polite chatter around me or the hum of the rotating fan blades. Only one thing has my attention now.

Woman from London missing in South West Scotland

She has a beautifully symmetrical face covered in freckles. It feels as though she's walked right past me. I can almost smell her perfume.

Like I said, the case chooses you.

13
Ruth

5 June

I'm on my way to the station when I notice someone waving frantically at me from outside the corner shop in Braeside. A young man I've never seen before. Judging by his enormous backpack, he's only just arrived in town.

I pull over and he comes rushing up as soon as I start lowering the window. He must have walked here all the way from the station wearing that rucksack because he's pink in the face and slightly out of breath as he peers into the car.

'Detective Lindsey, right?' he calls. He's American.

'That's me.'

'Do you have a moment to talk about Lily?' he pants out.

My heart's racing. Has he just come back from hiking? Maybe he's seen her in the mountains.

'Certainly,' I say, getting out and shutting the door behind me. 'Go ahead.'

The man lowers his backpack and rummages around inside. His hand reappears clutching a notebook and pen. He heaves the bag back onto his shoulders.

'Is there anything you can tell me about her disappearance?'

I glance down from his expectant face to his pen, poised on the paper.

'Excuse me?'

'What clues have you found so far?'

I let out an exasperated sigh. 'Oh right, a reporter, are you? Look, you need to contact the press office—'

'No. No, I'm not a journalist. I'm a content creator.'

'Uh huh.' I've never heard that one before.

'I'm investigating the case. Have you seen anyone strange around here lately?'

I blink, taking in the young man's multicoloured trainers and the star tattoo curving up his neck.

'Sorry, you… where you've come from?'

'Oh, I'm from Florida.'

He gives me a tranquil smile.

'You came here,' I say, speaking slowly, 'from Florida.'

'Sure did.'

'To investigate Lily's disappearance.'

'Yep.'

'Right. You don't know Lily?'

'No. Anyway, if you want to have an interview, I think that would be great, you know, me and you, we can talk about the case, just give people the facts, you know. I think people need the facts.'

'The facts?'

He says this as if I have everything needed to find Lily and I've been withholding the information this whole time. When in reality we've been pretty upfront with the public about what little we know – where she was last seen, what she was wearing and what routes she may have taken up the mountain.

'As I said, you can ask our press office any questions.'

He backs away, raising his hand. 'Look, that's okay, that's fine. Like I said, I just think people need the facts. That's why I'm here.'

I watch the man continue walking up into town. This time he takes his phone out of his pocket and holds it at arm's length, filming his surroundings, looking entirely in a world of his own.

14

'SOMETHING WEIRD JUST HAPPENED to me,' I announce to the office.

PC Giblin looks up from his computer screen. 'Was it one of the people from TikTok?'

He makes it sound like they're from another land – another planet.

'I guess so.'

He nods. 'Yeah, they tried talking to me as well. Shot over to me in the café the moment they saw the uniform.'

PC Hughes, an avid fell runner, with the skinny build to match, walks over holding a cup of tea. 'You know, we've had over two hundred calls since we issued the appeal. Very few of them are from local people. We've had calls from London, Manchester, the US, Canada. There's been a lot of engagement on social media as well.'

Giblin nods. 'I was looking at Lily's last Instagram post.'

Giblin, who is in his early thirties, is on his phone constantly so this doesn't surprise me.

He continues: 'When I first checked I swear it had something like two hundred likes. Now it has thirty thousand.'

'You're joking,' I say.

He slides his phone open and hands it to me. I'm looking at her last Instagram reel. Sure enough: 32,000 likes.

'Any patterns in what people are reporting on the helpline?'

Hughes replies: 'One person called in suggesting we look at the men she'd dated—'

'Very helpful,' I scoff.

'Another said we need to investigate whether she was kidnapped by a Russian gangster who wanted her parents' crypto fortune.'

Around the room there are titters, eye rolls, mutterings. But Thompson, standing outside his private office, is unphased. Raising his voice above the noise, he says: 'Getting a missing persons case in the public eye is half the battle. A thousand calls is worth it in my mind.'

A thousand calls. I look around our small team. There's no getting around it. Someone will have to go through the transcripts of every single one, summarising its contents and flagging anything to the team. We'll have to chase up sightings even though we know they're bullshit. I feel angry just thinking about the time we'll waste that could otherwise be spent on genuine leads.

Still. All the more reason to find Lily as quickly as possible.

'So apart from useless calls, what else have you got for me?' I ask.

'We've got access to Lily's financial records,' says Giblin. 'She hasn't used any of her cards since she went to Spar the day she was reported missing.'

Even though I saw this coming, my heart still sinks. So she isn't holed up in some city just to get away from her parents. She's out there somewhere.

I come round to look at Giblin's computer screen as he scrolls through the list.

'Only one large transaction,' he says. 'She withdrew four thousand pounds in cash at the bank three days before she went missing.'

'And this was from her savings?'

'From what looks like her inheritance, yes.'

'Strange,' I mutter.

'It's not that unusual,' says Giblin. 'I keep a couple of hundred underneath my bed in case there's a major blackout.'

'You've been watching too many films,' says Hughes.

'You should too!' Giblin replies.

As Giblin and Hughes debate the importance of holding cash during an apocalypse, I chew my lip. What would Lily need four thousand pounds in cash for? The only thing that comes to mind is travel. Had she taken this with her when she left? Or had she already spent it?

I comb through the list, searching for any other unusual transactions. Then I spot a name I recognise.

'The Anchor? That's far away,' I say. 'Forty minutes' drive from Braeside. In Newbank.'

She went there a month ago, before her family had arrived in town, and again on 26 May.

'Wait,' says Giblin, opening his phone. 'Is this the place?'

He shows a photo on Instagram of Lily posing with a drink in hand, on the same day the first transaction was made in early May.

'Yeah, that's it,' I reply. 'So she must have been out with someone.'

'On a date?'

'Potentially. We'll check it out.'

'Ah,' says the superintendent from the window. 'Here he is. Our new DI. Max Tolmie.'

I join him at the window. It's our saviour. Striding up towards the station, an expensive-looking satchel slung casually over one shoulder, the sun shining on his smooth, wrinkle-free forehead. I know from stalking him on social media last night that he's in his early thirties. But he looks so green he could be 25, if you ask me.

Giblin appears at my shoulder.

'Nice of him to end his grad scheme early to come and help us,' he sniggers.

15

As we drive to the Shorehouse together, Max stares at the rolling hills with confusion, as if he can't quite believe he's here.

'It must have been a while since you had a major crime round here,' he says. 'What is it mainly – agricultural theft?'

I tighten my hands around the steering wheel. Statistically, that is correct but I don't want to reinforce his preconceived notions about living out here.

'You get domestic violence and drugs everywhere.' Changing the subject, I say: 'So you're from Edinburgh? How long have you been a DI there?'

'Four years.'

I detect a note of pride in his voice. I try to ignore the pang of nostalgia in my chest. Sometimes I miss my old obsession with rank. The fixation on the next promotion – the rush of adrenaline when you got there. But I am more my own boss here. In the city, I worked under near constant supervision – now I manage my own time, for the most part.

'You were a DI on the Major Investigations Team in Glasgow, weren't you?' he says.

'Yes.'

'That's cool.'

He doesn't say this in a fawning way. He says it like he's

discovered I'm into the same niche indie band as him – like I've spent my whole career waiting for his approval.

'I came here four years ago,' I add.

'Why did you leave?' he asks.

'Here we are,' I say, turning into the Howards' drive.

Vanessa and Martyn are waiting for us inside. The family liaison officer is perched on the end of their cream sofa, clutching a mug of tea and looking terrified about spilling any.

'This is DI Tolmie,' I say. 'He's going to be investigating the case with me. We just wanted to ask a few more questions if that's all right.'

The couple nod listlessly.

'Does Lily usually come up by herself for a couple of months like this?' asks Max.

'No. It was the first time, actually,' says Martyn. 'I think she'd just started reconnecting with the area.'

'How often did Lily come to Scotland?'

'We used to come up a lot as a family. But this was her first trip here for a long time.'

'Any reason why that changed?'

'I don't know, life got busy, I suppose. Or she just lost appreciation for it. You can fall in and out of love with a place, can't you.'

'Can you remember when she stopped coming up as frequently?'

'Not long after we opened the restaurant, I think,' says Martyn.

'When was that?'

'Three years ago. Almost exactly. That was why we came up this week. To mark three years since we opened.'

Until this moment Vanessa has been staring into the empty fireplace with a lost expression, kneading her hands fitfully in front of her mouth. But Martyn's comment seems to cut through her trance. 'Well, that isn't the only reason we came up,' she says.

She turns to face him, hissing: 'I told you. There was a way to say it, Martyn.'

'A way to say it?' Max repeats carefully.

Vanessa seems to have only just remembered we're here. She gives Max an uncharacteristically sheepish look before continuing: 'We weren't just here to celebrate. We were hoping to talk some sense into Lily. It had been almost a year since she'd stopped teaching. She was done with her travelling and as far as we could tell she was just…'

'Spending her grandfather's inheritance,' Martyn mutters.

'She just needed some direction,' Vanessa interjects through gritted teeth.

'The money wasn't going to last forever.' Martyn directs this at me, like he's imploring me to see sense. 'And really we wanted her to be investing that for her future. So you see we felt we had to intervene.'

'And did you?'

'This is what I'm saying,' replies Vanessa. 'We had a plan about how we were going to address it. We were going to sit her down one morning and show her a few jobs we'd found. We weren't going to criticise her at all. That was the plan. But you just couldn't control yourself, could you?'

She turns to me, her eyes bright with fury. 'At dinner, two nights before she disappeared, he makes some disparaging comment about how there's no money in the arts, she says it's not about that for her, and within five minutes it's all coming out – you accusing her of slouching around, pissing her inheritance up the wall, and she's telling you she never wanted what we wanted for her anyway—'

'That's not why she left, Vanessa,' Martyn growls.

'You drove her away!' Vanessa shrieks. 'That's why she went on that hike. She wanted space, she wanted space from us. If you could have just been soft on her, for once.'

'And this was two nights before she left?' I ask.

Vanessa nods tearfully. The room, with its unlit candles and antique brass chandelier, feels ice-cold. Martyn is completely still. But I have a bad feeling he's just controlling his temper until we've gone.

It's almost a relief when the front door cracks open.

Vanessa straightens up and stretches out her arms. 'Toby!'

Like his sister, Toby is very good-looking – but much less elegant, with a stocky build and a constant frown. He looks despondent as he drops his backpack by the entrance to the room and turns to face us.

'We were hoping to ask you some questions, Toby,' I say.

'Yeah. Okay.'

He sits down next to his mother. She reaches out and squeezes his shoulder, as if reassuring herself that one of her children is still here.

'We've had a look at Lily's financial records,' I say. 'We can see she hasn't used any of her cards since she went to Spar the day she disappeared. We also saw she withdrew four thousand pounds in cash a few days earlier.'

'Four thousand pounds?' Martyn repeats loudly.

'Do any of you know why she would have done that?' I ask.

All three of them stare at me in confusion.

Vanessa turns to her husband. 'What if she was planning to go somewhere, Martyn?' she says, panicking. 'What if someone blackmailed her?'

'Mum,' says Toby, trying to calm her down.

'If any reason comes to mind, just call the station and let us know,' I say. 'Where were you all on the 2nd of June?'

'We were all here,' replies Vanessa.

'Do you have any reason to think Lily might have hurt herself?'

Toby is staring misty-eyed out of the window.

'I think she could have done,' he says.

'No, she wouldn't,' says Martyn sharply.

Ignoring Martyn, I ask Toby: 'Why do you say that?'

'She wasn't in a very good place.'

'Why?'

He shrugs. 'I don't think there's always one single reason, is there? She had a lot on her mind. Worrying about what she wanted to do with her life.'

'That doesn't mean she was a risk to herself, Toby,' snaps Martyn. 'For God's sake.'

'I'm not saying you were the reason, Dad,' Toby says, impatient.

Vanessa and Martyn are avoiding looking at me. I'm starting to understand why Lily might have needed that melatonin to help her sleep here.

16

'Creepy family,' says Max as soon as we're out of earshot of the house.

'Martyn's tone surprised me,' I say, walking back to the car. 'Who cares if Lily was pissing away her inheritance? His daughter's missing.'

Usually parents don't have a single bad word to say about their missing children. Instead, they punish themselves for every trivial family conflict they ever had. Apparently not the case for Martyn.

'Did you say they don't have any security cameras?'

'No.'

'Seems weird,' he says, looking up at the Shorehouse. 'A holiday home worth, I'm guessing, over £1 million. And they don't have cameras?'

I shrug. 'They have a gardener who checks in regularly, maybe they didn't see the need. Besides, officers searched the place. There's nothing.'

'Interesting she stopped coming up so much a few years ago. Do you think something happened?' asks Max.

'Maybe,' I say. 'One for us to ask her friend Georgia.'

Our next stop is the Anchor, in the small coastal town of Newbank. At this time of day, it's almost completely empty apart from an older couple having fish and chips on one of the tables outside, overlooking the bay. We quickly find out they don't have CCTV. Nor does the manager or the bartender remember seeing

Lily in the pub, but they tell us they'll ask someone else who was on shift that day. Our next best hope is the CCTV footage from the street outside and the closest car park.

I find it strange that Georgia didn't seem to know anything about a mystery man, so afterwards we head to the Nag's Head back in Braeside. Walking down the high street, we pass Iain, one of the elderly residents. I introduce him to the new DI then ask him how his wife is doing in the care home. Not well is the answer, and by the looks of things neither is he, living alone. I tell him I'll go round on Saturday afternoon and make a mental note to bring some eggs, bread, that kind of thing. Max spends this entire interaction just standing there like a fart in a trance. Once we part ways and head down the street, he turns and looks at me with faint surprise.

'You know everyone,' he says.

'It's not hard. Give it a couple of weeks and you will too.'

'Is that your job? To check on him?' Max looks as if he's still struggling to process what he just saw. 'Isn't there a social worker who can do that?'

'This isn't Edinburgh. People actually know their neighbours' names here. We look out for each other.'

Max is scanning the street. 'So?'

'So what?'

'Got a hunch? You must do, if you know everyone in Braeside.'

'A lot of people here are good people. I wouldn't say we have many arseholes.'

'Except people sometimes leave dead animals in each other's gardens?' Max is staring at me blankly.

'Well, that's one incident.'

'That's just funny here?' he continues.

I grit my teeth. For some reason, I feel obliged to paint the town in a good light. 'So there's clearly some… resentments,' I say. 'But you've had a look around. It's mainly retired people and a couple of families, right?'

The Nag's Head is by far the best pub in town. Although saying that, there are only two. It's big enough you can find a quiet corner at almost any time of year, even in the summer months when tourists are passing through.

'I met the family who run it this morning,' says Max. 'The Reids?'

'Really?'

He nods. 'This is where I'm staying at the moment.'

'Oh, right.' It hadn't occurred to me he'd base himself here. 'I've heard the rooms are nice.'

'It's central,' Max replies.

Georgia is working behind the bar with her dad. Max inspects the local paper, which lies open on the bar. I catch sight of an advert for a local crematorium right beside one for fishing gear.

Georgia finishes serving an old man a pint and heads over, looking at me with wide, anxious eyes.

'Is there any news?' she asks.

'Sorry, Georgia. No, there isn't. I just wanted to check a couple of things with you.'

'Of course.'

'Did you go with Lily to the Anchor this summer? The pub in Newbank.'

She frowns. 'No.'

'What about Harris?'

'I don't think so. I have trouble making Harris go anywhere that isn't a twenty-minute drive away. So Lily went there?'

'About a month ago. And again on the 26th.'

Georgia still looks bewildered.

I continue: 'You said Lily wasn't seeing anyone. Are you sure about that?'

Georgia frowns. 'Yeah. I mean. As far as I was aware, she wasn't.'

'But she'd have told you if she was?'

'I like to think so. Although she'd been keeping to herself lately. Maybe she just didn't feel like telling me.'

'There was something else we wanted to ask you,' says Max. 'Apparently Lily used to come up here a lot. But she stopped visiting so frequently about three years ago. Was there any reason why?'

Georgia's eyelashes flutter. 'I'm not sure. I guess she was just too busy.'

Declan Reid, her dad, heads down the bar towards us. He is a difficult one to miss, Declan. Six-foot with a large rectangular head, no hair. 'This about Lily, is it? Can I help?'

'Declan, do you remember seeing Lily in here at all?'

'A couple of times with Georgia and Harris.'

'You never saw her on a date?'

'Who's she going to date round here, Ruth? Most people are a hundred-years-old.'

'You get people hiking though, right? Young men.'

'Sorry, Ruth. If she was, I never saw her with anyone.'

'What about on the day she went missing? Did you see anyone acting strangely?'

'On the 2nd of June? It was pretty quiet, to be honest with you. Craig was my only customer for the first couple of hours of the day. He left around lunchtime.' He pauses. 'Not sure Kirsty would be pleased about him drinking on the job, so maybe keep that between us.'

I raise an eyebrow.

He glances around the pub. 'Ruth, there is one thing that's strange. I've seen all sorts here since she went missing. We'll be fully booked up all summer at this rate.'

'Don't you only have four rooms?'

'Still, I've never seen it like this.'

Once Declan and Georgia have returned to the other customers, I say to Max, 'These trips to the Anchor are bugging me.'

'After we get the data from her dating apps, we might see she matched with someone out of town who suggested that pub.'

'Yeah, but why wouldn't she mention that to her friend here?'

He shrugs. 'I don't tell my friends whenever I go on a date.'

'Well, women usually do. Especially if they're living by themselves like Lily was.'

My head's so frazzled, I'm no longer thinking clearly. I check my phone.

'Well, it's six o'clock. Want to get a drink? Celebrate your first day.'

He blinks at me like I've just suggested we throw ourselves into the path of an oncoming car.

Then he realises I'm serious and tries to recover. 'Oh, I'm actually busy.' After a moment, he adds: 'I have a video call with a friend.'

We stare at each other.

'Right. Have a good one then.'

17

6 June

'And then he goes "oh, I'm actually busy."'

I wiggle my hips in an awkward dance.

Encircling me in her beach towel, Kirsty narrows her eyes with suspicion.

'Yeah, right,' she says.

'Exactly. Busy in the town where he doesn't know anyone.' I pull up the rest of my swimsuit. 'Okay, done.'

We switch, me holding up the towel for her as she shimmies out of her jeans. The sun is hidden by the clouds this morning and a cool wind crosses the beach, spreading goosebumps over my exposed skin. It may be summer but it doesn't always feel like it here.

'So he clearly realises I know he doesn't have any plans and he goes, "I have a video call with a friend."'

'That could be true, I guess.'

'No way. And even if he does have a video call scheduled – which he almost certainly doesn't – he has time for a quick drink. He's literally staying in the pub. Upstairs.'

Kirsty tugs off her t-shirt and shakes her head in disapproval. 'The drink is obligatory when you're new.'

'I know, right.' I take the t-shirt and hand her the swimsuit. 'I just forgot the arrogance of these city boys. You'd think they were here to teach an uncontacted tribe how to make fire.'

'Little does he know you were investigating murders when he was in nappies,' she says, manoeuvring into her swimsuit.

'Hey, the age gap's not that big.'

She straightens up, finished, and I release the towel as she shakes out her hair before scooping it up into a high bun. I take a hairband from my wrist and start tying mine up as well.

'He does sound like an arsehole,' Kirsty says. 'But give him a chance. It was his first day.'

Gathering up her hair makes the skin tighten around her eyes. To my surprise, I see Kirsty is smirking to herself.

'What?'

'Nothing, it's just—' Hair up, she shoots me a sideways glance, amused. 'You hate new people.'

I accidentally pull a hair from its roots, pinching my scalp.

'What?' I scrunch up my face. 'No, I don't.'

'Yeah you do,' she says, putting her hands on her hips. 'That's why you moved somewhere with a rapidly declining population.'

'So did you.'

She shakes her head. 'Completely different. My husband dragged me here, as you know. You came willingly.'

I'd been enjoying ranting about Max but now I'm confused and annoyed.

'That's ridiculous,' I say. 'I like new people.'

But Kirsty is looking out to the waves.

'Ready?' she says, adjusting her shoulder straps.

I nod and we advance down the empty beach. Fragments of shell and stone dig into the soles of my bare feet. Neither of us hesitate before wading into the water. I'm a strong believer that there is no point edging in gradually, waiting for your body to adjust. It is better – more fun – to plunge yourself in.

Immediately I shoot off in one direction, my breath coming out in short sharp gasps. I don't slow down until I start to feel it: a little ball of warmth growing in my stomach – as if I've just gulped down a bowl of hot soup – that means my body is generating heat. For the next thirty minutes, the cold will be gone. I will belong to this world, not the land.

I roll over, swimming on my back, and feel the stress of the last few days lift away. Kirsty moves gracefully through the water towards me. The hills rear up all around Sunkhead Bay, sheltering us. You can just about see the town nestled at the base of the mountains, peeking out over the surrounding forests. The mountains look paint-splattered with purple heather and rust-coloured grass. This for me is the best view of Braeside. There is the church steeple. The blue window frames and grey slate roof of Kirsty's café. Sheep, tiny black-and-white flecks on the hillside. Everything in its place.

I take in a deep breath of salty air. For these precious moments the world is still. This is our home, I think. Our town.

Kirsty's comment plays on my mind as I drive home for a warm shower before work.

Maybe it's true. Maybe I have become stuck in my ways since moving here. But it's hard not to. Living alone, you get used to having full control over your routine. Especially in a place like Braeside, where so little happens. It couldn't be more different from Glasgow. In Glasgow, the threat of danger was like static electricity. Hovering constantly around the edges. I would get home late from a homicide investigation to a neighbour's Facebook post saying they'd been burgled down the road. I would put Molly to bed and check the locks on the doors twice in one evening. I would wake up two, three times a night to any disturbance outside, from sirens to foxes to the sound of a car idling. It wasn't the worst neighbourhood. I was just alert to the dangers in a way Connor wasn't, in a way I hadn't been until Molly came along.

Funny to think now. We never were burgled. Neither of us ever got mugged coming home or had our phones stolen. None of the scenarios I played out in my head ever came true. There was no trouble at all besides that which I investigated every day as part of my job. And that which I let walk straight through my front door and into my home one summer.

I remember thinking that I didn't like his mouth. Long and lipless, like a sculptor had put a knife in a head of clay and sliced sideways in an uneven line.

He didn't drink tea so I'd given him one of the Diet Cokes usually reserved for early morning starts when I didn't have time to make a coffee. For some reason that sticks in my mind. The cold aluminium can perspiring under my fingertips as I handed it over. Him taking small delicate sips on our sofa.

He had been polite and quiet. I remember afterwards telling Connor that he seemed older than he was. Something about the confident hand on her knee. His directness when he answered questions, like Connor probing into why he wasn't going to university: 'Academia's just not the one for me,' with a calm shake of his head. And also, I think, her body language, body tucked towards his, head attentively tilted, willing him to make a good impression. Maybe it would be him, I thought. You never know. I always wanted her to find someone strong, and this young man seemed strong.

I wish I could go back. I wish I could go back knowing what I know now.

I park up outside the house and shake the thought from my mind.

18

MAX HAS HIS HEAD buried in a file when I arrive at my desk.

'What's that?' I say, taking off my jacket and placing it on the back of my chair.

Max sits at the desk facing mine. He looks up and I catch a glimpse of the inside of his file. A photo shows a hare's hind legs lying rigid in dark grass.

'I've been speaking to Chloe, the Wildlife Crime Liaison Officer,' he says.

Here we go. I suppress a sigh as I sit down.

'Can you just talk me through what evidence you gathered? Whoever left this hare, they just vanished without a trace?'

'There was one piece of evidence. Footprints along the wall surrounding the Howards' garden. Men's size nine. Walking boots by the looks of it. They have a distinctive hexagonal logo on the heel. Neither Martyn, Toby nor the Howards' gardener have size nine feet so these belonged to someone outside the family. They could have been left by a delivery guy or something, but where they were planted was just right for someone throwing this hare over the wall.'

'And some of the animals had been shot, right?'

'The later ones.'

'So we need to find men in the area with shooting experience and identify someone with a matching shoe print,' says Max decisively.

'I didn't realise you were sent here to help solve the Great Bunny Murder of Braeside.'

His chair squeaks as he leans back to glare at me from across our desks. 'I don't understand why you're not taking this more seriously,' he says. 'Someone starts leaving dead animals at a family's home address, their daughter goes missing, and you don't think there could be a connection? You don't think that's concerning?'

'You may not have picked this up in your first twenty-four hours here,' I say, 'but the Howards weren't very popular, all right? If we found a dead rabbit in Lily's room on the day she disappeared, then fair enough, there's your connection. But right now, they're two completely separate incidents. We don't even know if Lily's disappearance involves a third party.'

Max pokes his tongue in his cheek and stares out the window but says nothing more. Relieved, I log in to my computer, wondering if the council has come back to us with CCTV footage from the car park near the Anchor. Not yet is the answer.

But then Max looks back at me, eyes narrowed. 'Are you sure you don't have an idea who might have done it?'

I squint at him. 'Are you suggesting,' I say, 'that I'm protecting someone because they're my friend?'

'No. It's just you seemed pretty friendly with everyone in town yesterday.'

'Seriously?' I say.

I grab my empty mug from my desk and get up, heading for the kitchen, bristling with anger. Unbelievable. Our second day and he accuses me of hiding information from my own team. Is it too early to ask the superintendent to swap someone else in?

As I pass Thompson's office, I notice movement out of the corner of my eye. He's waving at me through the glass walls. I poke my head inside.

'Yes?'

'The Howards are doing a public appeal for information this evening. I want at least one of you there.'

I nod. 'I can make it.'

No point inviting Max, he'll be too busy measuring the shoe size of everyone in town.

'It's important to show support for the family,' Thompson explains. 'But I also want you to see who else turns up. You never know, if someone was involved, they might be there. Make a note of any unusual behaviour.'

'Right,' I say.

I leave his office and continue carrying my mug to the kitchen. This is the first I've heard about a public appeal. Is anyone I know going? I use my free hand to check my phone. One message. My insides dissolve.

I haven't seen his name on my phone screen in years and the rush of nostalgia catches me off guard.

With a shaky thumb, I scroll down to briefly unfurl the whole text. I'm surprised he's written so much. But I can't bring myself to read the message in full so instead I scan the words, checking for any sign of an emergency. Finding none, I close the screen and put the phone in my pocket.

Then a memory hits me so hard it knocks the breath out of me.

I'm running. But I can't keep up with Connor as he pelts down the street, away from the court, his tie flying out behind him. Stopping briefly, I pull off my heeled shoes and toss them onto the pavement. Then I keep running in my socks, swerving to avoid passersby. I ignore the stares. I have to join Connor. Up ahead, he reaches the roadside where cars are slowing down in front of a red light. He singles theirs out and beats his palms against the window, roaring something inside. He's still shouting as the light turns green and the car pulls away. I watch it shrink into the distance, taking my heart with it. I'm half-aware of Connor yelling out one final time before reaching up and clutching the back of his head in despair.

When I get to the small kitchen in the station, there's no one there and I place my mug on the counter and lay my palm flat beside it. I take long, deep breaths.

I have enough to deal with right now without this as well.

19

IT IS THE KIND of sunset that appears to fill the sky with smoke and fire. I wait with the reporters by the dark obelisk that is Braeside's First World War memorial and look towards the light.

The search has ended for the day and the pedestrianised zone beside the Nag's Head is gradually filling up with people. Scrappy figures trudge up from the high street, some carrying empty water bottles, others with their arms around their children's shoulders. The TV crews have their cameras trained on the memorial, where everyone will finally hear the Howards speak in public.

Silence falls as their 4x4 rolls into a nearby parking space. But it ends the moment Vanessa's blonde head emerges from the car. The air is filled with the frantic clacking of the cameras. White flashes rain down on the couple, casting long shadows against the stone walls of the neighbouring houses as they walk side-by-side into the camera crews' lighting setup. It strikes me how small and out of place they look in this theatrical settling, like two reluctant children who've been forced to narrate the school play.

Vanessa swallows and lifts her chin, looking directly into one of the cameras. Even her tanned complexion looks washed out in the bright lights, and her eyes like chips of blue ice.

'I just wanted to personally thank you all for coming out here every day and searching for our daughter,' she says. 'It really does mean the world to us.'

A photographer bends down on one knee to get a closer shot, crossing the invisible line we've drawn between the family and the press. I shoot him a warning look and he steps back sheepishly.

Vanessa continues: 'Lily has now been missing for five days. We are extremely concerned for her well-being. We just want her to come home.'

Martyn speaks up, his voice a low rumble in contrast to Vanessa's. 'If you've walked around the Devil's Hand since the 2nd of June, please think about who else you saw walking. If you live in Braeside or the surrounding area – or you've recently driven through it – please check any dashcam footage or security cameras you have. Any sightings of Lily or someone acting strangely could help the police with their search.'

I scan the crowd. The lightning flashes from the cameras bounce off their faces. Craig and Kirsty, Declan, Georgia and Harris – they've all come out to show their support for the family. Their jaws are clenched, their eyes shining with emotion. Most of the people here have probably never even spoken to Vanessa and Martyn in their lives. But here they are, in solidarity. It is a beautiful moment. A reminder that Lily is still a part of this community.

Something catches my eye like a snag in a pattern. At the front of the crowd, but tucked away to the far right, are Stuart and Claire Marsh. They are holding hands but Stuart is watching Vanessa and Martyn with a haunted expression, lips pressed together. He looks like he is on the verge of crying.

A buzz in my pocket knocks me off focus. I retreat towards the houses, only answering once I know I'm out of earshot.

It's Max. 'I just wanted to let you know straight away,' he says.

'Go for it,' I say, looking back at the strange scene.

Vanessa and Martyn have stopped speaking. People start to trickle away, but the lights and the cameras follow the couple all the way back to their car.

'We've got the CCTV from the car park near the Anchor on the 26th of May. We can see Lily in someone's car. We've got the vehicle registration number. It's Stuart Marsh's car.'

20

7 June

I ARRIVE AT THE Marshes' house early, before Stuart can leave for work. The door opens to reveal Claire, dressed in a maxi dress with her hair freshly blow-dried. My throat tightens.

'Morning, Ruth. Everything okay?'

'Could I speak to your husband please?'

'Stuart?' She blinks in surprise. 'Uh, yeah, of course.'

She calls his name into the house, her voice filled with uncertainty.

I hear floorboards creaking and Stuart comes rushing downstairs. But all the urgency drains out of him when he sees me. Now he's moving in slow motion and I can tell from the horror in his eyes that he knows exactly why I'm here.

Claire is frozen in place with her hand still holding the door open. 'What's this about?' she asks me.

'I can't say at the moment, I'm afraid.'

I head towards the back garden with Stuart. A toy car and a plushie dinosaur serve as tripping hazards on our way through the kitchen extension. Their son Brodie's drawings cover the fridge as well as a huge calendar filled with birthdays, sleepovers and family get-togethers. I have the horrible feeling that I am about to set off a bomb in the middle of this family's house. Blow up the happy chaos that Claire spends every day of her life trying to bring into order.

Stuart walks out first. He is silent but I can tell he's panicking. The moment I slide the glass doors shut, his eyes drift behind me. Looking over my shoulder, I see that Claire has come into the kitchen for a glass of water. Although her gaze is down, I can see her face is creased with worry as she turns on the tap.

I wait til she's gone before starting.

'Where were you at seven o'clock on the 26th of May?'

'I was at Craig's,' he says immediately.

'Don't lie to me.'

I realise that he's shaking. 'Please don't do this, Ruth,' he breathes out.

'Do you want to go somewhere else to talk about this?'

He shakes his head. 'I don't want people to see me with you – in the car.'

'All right. Here, then.'

He places his hands on his hips, trying to control his breathing.

'How did you meet Lily?'

'I never paid her any mind until this summer. Didn't even know who she was at first. Until she told me her name.'

'Where? When?'

His eyelids flutter as he realises how this is going to go down. With me forcing him to spell out every humiliating detail.

'You know the viewing point near The Lighthouse?

I nod.

'Well, I like to go there sometimes when I need a break from things. Which is…' he lets out a frustrated sigh, 'fairly often at the moment.'

I'm guessing by this he means a young kid, work, maybe marital issues. But I don't want to interrupt his train of thought so I stay quiet.

'I went up one evening after work. And she was there. Sat on a blanket on the grass, painting the coast. I said something like, "That's really good." You know, it *was*. And it was just us two there, it felt weird not to say anything. I wasn't trying to come onto her.

'We got chatting for a bit. And that's when I realised who she was. She said she was in town for a few months, just taking a break. Then as I said I should be heading back, she scribbled something down on the corner of her sketchbook and tore it off. Stood up and handed it to me. It had her number on it. She said, "Listen, I don't really know many people here, so if you ever want to get a drink, let me know." That's when I could've said, "I'm married." *Should've* said,' he corrects. 'But I didn't.'

'When was this?'

'About a month ago. I told myself it was nothing. That I'd been tired and that's why I hadn't said I was married. But obviously that wasn't true. Over the next few days, I couldn't stop thinking about her. I hadn't had that kind of attention since I was a teenager. I think that's what it was.' He shook his head and looked over the fence. 'God, I'm so pathetic.'

I don't say anything. It's obvious from my manner that I agree. As Stuart stares into the trees, I study him. He's wearing a short-sleeved t-shirt that shows off the well-defined muscles in his arms. He's about 30 and he takes good care of himself. From Lily's perspective, in a town with few people under 40, he was probably the most eligible date she'd seen in months.

'How many times did you meet up?'

'Does it matter?' he says impatiently.

'Yes. If someone tells me they saw Lily with a man in a pub last month, I need to know it was you before I waste my time looking into it.'

He rubs his forehead. 'It was just four times.'

'Where?'

'We went to the Anchor. I knew the chances of someone recognising me there would have been slim. Another time we went for a coastal walk. The next time we went to her house.'

'Can you tell me the exact dates?'

'Not off the top of my head. I can look through my phone and work it out.'

'Did you have sex?'

'Christ, Ruth.'

'It matters.'

'Yeah, we did. You need to know what positions as well?'

'That's three times. Where'd you see her the fourth time?'

'The last time I saw her was the 26th of May. We met up for a drink at the Anchor again. About half an hour in, it started going wrong.

'She asked about my weekend and I said I was at my mum's. Immediately she says, "Hang on. You were at a friend's birthday, weren't you?" I was having to constantly make up reasons why I couldn't see her and explain what I was up to.

'I just said I'd misremembered. But she wouldn't let it go. "How do you forget something like that?" I'd even texted her on the day saying I was at this fictional birthday party, and she was going through these texts, showing me. Nothing would get her off the subject. Finally she says, "Let's just go. I don't want another drink." She's totally quiet as we head back to the car. And just as we're about to drive off, she looks at me and says, "You're with someone, aren't you?"

'It was awful. I didn't lie. I said, "Yeah, I'm married." I said I had kids as well. She looked at me like I was—' He shakes his head at the memory. 'I knew it was over. She said, "I can't do this. I don't want to get involved in someone else's marriage." She was furious. Said she felt like she'd been tricked into ripping up a family. I felt sick. I didn't even think about trying to fix things between me and her. I looked at the bay and thought about everything I'd risked for this. I wanted to scrub it all out.

'She said I should tell Claire. And I said, "Not a chance, no way." We argued about that for a while. Then… this might sound weird but we started talking about why I'd done it. She was very caring. She wanted to know what had made me do something like this. And I said I thought I was bored. I've spent half my life doing the same thing. You know what it's like here. It's stuck in time. I drove her home after that. We said our goodbyes. That's the last time I saw her. I swear Ruth.'

'Did she threaten to tell your wife?'

'No.' His eyes are still filled with panic. 'Ruth, please don't tell her. It was just a blip. I'll never do anything like that again.'

I let out a sigh of frustration, looking over the fence into the trees. Claire is a good person. She comes swimming sometimes with me and Kirsty. She doesn't deserve this.

'What do you think she's imagining right now, Stuart? If you don't tell her, I'll have to.'

He nods weakly. 'Okay. I will.'

I can't tell if he means it.

I continue: 'In the time you saw Lily, did she talk about wanting to go for a walk at the Devil's Hand?'

'She mentioned it. She would ask me about walks in the area and I told her I'd never tried that one but it was supposed to be beautiful.'

'Did she say anything about wanting to walk there on the 2nd of June?'

'No.'

I glare at him. 'You know what I'm going to ask you. What were you doing on the 2nd of June?'

'I went to see my mum. She lives about a fifteen-minute drive from Braeside. I can give you her address. I left early, at around nine, and got back after lunch.'

'And Claire?'

'She was at home looking after Brodie.'

I look back into the house. 'Is it all right if I take a look around?'

He nods, avoiding eye contact. I can tell he wants me gone.

As I head inside, I check my phone. 7 June. Tomorrow is the day. I feel the same thing I feel every year. A knot right underneath my ribcage.

21

Max and I let ourselves into Thompson's office. There's a new photo on his desk that shows one of his daughters clutching the family's border collie.

I nod at the photo. 'How's Milo getting on?'

The superintendent's daughters have been petitioning for a dog for years.

Thompson looks solemn. 'He's been diagnosed with separation anxiety,' he says.

'Don't all dogs have that?' says Max.

Thompson shakes his head. 'Milo is a severe case.'

'Poor thing,' I say. 'I'm not sure the cat even notices I'm home half the time.'

'We'll need to make some adjustments to our lifestyle,' says Thompson. 'But you know, the girls adore him.'

He sounds secretly disappointed the vet didn't suggest immediate euthanasia. He shakes his head, dismissing the conversation, and puts his hands on the desk. 'So… what do we think?'

'I took a look around the property. There's no signs of a struggle and I didn't find anything that looked like it belonged to Lily. But we'd need to do a more thorough check to be sure.

'On the day Lily went missing, Stuart claims he was seeing his mum from nine o'clock to early that afternoon. So we'll need to check his alibi.

'There's something else as well. Stuart had a copy of the local paper on his table. He put an ad in the paper about his parents' place. He's been trying to sell it since his dad died. It's an old farm cottage.'

Thompson nods, understanding. But Max squints at me.

'Why is that interesting?' he says.

'It's interesting,' I say, 'because it's up in the hills, about half an hour by foot from where we think Lily started walking.'

Max raises his eyebrows.

I hate how excited they both look now.

'Look, I know Stuart and I just can't see it,' I say.

'We know he's a liar, don't we?' Thompson points out.

'But I don't think he's violent,' I reply. 'It sounded like they ended on good terms, and I believe him. One other thing.' I look at Max. 'I checked Stuart's shoes when I was looking around. Size ten. So he isn't our bunny killer, you'll be disappointed to hear.'

Max glares at me.

Thompson ignores this. 'Even if you don't see it, he's the first suspect we've had. Talk to Stuart's mum. Trace his car's movements on the 2nd of June, and the days before. And get a warrant to search both properties. That might come back today if we're quick. Then report back to me first thing tomorrow morning.'

'I'm not here tomorrow morning, sir,' I say.

He stares at me with astonishment.

'Annual leave,' I explain. 'It's been in the calendar for months.'

'Can you move it? Time is precious right now.'

'Hospital appointment,' I lie. 'I'm sorry. I have to go.'

For a moment Thompson's eyes bore into mine. Then he says: 'Okay. Max, you deal with it.'

'That's fine,' Max replies.

Thompson returns to his computer, disgruntled. Max and I head back to our desks. I try to read my emails but they dissolve in front of me. I hate lying and I know I sounded desperate there, unlike myself. I glance at Max and notice he's avoiding my gaze – embarrassed for me maybe, or confused by my outburst.

Forget about it, I think.

Tomorrow is a day I can't afford to miss.

22

8 June

It's an hour-and-a-half drive to the meeting place.

The presents sit on the backseat in an open cardboard box. I wrapped them last night in turquoise wrapping paper and finished each one with a golden bow. Two of them I had to wrap twice. The Sellotape had bunched up and the paper creased on one side, forcing me to start again.

The meeting place is an almost-always empty road shielded on one side by a hill covered in heather. Up ahead, a small old bridge made out of grey stone curves over a rushing river. After that the road disappears behind a crowd of conifer trees. I park on the roadside and wait.

He is never on time, which I'm certain is deliberate – a power move. But I think he also slows down and waits ahead of the bridge, behind the trees, peering through just to make sure I've arrived alone.

Ten minutes pass. I sit up straight when I see his dusty car emerge over the bridge. He parks on the roadside some 15 metres ahead of me. I peer through his windscreen, desperate to see if anyone's in the passenger seat beside him. But no, there's no one there. There never is. And when he gets out, he gets out alone, only one car door opening and closing. Even though this happens every time, my heart sinks.

He walks towards my car with a bag for life folded up in one hand. I scan him for signs they're struggling. But he looks the same as ever. Blue jeans and a fashionable jacket. His hair, the colour of dirty straw, lies flat on his head.

I roll down the window. 'How are you?'

'I'm well, thank you.'

'The presents are on the back seat.'

And so the annual ritual begins. He peers past me into the car, then steps to the side and opens the back door.

He picks up the card first. He takes out a penknife and slices open the envelope. Reads my card by the side of the road with the officiousness of a passport inspector. Satisfied, he places it back inside the envelope and turns his attention to the presents.

I stare into the dark-green trees in the near distance and listen to the sound of his penknife gliding through the wrapping paper. One by one, he checks each gift – unpicking Sellotape, opening cardboard boxes and feeling along seams – before carefully resealing everything. I never understand exactly what he is looking for. Tracking devices, I assume. Secret messages. Telephone numbers.

One year I bought her jewellery. But I became afraid he would either sell it or say it was from him. These remain possibilities with every present I bring. Now I try and pick things strategically that he would clearly not think to buy himself. This year, I have bought luxury haircare, two novels, a jewellery box and a painting of Braeside bought from a local artist.

I've passed the test. He loads the presents into the carrier bag and shuts the door behind him.

I lean towards the rolled-down window.

'How is she?'

I ask every time and every time I get the same response.

'She's doing very well,' he says. He thinks for a moment, then adds: 'She doesn't use Facebook anymore.'

'What?'

'Facebook. You message her sometimes on Facebook. But we don't have social media anymore.'

I don't know what to say. I know he reads every message I send. But I'm shocked he would almost own up to it like this.

'Is email okay?'

'Email's fine.'

'Will you please tell her that I would love to see her?'

I ask this every time as well.

He nods.

I continue: 'There's a pub in the town near here, about fifteen minutes away. It's well-reviewed. Does very good food. If this is convenient for you, we could meet there – the three of us. I'll pay, of course.'

He stares at me with his slate-coloured eyes. In these moments he is almost soft. Because he is at his most comfortable right now. In control.

'I'll let her know,' he replies.

Once I'm close to home I follow the stretch of coastline. There is no wind today. The sea is as flat and reflective as a sheet of steel. I wonder sometimes if you can die from hate.

Months after she left, she had been caught on a CCTV camera in a fish and chip shop. The relief I felt when I saw that grainy footage of her in a grey cardigan, studying the menu behind the bar, was like nothing I've felt before or since. But it raised a hundred questions. Why hadn't she called home? Was she with him? Was that why she hadn't called – was he stopping her?

The sergeant on the case tracked her down and, after a brief phone call, got her to agree to a meeting one-on-one. It had the impact of closing the case and breaking my heart into a thousand pieces.

Yes, she was with her boyfriend.

Yes, she was fine.
No, she didn't want to speak to her mum.
No, she wouldn't be coming home.

23

I SPLASH COLD WATER on my face in the bathroom. Then I run a hand through my hair, trying to banish the last few hours from my mind. Now I'm back home, with a hungry Douglas circling my ankles, I can start to forget. But what I really need is to get out. Clear my head.

I set off on a walk that takes me across farmland, fields of bracken and through dense woods. Left to my own devices, I could walk all day. When I was living in Glasgow and work became too much, I used to come here and walk until I'd flushed the city out of my system.

But today my walk isn't recreational. My eyes scan the vegetation constantly for items of Lily's clothing. I'm half-convinced that at any moment I'll see a pale hand lying motionless beneath the ferns. Other people in town haven't stopped searching for her – so how, in good conscience, can I?

I move deeper into the woods. Here the trees are short, so the canopy starts not far above your head. The forest floor is carpeted with spongy, emerald-green moss, interrupted only by leaf litter and a single fungus, fairy-tale red.

I stand still, breathing in the damp smell of the trees. These are so old that their bark has fissured and cracked like the skin of an elephant. I have always loved it here. The closeness of the trees. The solitude. The feeling you could be the only person in the world.

A twig snaps somewhere up ahead. I follow the sound until I see the sliced-up figure of a person between the trees. A white t-shirt. Yellow shorts. Red cap.

Suddenly my attention is hyperfocused on this person up ahead. I walk over the uneven ground towards them. The gaps between the trees widen, allowing me to see them in full. It's a young man, probably in his twenties. Head tilted back, staring up at something in the canopy.

And then I realise where we are.

It's the tree from Lily's Instagram. What was the caption? *Found the most beautiful tree in Scotland.* And it is a beauty – a yew tree with multiple trunks and thick branches winding up into the canopy. It is covered in baby blue ribbons.

As I approach, he pulls out his phone, holds it at arm's length and – to my horror – snaps a selfie with the now instantly recognisable tree in the background.

Suddenly he spots me. I hold up my badge and he recoils, pocketing his phone. As I approach, he straightens up, face now flushed with embarrassment.

'What are you doing?' I ask.

'Oh – I'm not – sorry, I just wanted to see it for myself.'

I squint at him, then at the tree. The ribbons hang down like vines. Visitors have left bouquets of yellow and white flowers at the base of the trunk, where they sit discolouring beside placards with handwritten notes. *Come home, Lily*, reads one.

'Can I get your name please?'

His eyes widen in alarm. 'Isaac Morton.'

'And you're from?'

'Leicester.'

I make a note on my phone. 'Long way to travel,' I say. 'Did you know Lily?'

'No. I just wanted to help.'

And take pictures? I almost say, but I bite my lip.

'Can I go now?' he asks.

I nod. He steps around me carefully, like a deer creeping past a sleeping dog.

As I watch him stumble into the forest – disappearing and reappearing behind tree trunks, until I can only make out a fleeting glimpse of his white t-shirt – a hole opens up in my chest. I'll ask someone to check him out when I get to the station, of course. But deep down I believe him. He's just another true crime tourist. It bothers me that I can't get away from them even here, in this lonely place.

What possesses these people to come to the Devil's Hand? This is where a chasm opened up and swallowed a woman whole. And all anyone wants to do is drive up to peer over the edge.

I had planned on following the loop round. But I decide to keep walking towards the mountain range. So many ribbons on that tree. This place must be crawling with them.

And sure enough, as I emerge from the forest and into a tussocky field on the south side of Brecken Head, one of the smaller peaks in the Devil's Hand, I find them. Packs of walkers following the route Lily took. Some of them carrying GoPros on selfie sticks, others stopping to take photographs on their phones. It's a swarm.

And that's when I see her.

24
Mia

8 June

I LOWER MY PHONE.

Something about the way she's standing tells me she's police. Maybe it's the posture. Dead straight. Militaristic.

I knew she was there because I felt the burning sensation of a person's eyes on my skin. I had turned around to take a picture of the golden curve of the hillside rolling down beneath me, the coast glittering in the distance, and there she was. At the bottom of Brecken Head. A lone figure staring up at me. Even from here I can tell she's not smiling. She has an intensity that makes my stomach squirm and my skin catch fire. I feel like an insect under a magnifying glass.

As soon as I saw that first news story in the salon about Lily's disappearance, I was hooked. After my shift finished, I went home and read everything I could about it. One of the first things I did was go looking for a forum. If a case has attracted any interest, there'll be a thread – and sure enough, I found one. The latest post was seven-minutes-old.

HoundoftheBaskervilles: based on the details surrounding Lily's disappearance and the weather conditions, I have analysed the situation and I think the most likely cause of death is death by heat stroke

Puzzlez001: we don't even know she is dead
MissMarple77: it is easy to get someone alone up in those hills

Then I went on TikTok and searched for her name. She was everywhere. I didn't know how I'd missed her. Videos appeared of random university students saying they were going to buy a train ticket and search for her. Some of them were there already. Filming themselves traipsing through beautiful countryside. Envy bubbled up inside me. I knew this case was mine. I needed to act quickly.

There was just the small issue of the salon. I called my manager and explained I wouldn't be able to work my next few shifts. I said it was for personal reasons but I kept my voice low and my explanation vague. Hopefully it sounded like I'd experienced a death in the family or a mental breakdown. She seemed pissed off – the salon was already short-staffed. But she accepted what I was saying and told me to call in a few weeks' time.

When I got off the call, my hands were trembling. It felt risky abandoning the job like this. But I had no idea how long I'd be gone for. Lily could be found tomorrow or in a few months' time for all I knew. And I'd prepared for this exact situation. I'd saved up some money for an investigation like this.

I bought a one-way ticket to Carlisle. From there I boarded another train and waited half an hour for a bus which then spent another 30 minutes crawling through the remote countryside towards Braeside. By the time I arrived, I was desperate to get moving.

The photographs I had seen showed a peaceful town. But I stepped off the bus into a crowd of people. There were police officers, reporters and – I assumed from their youthful faces and weather-inappropriate clothing – out-of-towners like me who'd turned up to join the search. It looked like a film set. As I dragged my wheelie case up the high street, I heard a burst of noise from a police radio somewhere in the crowd. The atmosphere was electric.

The walk to the hostel was longer than I had expected. By the time I arrived, it was late and I was exhausted. The number of travellers in the reception only added to my sense of stress. Because I knew they were all up for the same reason I was. I retreated to my room, which was completely featureless apart from the window looking onto the hills.

It is very important for me, once I start working on a case, to schedule in time for a cry. I open photos of the victim on my laptop, photos of their family, and if there's video footage yet of the family's pleas for help I start playing that too, out of my earphones – the sound of the mother crying, begging someone to come forward – and I try to imagine I'm part of that family, and my son or my brother has gone missing. I'll focus on it until it feels real, until my eyelids are swelling and I'm crying like a baby at the foot of my bed, hands over my face, feeling like the world is this terrible dark place and I'm falling into it. Afterwards, it's like I've been cleansed.

But this time a notification on my phone interrupted my crying. Lily's mother had uploaded a video from her garden. I searched for similarities with her daughter but struggled to find any. Vanessa was more angular, with steeply arched eyebrows and a fake tan. As she addressed the camera, she held herself with poise but her trembling voice betrayed her emotion.

'If you saw something, or if you know anything about where she might be right now, please come forward. Even if it seems small, it could really help us find our daughter.'

She drew in a shaky breath before continuing.

'If you're with Lily, please let her come home. Please don't hurt her. She's a good person.'

That got me. I pulled a tissue out of the box perched on the bedside table and blew hard into it.

'The only thing we want is to find Lily safe and well, as soon as possible. That's why I'm giving a fifty thousand pound reward to whoever provides information that proves critical in finding our daughter.'

My crying ebbed into sniffles. The room swam around me as I contemplated the number. Fifty grand. I could give up working for the salon, at least for a little. Go travelling. Maybe make a true crime documentary.

Feeling rejuvenated, I looked at Lily's Instagram through a more analytical lens. Lily was prolific there, which made my job easier. From someone who posted so regularly, it was striking to see her digital life come to an abrupt end.

As I scrolled back through her photos, yearning filled my chest. I found one post from several years ago – a carousel showcasing her holiday in Braeside. Lily on the hills, drinking cocktails with her mum, swimming in the sea with her brother. *Home, sweet home* read the caption. There were thousands of likes. Lily's posts usually performed well but this was exceptional. That was because distant friends and mourners had come here to pay their respects. I clicked on the comments. *Praying she gets home safe*, said one. *The poor family*, said another.

I opened a spreadsheet on my laptop, navigated back up to the top of her Instagram, and began cataloguing the users who liked and commented on her posts most frequently, in order. It was boring work. But after an hour, I'd got through about thirty posts. I looked at the users ranked at the top of the sheet. Some names I recognised as those of her friends and family. Others I didn't. I looked through their profiles. Were they friends of the past? Hangers-on? Weird internet stalkers? I had no idea. But once I had a sense of her social network, it'd be easier to identify anyone strange.

Satisfied, I saved and closed the spreadsheet. It was eleven o'clock at night. I took one last look at Lily's smile, shining through the screen, before getting ready for bed. A tree gently rattled its branches against the side of the hostel, like a hand scraping the window, asking to be let in.

I got up early the next day, hoping to get a head start on the others. I picked out a cute yellow sports bra and paired it with blue-grey leggings. This seemed like a good opportunity to show off my midriff on camera.

I usually have a smoothie in the morning to increase my fruit and vegetable count. But there was nothing like that in the hostel's dining area – just fried food and baked beans – so I settled instead for oats, the least offensive breakfast item there.

Then I started walking to the range of hills called the Devil's Hand. The grass here was thick with springy moss and mountain flowers. I'd never searched for a missing person in real life. In fact, I'd never even gone out by myself like this before. Never packed a bag for the day and set off with the sole intention of being alone in nature for hours.

The footpath was not very tourist-friendly. I picked my way over the smooth rocks that stuck out of the earth, almost piled on top of each other in a haphazard, clumsily built staircase, taking good care because I couldn't afford to twist my ankle out here.

I checked my make-up in my phone camera. The natural light was amazing. My skin looked completely clear. I filmed a thirty-second TikTok giving a quick update to my followers. Once I'd posted it, I looked around and then it hit me – how alone I was out in this wilderness.

Sweat beaded on my forehead. I could feel my mascara sticking to my skin. I'd need to reapply if I filmed anything else. My calves began to ache. I was barely twenty minutes into my walk and already I felt out of my depth.

In London, constant noise spilled from the street outside into my flat – car alarms, pub music, arguments in the street. Here, there was nothing. Not even birdsong. Just the trickle of a stream up ahead and the sound of my own plodding footsteps. This was what people craved, the silence of the great outdoors. I had expected to love it. But I found it disconcerting.

The shrubbery ducked down, allowing a huge green mountain to rear up. It looked somehow like it was within touching distance and hundreds of miles away at the same time. On the slope, a jagged pool perfectly reflected the clouds above, like a piece of sky that had fallen down to earth.

I was waiting to feel rejuvenated. That was what I was supposed to feel, wasn't it? People came to beautiful places like this to unwind. So why was my heart beating at a thousand miles an hour?

I breathed in through my nose and out through my mouth. There was a phrase my online therapist had taught me to repeat to myself. *My inner reality creates my outer reality.* She said our negative thoughts made the world seem more threatening than it really was. I repeated this phrase to myself as I followed the path up the mountain, wishing something would bring me fully into the present moment. The urge to check my phone was strong. Being online softened things, made them somehow easier to manage.

I needed to stop somewhere and take a break. The path began running alongside a shallow stream. Maybe this was what I needed. I forced myself to follow the stepping stones into the middle of the stream. I felt hyper-aware of myself, like I was watching someone else crouch down and trail their fingers in the running water. Despite the summer heat, it was ice-cold. I pressed my cool fingertips to my forehead and breathed out deeply – in one two three, out one two three.

My mum was very connected with the natural world. She would seek out patches of sunlight the way plants grew in its direction. On holiday, when I was little and bored, I would try to rouse her from the sun lounger. But she would wave me away, lift her chin and angle her face to the sun like a flower. It was strange to see her so peaceful. I remember feeling envy. For her or the sun, I wasn't sure. Her bleached hair would glow bright, like a band of gold.

My inner reality creates my outer reality. My inner reality creates my outer reality.

'Hey!'

The voice ripped through me. I jumped up so quickly that I lost my footing. I lurched forward to right myself just before I could fall into the water.

A ginger man in his twenties was bounding along the path towards me. He came to a stop beside the water, shielding his eyes from the sun with his hand. 'You feeling okay?' he asked.

I stood very still, reminded that a woman my age recently went missing in this area – and there was no way out of the water except along the pebbles that led straight to this man.

'I'm fine. Just the heat.'

A purple-haired woman trudged up the path behind him, ill-dressed for the weather in a band t-shirt and panting heavily. This calmed me down. They looked like companions. But the ginger man was too busy beaming at me to acknowledge his friend.

'Yeah, it's boiling. It's you, right? BlackBird? You solved the Hayley Pieterson case?'

Suddenly I realised. I'd seen this guy before. He was one of the YouTubers who said they were coming up here. Another sleuth, fairly new in the community. Embarrassment churned in my stomach as I realised he'd just seen me crouching on the balls of my feet in a moment of total vulnerability.

'That's me,' I replied, straightening up.

'I'm actually a sleuth as well,' he said.

The purple-haired woman frowned at him.

'Sorry, *we're* sleuths,' he said hurriedly, gesturing between them. 'I'm Ollie and this is Becca. We met yesterday.'

'Nice to meet you,' said Becca automatically.

He continued: 'I saw from your post that you were coming up here. We'll find her in no time with you looking into this.'

I laughed politely.

'Do you want to search together?'

I clenched and unclenched my sweaty hands. I never worked

well with other people. But I'd hated being out here so much, the idea of going on alone didn't appeal to me at all. I glanced up at the mountain, then back at Ollie and Becca.

'I would like that. Thank you.'

The woman at the bottom of the mountain with the militaristic posture is still watching me. Is she going to do something? Is she going to come up here?

'Mia! Hey, you all good?'

It's Ollie. Calling me again. I have to tear myself away and continue up the mountain. But with each step, I still feel her gaze on my back, like sunburn.

25

Ruth

'THEY'RE EVERYWHERE,' SAYS KIRSTY.

I'd asked Kirsty to come over as soon as I got home. I let my frustration out by aggressively tidying up the dishes from dinner.

She continues: 'The café was heaving today. Can you believe someone goes missing here and we actually become more popular?'

'Bunch of grief tourists. They weren't even wearing proper walking boots. You should've seen them. These eejts were going up the mountain in their white trainers.' I load the dishwasher angrily. 'You know what's going to happen? One of them's going to get lost and we'll have to send out officers looking for them instead of Lily.'

'There's plenty of experienced people searching those mountains now. Mountain Rescue won't let them do anything stupid.'

'Mountain Rescue's got enough on their hands. They don't need to look out for a bunch of idiot Americans and Londoners with a bloody superhero complex.' I tip the remains of the cold coffee down the sink. 'These people want to play detective so badly, why don't they just become one?'

'Because you make it look so great, don't you? Just try and ignore them. Focus on doing your job.' I can feel Kirsty's concerned glare boring into my back. 'Why's this bothering you so much?'

I look up from the sink and stare out of the window, the memory coming back to me.

'I saw this girl.'

'Huh?'

'She was… smiling.'

All day I haven't stopped thinking about her. The girl on the mountain. She must have been around Lily's age. First I'd been struck by her beauty. Her elegant shoulders, exposed by a bright-yellow sports bra, her glossy black hair. But what had really gotten to me was the serene look on her face. She was smiling. A woman around her age was missing. And she was smiling. Why on earth had she come here?

'I've been meaning to ask,' says Kirsty, 'how was it today?'

The meeting place. The conifer trees and the old stone bridge. I don't like to think about it when I'm not there. Let alone talk about it. 'The same as it always is,' I reply.

'Did he say anything about her?'

'No.'

Kirsty goes quiet. She knows I find it hard to discuss.

Heat crawls up my neck. There is something I do want to talk to her about. Compared to everything that's happened today, it's trivial. Pathetic.

'Connor messaged.'

Kirsty frowns. 'Really? What did he say?'

'He says he saw the case on the news. He wants to meet up'

Kirsty's eyes widen. I look out the window, feeling overwhelmed by the emotion that's hit me, wanting it to pass.

I had read the text when I got home, not long before Kirsty arrived. Then I'd read it four more times after that, imagining his fingers typing out the message. Had he agonised over every word, like I would? Or bashed it out and pressed send without even thinking?

Before Kirsty can say anything, I blurt out: 'Does anyone else want to come here, you know what I mean? Everyone and their granny wants to help search for her, apparently.'

Kirsty's look of surprise has softened. 'It must remind him of what happened,' she says quietly.

Kirsty is the only person who talks to me about these things and she handles it as sensitively as anyone could, but I still tense up with discomfort.

Noticing this, Kirsty moves on. 'Did he say anything else?'

I bite my lip. 'Yeah. Do I want to go for a coffee or a pint after?'

Anger rises inside me at the flash of excitement in Kirsty's eyes, which she tries and fails to hide. This is why I didn't want to tell her. I know she wishes Connor and I would get back together. She never says this out loud. But I know it's true because she always said Connor was a great husband when we were together, which was a fair observation. And she's never said anything that bad about him since we broke up. Deep down, she can't get over the idea we're soulmates, no matter how hard I try and explain why there's no going back.

Cautiously, she asks: 'How does that make you feel?'

I scratch at the base of my ponytail. 'Not good. I wish he hadn't. Not now, especially.'

I don't want to say this, but how I feel depends on his intentions. I avoid thinking or ever talking about Connor because of the magnitude of what we went through. For me it's like looking directly at the sun. The idea that it isn't like that for him makes me feel sick.

'Wouldn't it be good to see him? Clear the air.'

'I don't know. What is there to say?'

The chair legs screech as Kirsty gets up. 'Come on, let's head out. Get you a drink.'

'No, I want a clear head for work tomorrow.'

'It'll take your mind off things.'

The plughole is dotted with this morning's coffee grounds. I turn on the tap and flush them all away.

*

It's about 8.30 in the evening. As we walk up the high street, a familiar golden light at the top of the hill grows steadily brighter. Warmth spreads through my chest as the lantern above the pub door materialises, illuminating the sign for the Nag's Head. Kirsty's right. This will help me unwind. I start to salivate, imagining that first refreshing sip of cold lager.

We're approaching the door when I notice the window seat is taken, and my heart deflates. The window seat is the coldest and smallest seat in the house. If somebody's already sat there, then there's no hope of us getting a table. I begin to notice the chatter carrying through the walls. The front door creaks open and a lanky young man is carried out on a tide of young voices. He shuts the door behind him and stands by one of the few outdoor pub tables vaping and scrolling on his phone. The glow of the screen turns his face into a blue disk. With a jolt of surprise, I recognise the man from earlier. The one from Florida. He hasn't seen me. He's too engrossed in his phone.

Kirsty squeezes my arm.

'We'll go to the Coach and Horses,' she says.

The indignity. Locked out of your own local by a bunch of tourists. Kirsty steers me away, on the tragic walk towards the Braeside's second (and distinctly second-best) watering hole. I peer over my shoulder into the window of the Nag's Head. A radiant face stands out among the crowd.

The girl from the mountain is sat inside, smiling.

26
Mia

The Nag's Head falls silent almost the moment we step through the door. No one moves apart a black Labrador, whose tail is repeatedly thwacking a table leg as he eyes up his owner's steak pie.

We buy our drinks and find a table.

'I think we did well,' says Becca, sipping her lemonade. 'We covered a lot of ground today.'

I can't say I agree. Five hours of wandering around aimlessly, finding nothing. There's got to be a better way to investigate this case.

We hush up when a huge, six-foot man plants himself down in the armchair next to us.

'Where are you guys from?' he asks.

The other two reel off their hometowns.

'London,' I say reluctantly.

'This is a change of pace for you then, isn't it?' the newcomer laughs.

I don't like how this guy is settling into our conversation.

He continues: 'You guys are coming from all over. Never seen the place so popular. It's touched people, hasn't it?'

Ollie asks: 'And you? You live here?'

He nods. 'This is my pub,' he says, by way of explanation. 'I'm Declan, by the way.'

And suddenly it all adds up. The overfriendliness. The concern for local tourism and how the outside world views Braeside. How could I have been so stupid? This is probably a pillar of the community – somebody potentially crucial for the investigation – and I almost ignored him. 'Oh,' I say, automatically pointing my knees in his direction. 'It's lovely.'

He smiles at me. 'Family operation. That's my wife behind the bar. My daughter Georgia works here too. She knows Lily well.'

'I'm so sorry,' I say.

He nods. 'She's a good person. I really hope she's okay.'

And just like that, it's like we've received a blessing from the town spokesperson and other curious neighbours start to trickle over. A lady who says she teaches in the local secondary school tells us that people like us restore her faith in the youth of today. A couple of older men who are clearly regulars watch from a distance, nursing their beers, keeping their voices low and their conversation sparse, as though waiting for an opportunity to join ours instead. Suddenly we are the bright new things. The centre of attention.

The wine has gone straight to my head, making me feel jittery and alive. The lights are collecting in my eyelashes.

Ollie laughs at my jokes more loudly than anyone else, keeps his eyes trained on me long after either of us have finished speaking. Are we going to sleep together? Would that be a good idea? I don't know. I'm not really attracted to him. But he's so keen, maybe he'd be really energetic.

Becca has been talking to a couple of locals separately. She returns glowing with excitement.

'Apparently there's a rumour that Lily went for a drink at the Anchor with someone a few times. But no one knows who with.'

My phone buzzes. I check it discreetly, keeping the screen close to my chest.

YOU SHOULD KILL YOURSELF YOU EVIL BITCH

A new number. How does she always text from a new number? How many Sim cards is she buying?

I swipe the message away, pocket my phone and clear my throat.

'That's very interesting,' I say.

'The other thing I learned is the Howard family aren't really part of the community. Apparently.'

'Yeah, it seems that way,' says Ollie. 'Someone needs to get close to them.'

Becca shakes her head. 'I don't know. I think the best we can do is search the hills. It's clear that's where she is.'

I disagree, but I keep my mouth shut. The more progress we make towards finding Lily the better, of course. But this isn't a team effort. Only one person's going to solve this case. I have no intention of going back up those hills. Here is where the secrets are.

I've never liked drinking – the way it makes the world spin. I head over to the bar, where Declan is now working, and ask for a tap water.

'You say your daughter knows Lily well?'

'Yeah, they've been friends since they were teenagers,' he replies, pouring me a glass.

'So she must have a theory about what's happened?'

He grimaces. 'Look, she's really shocked. Lily wasn't the type to do something stupid like go off-grid for a couple of days.'

I take a sip of water and ask, 'Was there anything strange about her disappearance that I should know about?'

He studies the ceiling, thinking. 'She did send a weird message to Georgia that morning. And that's the last anyone's heard of her.'

'What did it say?'

'Let me think. Georgia did send it to me. It said something like, "I feel free now".' He shakes his head. 'It makes you worry but then… I really don't think she was the type, you know?'

My heartbeat speeds up. 'Do you mind forwarding that to me on WhatsApp?'

He hesitates and I worry I've gone too far too quickly. But then he sighs and pulls out his phone. 'I guess we need all the help we can get,' he says.

I give him my number and moments later the message appears on my phone. Electricity creeps over my skin. *For the first time in a long time, I feel free.*

As he watches me read, Declan says with a note of caution in his voice, 'Just so you know, a lot of people here are quite guarded. Not used to strangers. I'd say be careful before poking around, you know what I mean?'

'Yeah, I get you,' I say.

But my mind is elsewhere. I stare at the slightly damp surface of the bar. Maybe she has had some kind of breakdown. Maybe she really is just wandering around the hills by herself. But if she is – or if she's killed herself – wouldn't Mountain Rescue have found her by now?

This is the kind of information the police will choose to withhold about a case. I'll set it free. I'll release it into the world. It's better to have many minds on something like this. Plus, I really should post something good soon.

The pub door opens and a broad-shouldered man walks in. It feels as though the centre of gravity in the room has shifted. He orders a whisky. I hear Declan tell him it's on the house. Once he's been served, the man, who is probably in his mid-twenties, takes his drink to a booth by himself, knocks back the first sip and nurses his temples, breathing hard. I can tell from the way his t-shirt vibrates, his ribcage is moving up and down, that he's fighting back tears. God. So attractive when men aren't afraid to show their emotions.

Declan rescues a couple of empty pint glasses scattered around the room and returns to the bar with them clinking between his fingers. People continue their conversations but really they're all watching this newcomer with a combination of pity and fascination.

'Who's that?' I whisper as Declan deposits them in the sink behind him.

'Who? Oh. Lily's older brother. Toby,' he says. He shakes his head. 'Been out all day looking for her. Poor fucker.'

He retreats down the bar to serve someone else. As subtly as I can, I look sideways at the brother. I try to spot the resemblance. They are both beautiful but in distinctly masculine and feminine ways; they look nothing alike. The rest of the whisky is already gone. His fingers knotted in his hair. The sweat and dirt of the day still gleaming on his muscled arms.

I walk carefully from the bar to his booth.

Toby's red-rimmed eyes drift up to me.

'Can I get you another of those?' I ask.

27
Ruth

9 June

THE SOUND OF MY alarm snaps me out of a deep sleep. I grope blindly on my bedside table for the right button to turn it off, then lie back for a few moments, readying myself.

Three drinks with Kirsty. It didn't seem like much at the time. But coupled with the exhaustion of the week I'm left with dry eyes and a head full of cobwebs as I get dressed and plod downstairs.

I turn on the radio while I make myself a cup of tea. The roar of the kettle drowns out the chatter. Once it's boiled, I start to catch traces of the broadcast. They're talking about Lily.

Something about messages. I take a sip.

'For the first time in a long time, I feel free.'

I almost spit out my tea.

Lily's last text message. On the radio.

The radio presenter continues: 'That is the text Lily Howard sent on the day she went missing in the town of Braeside. The strange message has sparked concern among—'

'Jesus Christ,' I mutter, before necking the rest of my tea and heading out.

'Good day off?' asks Max as I follow him up the stairs into the station.

'Fine,' I say quickly. 'Did you search Stuart's parents' place?'

'We sent a couple of officers down. They didn't find anything.' His voice carries down to me, filled with disappointment. 'I've been trying to confirm Stuart's alibi. We ran his registration through ANPR. That shows him driving out of Braeside at around nine o'clock and coming back at around two o'clock, like he said. But he wasn't caught on many security cameras. So we still don't know exactly where he was around the time Lily went missing.'

'What did his mum say?'

'She said he was at hers. But I'm not sure we can trust her.'

'Why?'

'She's his mum, right? And she's just lost her husband. It's not insane she might lie to protect Stuart.'

That seems far-fetched to me, but I decide to leave it. 'What about the days after the 26th, the last time he saw Lily?'

'No visits to the Shorehouse or anything like that. I've sent you the footage so you can have a look through yourself. You know the area so you might spot something I missed.'

'Have you seen the news yet this morning?'

'The text message?'

'How did that get out?'

'I spoke to the comms team,' he says. 'Apparently the press contacted us late yesterday and we said we weren't commenting.'

'Sounds like the right move,' I reply.

Holding the door open for me at the top, Max shakes his head. 'Look, everyone's seen this text, it was only a matter of time before it got leaked. I think we should have pre-empted it. Released it beforehand.'

'We don't need to livestream everything we do on this case just to reassure the public.'

'About that—'

'You think we should?'

'No, I mean, there's something you should see.'

He pulls me to a stop in the middle of the corridor and gets out his phone, selects something, and hands the device over to me. It's a video of a pretty girl in her bedroom, backlit by a soft purple glow.

'Look, what you watch in your private time is your own business, Max.'

'Very funny. Look at the title.'

The video is named: *Last message Lily sent to her friend – REVEALED*. I look more closely at the girl. It takes a few moments for me to realise who I'm looking at. It's her. The girl from the mountain. From the pub. Or some ethereal version of her. Her make-up is flawless, her already youthful complexion cleared of any imperfections by the strong lighting, or perhaps edited away in post-production.

'This was uploaded last night,' he says.

He turns up the volume. Her soft voice comes out of the speaker: 'I've been speaking with people in the town and one of them shared this text message which Lily sent to Georgia, her oldest friend here.'

The conversation appears on screen. So this is where the media got it from.

The girl continues: 'I want to hear what your thoughts are on this. Was Lily having some kind of breakdown when she sent this? Or is it possible someone got a hold of her phone and sent it?'

The way people hold themselves in videos like this is always so strange to me. Self-consciously smirking into the camera, mannequin-like, all expression sacrificed so they can look composed.

'So people watch this?' I say.

'A lot of people. Hundreds of thousands.'

He points to the view count on the screen. My eyes widen.

'Does she get paid for this?'

'There'll be some revenue, sure. From advertising. Shopping.'

I squint at the screen. There is a tiny advert underneath the video.

'*Solve a cold case. Buy a t-shirt*?' I read.

I shoot Max an incredulous look. He shrugs hopelessly.

'Jesus Christ,' I say. 'And what does "BlackBird" even mean?'

Every other t-shirt is emblazoned with this word, sometimes accompanied by a simple drawing of the bird, like a logo.

'That's her username. Or sleuthing name or whatever.'

'I hate that so much. What is she, a superhero?' I straighten up, putting my hands on my hips. 'Should we do something? Interview her, give her a warning?'

'About what?'

'I mean, isn't she obstructing the investigation by sharing that?'

'It's not that sensitive what she's posted. Also, do you know how many videos there are like this? You want to caution hundreds of people posting online?' He pockets his phone. 'None of this has been helped by the Howards offering a fifty grand reward to the person who finds Lily.'

I rub my face, really regretting the three drinks now. 'The family liaison officer specifically advised the Howards *not* to do that.'

'Well, apparently they didn't listen.'

I shake my head. 'I'll talk to Vanessa. See if she's okay. Maybe get her to retract this stupid reward.'

28

PARENTS OF MISSING CHILDREN are usually filled with desperate relief when a detective shows up on their doorstep. But Vanessa just glares at me. I follow her into the kitchen, all gleaming marble surfaces. I've never seen her without make-up like this before. Her eyes look small and red.

'I was hoping to speak to you about all the attention Lily's disappearance is getting,' I say. 'All the people who've arrived in the town. I just wanted to check—'

Behind Vanessa appears the slender figure of a young woman. My heart stops. But no, it's not Lily. This woman has straight black hair, a small knowing smile, a narrow chin and swimming blue eyes that overwhelm the rest of her face. It's her. The smiling girl. 'BlackBird'.

I look between them, waiting for an explanation.

'Have you met Mia Chaplin yet?' Vanessa asks.

'Not in person no,' I say, looking over her shoulder at the woman. 'But I've seen some of your… content.'

For a second her eyes glow with childlike delight, as if I've given her a compliment.

'I've been meeting a lot of the locals,' she says.

'So you have,' I say, looking again at Vanessa.

'You're the local detective.'

'Inspector Lindsey,' I clarify.

Vanessa interjects: 'Mia is going to be staying with us while she investigates Lily's disappearance.'

My mouth falls open.

Mia throws me a tranquil smile from the doorway. But she stays exactly where she is. Holding herself like a teenager, hovering on the edge of the conversation.

'Is it all right if I speak with you alone, Vanessa?'

Vanessa shares a look with Mia. A twitch in her upper lip tells me Mia's offended but she slinks out of the room. Through the doorway I watch her shadow travel up the staircase. Already I don't trust her not to lurk outside the door and listen.

I lower my voice. 'Have you spoken to the family liaison officer about this?'

'I decide who stays in my own home.'

'But why does she have to stay here?'

'She's come all this way to help look for my daughter. The least I could do is put her up. Not have her spending silly money staying in some grotty youth hostel.'

I clasp my hands together, trying to calm myself down. 'I came to talk to you about all the attention the case is getting. You must be receiving a lot of unsolicited messages right now. Have any been distressing?'

'I'm not really looking at social media very much. I'm busy looking for my daughter.'

'Because there are things we can do if anyone's said anything upsetting to you.'

'I'm fine. Thank you.'

I can't believe this is happening. I can tell Vanessa wants me gone. But I can't just leave her like this.

'Are you sure this is the best idea right now?' I say. 'Up at the station we're concerned about the influence people like her are having on the case. I would advise you not to have such a close relationship with Mia.'

'She's raising awareness. Frankly she's doing more than you lot are.'

'But is she really doing it out of the goodness of her heart, Vanessa? Or is she doing it for likes on social media? For the money?'

Vanessa looks away.

'We told you not to offer a reward,' I continue. 'It'll just make more people send information that isn't useful.'

'I'll make my own decisions about that, thank you very much,' she snaps.

'You're in a vulnerable place right now, Vanessa –'

'I think it's time for you to go if that's all you have to say.'

Vanessa tightens her hands around the back of a chair. She looks tiny to me right now in this huge kitchen.

I swallow. 'I'll be back to give you an update on the investigation.' I can't help adding: 'We are trying, Vanessa. I promise you we are.'

Through the doorway a long shadow stretches up the living room wall. Mia is standing at the top of the stairs, waiting for me to leave.

29
Mia

Once the door has closed, I move slowly and quietly downstairs. Vanessa emerges from the kitchen into the living room.

'I'm sorry about her,' she says.

'They're always like this.'

I try to hide how shaken I am. During our interaction, Vanessa was smiling at me with encouragement. DI Lindsey was not. DI Lindsey had a probing gaze. Clear grey eyes, the colour of the sea. Instantly I was reminded of Mrs Parsons, the teacher I hated at school. The one who kept tabs on uncompleted homework, who ignored every excuse I ever gave.

I need to keep this person at bay.

'Have you dealt with many police officers in your investigations?'

'Oh yeah. You'd think they'd want the extra pair of hands.' I shrug. 'But that's not how they see it.'

Vanessa lowers herself into the sofa facing the fireplace. 'She makes me so angry. But I think she's well-meaning.'

Should I? Can I?

'Well…' I begin.

Vanessa turns her face towards me. 'What's your reading of her?'

'My reading?' Through the window a couple of seagulls glide down to the beach. 'Based on first impressions, to be honest, I would say she's jealous of you.'

Vanessa's eyes widen.

'You have so much. A beautiful house. A loving family. An amazing daughter. It's obvious she has a grudge. Perhaps that's why.'

'Gosh. Gosh, that's so funny. That would make sense because...'

She's about to tell me something important. Excitement pulses through me.

But something makes her decide against it. Instead she just says, 'You're very perceptive.'

'I'll only say, with someone like that, someone you have a history with, someone who feels resentment... are they really going to look at Lily's disappearance clearly, without bias? You have to be careful.'

Motion outside the window catches Vanessa's attention.

'Toby's back. I wonder if he found anything.'

I can see only a segment of the brother's face in the window. Frowning in concentration as he lights a cigarette.

'I'll ask him,' I say, and head for the door.

He stands against the wall of the house, boots streaked with mud, backpack lying on the porch, an empty water bottle next to him. Back from another search.

He looks annoyed that I've disturbed him.

'Want one?' he asks, gesturing with the cigarette.

I shake my head.

He goes back to smoking.

'Thank you again for putting me in touch with your mum,' I say.

'That's okay. Like I said, I'd heard of you. I thought with your experience, you know. We need all the help we can get.' He rubs his forehead. 'Sorry, I don't remember what else we spoke about, to be honest. My head's sort of fucked right now.'

'Of course,' I reply.

He doesn't sound that posh considering his parents' wealth. Surely he went to a good school. He must have roughed up his accent over time, deliberately chipping away the RP inherited from his parents and his privately educated peers.

He turns around, rests his hands on his hips, studying the wall of the house, and slowly releases a stream of smoke into the air.

When he next looks at me, his face has hardened.

'Vanessa says you're staying,' he says.

'Yes.'

'Just be careful with her, all right,' he says. 'She's not in a good place right now.'

'Of course.'

'So what are you looking into today?'

Embarrassment rushes through me. I got up at 11 o'clock today. I haven't started work yet. Quickly, I say: 'There's a rumour Lily was dating someone in the town. I'm going to find out who it is.'

He looks unconvinced. Where is the man I spoke to yesterday? Last night he was distracted but pliable, typing my number into his phone while his shoulder brushed mine in the booth.

'Do you want to go for a drink tonight?'

He blinks at me in frustration. Wipes sweat away from his face, breathes smoke into the wind.

'I don't think now's the best time,' he says flatly.

So last night it was appropriate to drink three whiskies, but now it's not?

I can already sense this family is going to be hard work.

30

r/LilyHoward

Did you hear? Lily was dating someone
Who?
Does anyone know?
Rumour is the police have interviewed him
Apparently they met at a local pub. If we look through Lily's photos we might find something
Does anyone know where this guy lives?

31

Stuart

10 June

STUART BRUSHES, SPITS AND then inspects his teeth in the mirror. A high-pitched shriek of delight sails in through the open window. His son is playing while his wife waters their garden. Warmth spreads around his chest. He smiles to himself. For the first time in weeks, things are returning to normal.

Ruth's visit had scared the shit out of him. But after she'd gone, it was like a weight had lifted. He'd needed to tell someone. And now he has explained himself, hopefully this will all go away.

He moves closer to the window and looks down into the garden, where his son is running rings around Claire, trying to get under the hosepipe's spray while she does sweeps of the garden. He loves her broad hips, the way she holds herself. This morning was the first time in weeks they'd had sex with no interruptions or distractions, and the memory of it is still floating through him, creating a faint buzz that hovers over his temples.

She can never, ever know. He is almost certain that, deep down, she wouldn't want to know. All things considered, this is the best thing for all of them.

His phone buzzes loudly and aggressively on the tiled windowsill.

There's just one message.

Mate have you seen this?

For a second he wonders if Craig has been hacked, because he never usually texts him with such urgency, and there's a hyperlink after the message.

But then he reads the link.

Who is Lily Howard's mystery man?

'What the fuck?' he mutters to himself, and clicks the link.

YouTube opens and a video starts playing. A black-haired girl he's never seen in his life is talking to camera. 'So we know from Lily's Instagram that she went to a pub in early May.'

The video cuts to a photo from her social media. He recognises it instantly. She'd taken the photos while she was waiting for him. He remembers feeling a rush of excitement when he found the post on Instagram, because it meant she'd had a good time. The light that evening was beautiful and Lily had photographed first the flowers on the table, sitting in a beam of golden light, and then herself, lit up by that same beam, smiling.

The girl says: 'I looked on Google Maps and managed to identify the pub from the interior. It's called the Anchor. A quick look on Facebook shows that a couple were celebrating an anniversary there at around the same time. They posted a photo and uploaded it that evening. Lily is just about visible in the background, having a drink with a man in a green shirt.'

He feels his insides dissolve. A horribly tanned middle-aged couple grin with their drinks. And behind them, near the windows, you can just make out Lily's red hair. Far away, but instantly recognisable.

What she says next makes him think he's going to be sick.

'Looks like they're on a date, right? So, who is this guy? Luckily, there's been cameras everywhere over the last week, so it didn't take long to find out. These are the images from the press conference Lily's parents held recently. See that man in the crowd? Well, isn't that the same green shirt we saw earlier?'

He watches the rest of the three-minute clip in horror as she calmly explains everything she's gleaned about him from the internet, including that he's married with a child.

'I think if the police aren't already looking at this guy, they should be.'

Is this real? Is this really out there?

But it is – 70,000 views, and it was only posted an hour ago.

And if Craig has already seen it… then surely others in town have as well.

Which means it's only a matter of time before Claire does too.

Outside, his son starts wailing.

He sticks out his neck and looks into the garden again.

Brodie is stumbling towards his mum, calling out, despondent, wondering why the fun has stopped. The hose hangs limp in Claire's hand, spraying water onto the same spot on the lawn. Her head is bent forwards as she stares, entranced, at something on her phone.

Oh my God. Oh no.

He bolts out of the bathroom. A toy car almost sends him flying as he skids down the stairs and through the house. When he bursts into the garden, Claire is heading back inside. They stop moments before crashing into each other. The look on her face goes right through him. Her eyes are squinting in the sunshine and her upper lip is curled with confusion, pain and – he knows – disgust.

I can explain, he wants to say.

But he can't. He says nothing. There is no sound apart from the now-joyful cries of their son bouncing up and down on the wet grass.

32
Mia

I itch with the desire to look at it again. I click the link and get a hit of dopamine. The number of views is already ten per cent higher than when I last checked an hour ago. This is one of the most successful posts I've ever made. It's been shared all over the place. Ollie sent me a text as soon as it went up, presumably after wetting himself with excitement. Smashed it! Maybe you've solved this already haha

My heart is pounding in my chest as I sit at the desk in my new room. I was very pleased to leave the hostel and come to stay with Vanessa. The house is more luxurious than anywhere I've stayed before. I like the sensation of my feet sinking into the plush carpets. The gigantic fridge. The fact I have a whole en suite to myself.

Sharing the post was risky, because now every other sleuth will be looking at Stuart as well. But it was worth it. I need to put my name on the map. Establish myself as *the* person investigating this case.

But I need to keep the momentum going. I tap my long nails on the desk in agitation. How else can I look into Stuart? I read through the notes I made for my video, combing through everything I dug up on his family.

Then I work it out. My next move.

33
Ruth

10 June

THE TOWN HAS STARTED to change. Parking spaces are limited because every street is bursting with new cars. The arrivals keep blocking driveways and stationing themselves down country lanes, desperate to stay close to town.

Unfamiliar faces now outnumber locals. When I go to the café, I find myself queuing up behind a couple of young English people and a TV crew on a break.

Why is this happening? I ask myself as I take my coffee back to the car. The mountain is bright in the morning light. I know the case has attracted national attention because Lily is beautiful and privileged. Still, what is it about her disappearance that has inspired this strange desire to participate? To play a role in the story? At first I thought people just wanted an excuse for a holiday up here. But now I'm not so sure. Now I'm wondering if this will be an inevitable part of every major case going forward. A team of Reddit users tagging along in search of clues the police have missed.

'Ruth!'

I turn around to see who's called my name. Claire is charging up the hill in her flip-flops, hands balled into fists, blue summer dress swinging around her knees.

By the time she reaches me, her face is flushed, eyes shining with anger.

'Why didn't you tell me, Ruth?'

'Claire—'

'That's why you interviewed him, isn't it? You should've told me.'

I've never heard Claire raise her voice before. My throat tightens as I'm filled with regret.

'I'm so sorry. He said he'd tell you.'

'Well, it's too late now, isn't it? Now everybody fucking knows.'

She whips past me, leaving me on the high street, wishing I could disappear through the pavement.

I screw up my eyes in confusion. *Now everybody knows?* How had it gotten out so quickly?

34

I LOOK AT MIA on the tiny screen. It's strange how much damage one video can do.

We're watching the clip in the office, all huddled around Giblin's phone. I hate how pleased with herself Mia looks as she painstakingly dismantles Stuart's life. I dig my nails into my palms. How could she have posted this without thinking about Claire? What if it turns out Stuart doesn't have anything to do with Lily's disappearance?

When the clip ends, Giblin is the first to speak. 'Do you think Stuart's wife will kill him first? Or a mob of angry women?'

'Have Stuart or Claire reported this?' I ask.

'Neither of them.'

'Do we need to talk to the person who uploaded it? It's harassment, no?' says Hughes.

'Definitely. She's staying with Vanessa at the moment. We need to get an officer over there.'

Max steps back. 'Are you kidding? We're meant to be looking for a missing woman. Why are we even watching this?'

Claire's distraught face flashes through my mind and I sit down, massaging my temples.

'You okay, Ruth?' asks Giblin.

'I've just really fucked it with Stuart's wife. I should've told her before this came out.'

'Well, you didn't know some moron was going to make a whole video about her husband's extramarital affairs.'

'Ruth?' One of the officers appears from the corridor.

'Yep?'

'Someone here to see you.'

35

TO MY SURPRISE DECLAN and Georgia are sat on the sofa waiting for me inside the Family Room.

'Hey, Ruth. We wanted to talk to you about something,' says Declan.

'Of course.' My heart races as I shut the door behind me. This must be serious if they've come to the station from Braeside, rather than knocking on my door. 'Is this about the text message?'

Georgia nods.

'Do you have any idea how it got out?' I ask.

'It's my fault,' says Declan. 'I showed it to that – what's she called? BlackBird?' He's red in the face with anger. 'I thought she was trying to help. I had no idea she was some sort of influencer. Why would someone even do that?' He shakes his head. 'Anyway, Ruth, we wanted to report something.'

'Report what?'

Georgia swallows nervously. 'Well, all day, I've had people messaging me on social media. Tagging me in things.'

'Saying what?'

'Saying I'm not telling the whole truth. Loads of them think it's weird I didn't call the police as soon as she sent me that message. Or they think I sent the message to myself, on her phone. They're suggesting that I had something to do with her disappearance. My own friend.'

Her eyes are welling up. Declan gives her an awkward, fatherly pat on the shoulder.

'Do you know any of the people sending you these messages?'

'I don't think so. I think it's trolls.'

'Have any of them been threatening?

'No. They just ask questions. Make accusations. It's horrible.'

'Can you do something, Ruth?' asks Declan. 'They can't be allowed to do this, can they?'

'Have you got the links to these posts? Screenshots of the messages they sent you?'

'Yes,' says Georgia.

'Send them to me. We'll look into it and see if we can find who's sending these messages. And if you haven't already, block the people messaging you. You don't need that in your life right now. Maybe take a break from social media for a while.'

Looking relieved, Georgia nods and leans back into her chair. But something stops her from getting up.

'I had one other question,' she says.

'Yes?'

'A couple of journalists have gotten in touch with me as well. Asking if I want to give an interview. Talk about Lily. Tell my side of the story. What do you think?'

'I don't think she should,' says Declan.

The idea makes me squirm. 'I don't know, Georgia. If you're getting this much attention just from that one message… Do you not think you'd be adding fuel to the fire?'

'But I could straighten things out,' says Georgia desperately. 'If they heard me explaining myself, maybe these people would see I don't have anything to do with it.'

'It's your decision,' I reply. 'But whatever you end up doing, be careful.'

As I see them out, Declan hangs back with me for a moment.

'What possesses these people, Ruth?' he says. 'She's going through enough as it is.'

36

IN THE AFTERNOON I go through all of the instances over the past month when Stuart's car was captured by an ANPR camera. Then I check the accompanying CCTV footage. It looks like Stuart was telling the truth about where and when he saw Lily. But we can't confirm the exact destinations of some of his more recent trips. On the morning of the 31st of May, he went to Hobkirk without Claire or Brodie. Could he have met her there? Or bought something?

It's getting late when Giblin calls out: 'She's just posted again.'

He's staring at his phone. Hughes gets up to join him.

Max, working opposite me, groans. 'Just ignore it, everyone.'

'She's live-streaming,' says Hughes, his eyes fixed on Giblin's screen.

An unfamiliar pop song bursts out of Giblin's phone. He squints at the screen. 'Where is that? It's definitely not the Howards' place.'

Chair legs squeak and two officers get up to watch the video, trying to guess Mia's location.

Eventually my curiosity gets the better of me. 'Let's have a look.'

Ignoring Max's judgemental look, I head to Giblin and watch the clip over his shoulder. Mia is walking around the hills. She smiles knowingly at the camera. A pop song plays over the video. There is just one caption: *The search is on…*

'Who watches this stuff?' snorts one of the officers.

'People with too much time on their hands,' another replies.

After just 20 seconds, the video ends. I feel a buzz of recognition.

'Play it again,' I say.

The clip repeats. Halfway through, Mia lowers the camera, tilting it up for a flattering angle, briefly revealing an object behind her.

'Stop.'

The clip freezes. There is a small stone outhouse with a collapsed roof in the background.

I know where she is.

And she isn't allowed to be there.

Got you.

I return to my desk, picking up my jacket from the back of my chair.

Max's forehead creases with worry. 'What are you doing?'

I look past him, straight at the officers. 'Hughes – come with me.'

37

The wooden gate squeaks open as I enter the property. Somewhere in the darkness, an animal shoots out from its hiding place in the ferns.

'Are you sure this is where she is?' Hughes asks behind me.

'She'll be here somewhere. I know it.'

The white-painted house gleams blue at this late hour. You can just make out the sunlight retreating over the hills in the distance. There are no other houses around.

I recognised Stuart's parents' house in Mia's video thanks to the strange outbuilding in the background. I remembered seeing that dilapidated structure in the ad in the local paper. She must have found the ad herself while digging for dirt on him.

I bet she thinks Stuart has Lily holed up here. Not realising we've already searched this place, and there's not a single piece of evidence to be found.

Silvery light flutters over the grass behind the house before disappearing.

Mia's torchlight.

'She's on the other side,' I say.

I follow the path up to the house and slide quietly along the side until I make it past the corner.

There she is – lurking behind the house, shining her torch into the windows.

'Mia,' I call.

Mia turns off her torchlight and freezes. She looks like a crow, hunched over defensively, balancing on her thin legs.

I reach into my pocket for a torch and shine it at her, marching over. 'I'm arresting you on suspicion of threatening behaviour. You do not have to say anything, but anything you do say will be noted and may be used in evidence. Do you understand?'

As I tell her this she sways on the spot.

'No,' she manages. 'No, I – I didn't threaten him—'

'Come with me. We're going to the station.'

The light from my torch makes her skin glow white against the darkness of the garden. I think for a second she's going to cry. Then she does something unexpected.

She takes a step back, gets out her phone and holds it in front of her.

'The police have just arrested me for trying to find Lily,' she tells it, her face gravely serious.

I can tell from her eyes that the camera's on me now. My right hand curls into a fist.

It takes all my self-restraint to say calmly and slowly: 'Put the phone down.'

'Why? What don't you want people to see?'

'Stop filming right now. You're on private property.'

I take a swipe at her, trying to bat the phone away. My hand barely makes contact but she twists away from me. 'The police are using force. They're using force. They're going to take me to the station.'

'Turn it off right now.'

She does, but not because I've told her. She turns it off because she's got what she wanted. To my surprise when I start walking back down the path, she trudges after me with her head bowed.

I open the car door for her and she climbs shakily inside. I join her in the back. As Hughes drives us down the country road it's silent apart from the gentle hum of the engine. There's no street lights out here and the only thing I can see is the occasional stretch of fence or hedge illuminated by the headlights.

Mia is staring out of the window. Maybe it's the vibrations of the car but I swear I can feel her shaking. Good. That weird altercation still has my heart crashing around in my chest. What is it that's so violating about being filmed? I think about that old superstition that a photograph can capture part of the soul. I get it. It feels like she might as well have reached over, plunged her hand into my handbag, and rummaged through my belongings. And now she's just sat there in a world of her own.

She murmurs something in the darkness.

'What?'

'You're making a mistake,' she repeats.

'Don't you call yourself an investigator? Don't you know that posting about Stuart Marsh and trespassing on his property could be considered harassment?'

Mia doesn't have anything to say to that. She is grimacing in pain. She leans forward against the seatbelt, her hair falling out in curtains on either side of her face.

'Oh my God,' she says. 'Oh my God, oh my God.'

Is she ill? About to throw up?

She claps her hands over her nose and mouth and starts to cry. High-pitched, unrestrained crying. I can't even tell if it's real. I manage to find Hughes' eyes in the rear-view mirror and see my own alarm reflected there. Jesus Christ.

I don't think I can bring myself to pat her on the back. Instead, I tell her: 'Deep breaths, Mia. Deep breaths.'

She doesn't respond. She just keeps crying.

It's going to be a long drive back to the station.

38

Mia

No, no, no. This is all wrong.

The police station. The detective leads me up to a reception desk, where another officer sits behind a transparent screen.

Now we're in the light, I can get a good look at DI Lindsey. To me she has the worn-out look of an ageing rockstar. Her hair is held in a ponytail with a black tie at the base of her scalp.

'Sarge, this is Mia.'

The sergeant looks at me through the screen. 'Okay, Mia, can I have your full name, date of birth and nationality please?'

'Mia Chaplin. Fourteenth of November 2001. British.'

'You're under arrest in connection with an allegation of threatening behaviour. Do you understand?'

'Yes.'

'Have you had your rights explained to you?'

'Yes.'

'And do you want a solicitor?'

Surely I don't need that – I've done nothing wrong. 'No,' I reply.

'You have the right to let someone know you're here. Is there someone you'd like to tell?'

'Vanessa Howard.'

Next to me, the detective jerks her head to the right, concealing an eye-roll.

'Do you have any health conditions? Are you taking any medication at the moment?'

I shake my head weakly, too shocked to say anything else.

I can't stop shaking as DI Lindsey takes me to the interview room. It's small and stuffy with green walls and an ugly striped carpet. A black box sits ominously at one end of the table.

DI Lindsey closes the door behind us.

39
Ruth

MIA IS STARING AT the ceiling with the gothic melodrama of a Virgin Mary, her mascara smeared into grey semi-circles under her eyes.

I say: 'Okay, we're in Interview Room Three. This interview is being recorded so if you could speak clearly for the microphones please.

'This evening we arrived to find you trespassing and filming on Mr Marsh's property. Had Mr Marsh given you permission to be on his property or film there?'

'No comment.'

'How did you get in?'

'It wasn't hard,' she mutters resentfully. 'I walked.'

'What were you doing there?'

'No comment.'

'Right. Do you remember posting a video of Mr Marsh's property on social media?'

I load up screenshots on my laptop and turn the screen towards her.

'This is you, isn't it? BlackBird.'

Her blue eyes search the page. She seems to perk up slightly.

I continue: 'Amateur detective investigating cold cases and on-going homicides and disappearances. That's what you do, isn't it?'

She says nothing.

'Your latest post was a livestream of the property. Only visible for twenty-four hours but luckily we can still watch it.'

I hit play.

'And prior to that, you posted a video suggesting that Mr Marsh was having an affair with the missing person Lily Howard. So I'm going to take a huge leap in the dark and say that you were doing more… investigating—' I drag out the word, emphasising my disdain, 'into Mr Marsh, is that right?'

'I was looking for Lily.'

'And why did you think she would be there?'

'He's a person of interest with connections to a missing girl. And he owns a house near where she went missing. Someone had to check.'

'Well, how kind of you to do our jobs for us. Can you tell me what your intention was when you posted about Mr Marsh's private life?'

'I was just reposting what was already in the public domain and joining the dots.'

'And telling tens of thousands of strangers.'

'He shouldn't cheat if he doesn't want to get caught.'

'What you posted has caused serious distress to Mr Marsh and his family.'

'I didn't mean to,' she mutters.

'Do you know what harassment is, Mia?'

A flush of pink enters Mia's otherwise pale cheeks.

'Yes,' she says weakly.

'You've entered Mr Marsh's private property without his permission and posted unwanted content about his private life on social media. That could be considered stalking or threatening behaviour.'

'No… it wasn't—'

'I'm not sure he would agree with that. Interview terminated.'

I reach across the table, and hit pause on the recorder. Then I sit back down, sinking into the chair.

I shouldn't. I shouldn't do it.

She's looking me up and down with alarm, worrying that I'm settling in for the long haul.

'You're from London?'

She nods.

'Does your mum know you're here?'

'She's dead.'

'Sorry to hear that. Your dad then?'

'Him too.' She continues: 'I'm a grown adult. I don't need someone's permission to be here. Can I go now?'

The interview's over. I should let her go. But how many more chances am I going to get? To say what's on my mind.

'What do you want exactly?' I squint at her.

'I just want to help,' she manages.

'Do you get a kick out of this?'

'What?'

'Because to tell you the truth, I don't think I do. I never was someone who loved the thrill of the chase. Not even when I was on the Major Investigations Team in Glasgow. If a job comes in, I just want to get it done. Get justice for the family.'

My foot is tapping underneath the table. I lean in and she leans back.

I continue: 'The way I see it, I'm a cleaner. I clean up around here. That's my job. I keep this place clean and tidy. You create a mess here, we have to clean it up. What do you know about that? Turning up to a place you don't even know. What sense of responsibility could you possibly feel?'

She opens her mouth to defend herself but I keep going.

'I know why you're really here. You people want to feel something. You see a mother's grief on the screen and it makes you feel something doesn't it? Because pain does that. It wakes you up. It reminds you you're alive. Part of this world. Well, if you feel numb, let me help diagnose that for you. It's a symptom of privilege. Because nothing that bad has ever happened to you, has it? And you want to know what it feels like. Well, one day you will know what it feels like. And when that happens, you'll look back on all these times you watched someone else suffer and longed to feel as deeply as that, and you'll see those moments for what they really were. A waste. A total waste.'

She's rocking slightly in her seat.

'The Howard family is going through the worst thing anyone can imagine. If you want to do the best thing for them, you'll get up tomorrow and you'll thank them for their hospitality, and you'll pack your bags, and you'll get the first train back to London.'

40
Mia

I SIT IN SILENCE as one of the officers drives me back to Vanessa's. I'm afraid of what she might say. But she makes me tea and toast and strokes my arm like I'm a sick child. My hand is shaking so much the toast vibrates up to my mouth every time I go to take a bite.

'That woman,' she growls. 'Arresting people like you when she should be finding Lily.'

I try to put on a brave face. 'It comes with the territory,' I say.

Once I'm in my room I go straight to the en suite and grip the edge of the marble sink. I hate how shit she's made me look. My eyeliner is smeared into grey streaks. That horrible woman. Horrible, horrible, horrible. Talking like she could peer into my soul. When she doesn't know a single thing about me. What I've been through.

My throat tightens and my lips vibrate and I sniff and I'm crying again, hot tears splashing down my cheeks and onto the sink. Only this time they're tears of anger.

I'll get her. She'll feel the fear and pain I felt today. This is just the start.

41
Ruth

11 June

THOMPSON CALLS ME INTO his office first thing. I know from the way he's slouching, like he wants to disappear into his desk, that this isn't going to be good.

'I've had a busy morning,' he says. 'The chief superintendent wanted to meet with me. To discuss this.'

He picks up his phone and plays a video. On the screen is a pale-faced figure looming out of the darkness. Embarrassment writhes inside me when I realise it's me. Christ. It's worse than I imagined. I look like a monster who's about to attack Mia as she cries out in distress.

'Sorry about that,' I mumble.

'Is this a valuable use of your time? When you need to find Lily Howard?'

'She was live-streaming. We needed to act quickly.'

'So send officers.'

I bite the inside of my mouth. He's right, of course. I could have sent a couple of officers to deal with this instead. But the thought hadn't even occurred to me.

'Look, I know I should have sent someone else. But I wanted to talk to her in person and warn her off doing something like this again. What's she going to do next – break into someone's house? It's my job to protect the community.'

'Your other job is to maintain the confidence of the public. And you appearing on some grainy footage arresting a YouTube influencer doesn't help with that.'

'She's living with the victim's family. She's a threat to this case.'

'She's staying with the Howards because you've lost their trust.'

It's the first time anyone has said this to me out loud and heat rushes to my face.

He continues: 'And now we've got videos like this doing the rounds on social media. None of this is helping. I know it's hard, but don't let these people film you. Just stay out of it.'

'What was I supposed to do? Look, we need to do something about this. I've never had anything this bad.'

'I'm well aware of that. We're releasing a statement later today warning people against spreading misinformation about the case. We'll reference the arrest as a deterrent.'

I scoff. 'That'll really help. Maybe if you say pretty please as well.' I clench my fists. 'We need more resources. We need some kind of… social media ban.'

'I'll decide what we need,' Thompson snaps. 'The best thing is for you to steer clear of these people, all right? Stay away from Black Cat or whatever she's called.'

There's a loud knock on the door. I straighten up, trying to compose myself.

Giblin enters the office, his face drained of colour. 'Sorry to interrupt. But it's the Underwater Search Team. They've found something.'

42

THE LOCH IS ABOUT half an hour's walk from the Devil's Hand. I step out onto the pebbled beach where the rest of the search team are waiting for the divers to return. In the middle of the loch sits an inflatable boat with an officer crouched inside. The neoprene-covered head of one diver bobs in the water beside him, tubes connecting his mask to an oxygen tank. Eventually another diver surfaces like a seal coming up for air. Then the two go down together.

'How did you find her?' I ask one of the members of the search team.

'The sonar didn't work; the bottom of the loch was too uneven. So we had to carry out grid searches. That was how.'

Squaring off sections of water. Groping in the darkness for the impression of a body. Miserable work. But this moment makes it all worthwhile. The recovery.

The divers reappear, holding something. The person's nose and forehead break the surface of the water.

Together the three men begin the delicate task of lifting the body into the boat and carrying her back to shore.

We've got you now, I think. *It's all right. We've got you now.*

43

Cold seeps out from the mortuary cabinet. I fold my arms over my chest to stop myself from shivering as the pathologist opens his laptop on one of the stainless steel tables to show me photographs from the post-mortem.

The moment I see the image, I wish I could unsee it.

But I know for sure. This is Lily.

'Her lungs weren't waterlogged,' the pathologist says. 'She didn't drown.'

I swallow, noticing my throat is completely dry.

'Her t-shirt was ripped. There were bruises on her arms and scratches on her back that look indicative of a struggle on the ground, with the aggressor on top.

'I believe the cause of death was asphyxiation. The bruising around the neck is consistent with strangulation. Her shoes and leggings were weighed down with rocks from around the loch.'

I shiver in the cold, imagining the scene in my head. Someone cramming slippery rocks into the bottom of her shoes. Clumsily angling them on to her white, unresponsive feet. Pushing the body over the edge of the old wooden pier.

44

THIS IS EXACTLY WHERE I didn't want to be.

Vanessa sits hunched over at the table in the Family Room. I open the folder and pull out the photograph taken a few hours earlier by forensics, sliding it across the table towards her.

The desperation in her face is difficult to bear. She stares at the photograph like she's staring down a deep well.

'Do you recognise these clothes as belonging to your daughter?'

Vanessa reaches out. Her fingers trace the shapes on the photograph with a tenderness that makes my throat clench up.

The skin around her mouth twitches. She manages: 'That – that doesn't mean—'

She doesn't finish the sentence.

'I've seen her, Vanessa. It is. I'm so sorry.'

Vanessa pushes her chair back. She starts to lean forward and for a moment I think she might vomit.

'You weren't fast enough,' she tells the floor.

'Vanessa—'

'You weren't fast enough,' she repeats.

She covers her mouth just as a low groan comes out of her. An animal sound. Then she gets up. She leaves the room in silence. A rush of air hits me when the door slams shut.

I start returning the photo to the folder. But it keeps slipping past the opening because I can't feel my hands. The walls close in around me. I try a few more times before giving up and clasping my hands over my face and squeezing my eyes shut.

*

Kirsty has cooked for me. I'm grateful for the company but I have no appetite. I force down every bite.

'There's no way it could be a suicide?' she asks.

I shake my head. 'The post-mortem ruled it out.'

'What about that text she sent?'

'Either it means something else. Or the killer sent it after he killed her.' I press a hand to my clammy forehead. 'I think it's the latter. I think they wanted us to think she killed herself.'

Kirsty picks up the saucepan, crusted with tomato sauce, and takes it to the sink. Alone at the table, I rub my forehead. I'm overheating. It feels like an iron band is fastened around my head, and someone is slowly tightening it.

Was Lily grabbed from behind moments into her walk? Or threatened into a car? Did the whole ordeal last only minutes? Or hours?

Suddenly Molly's face flashes through my mind.

I hear a clatter in the sink. I realise I'm clutching my head in my hands and Kirsty is sweeping across the room towards me.

'Hey, hey, hey,' she says. She rubs her hand in circles on my back.

Rubbing her back when she had a stomach bug. Brushing her hair as she lay on her front on the living room floor, drawing in her colouring book. Each of us lost in a peaceful trance.

I feel embarrassed she's having to look after me like this but I lean against Kirsty's stomach, trying to show her I'm grateful.

'Sorry. I just thought—' My mouth's completely dry and I swallow. 'I thought I was going to find her alive.'

'It's not your fault,' she says quietly.

I reach up and hold Kirsty's forearm. 'I thought she'd be alive,' I repeat, almost to myself this time.

45
Mia

11 June

I COULD GET USED to living with the Howards. My en suite bathroom has a deep sink below an ornate mirror. The light is extremely flattering – softening everything and turning my pale skin gold. I take four selfies and almost post one of them. Then I realise it might look insensitive so soon after my last post, which was a panoramic shot of the mountains with the caption Where is Lily?. So I head out onto the landing.

As I pass the window, admiring the dark hills across the bay, something catches my eye. Toby is down on the private beach, fully clothed, holding his head in his hands as the waves roll in. Excitement pulses through me. Maybe he'd like some company. A little nightcap perhaps—

And then I hear it, rising up through the silence of the house. The tiny, gasping breaths of a woman crying in the kitchen, followed by the unintelligible murmurings of her husband trying to comfort her.

My body goes cold.

No. No, no, no.

I rush through to my bedroom, where I left my phone charging, unlock the screen and check the news.

Human remains found in search for Lily Howard

All the blood drains out of my head.

No. This can't be it.

With trembling hands, I skim-read the news story. Details are scarce. But it's clear this isn't a mistake. They've really found her.

I leave my phone on the bed and walk backwards until my back touches the wall. I bend forward, clutching my stomach.

I'm supposed to find her.

The sound of Vanessa crying is still drifting up the staircase. I can't think straight. Overwhelmed, I leave my room and head upstairs.

Cautiously, I push open the door to Lily's room and step inside. The family hasn't touched this space since she went missing, and it still feels lived-in. Her clothes are slung over an armchair in the corner and ash is scattered in the incense holder on the desk. I gently sit down on the bed, spreading my fingers over the cold sheets. I look out of the small window, imagining her sitting here in this same spot, admiring the sea view. My chest feels like it's caving in.

I look around the room, finding one item of clothing on the armchair that gleams among the rest. It's green, with mesh around the collar. I've seen it before. She wore this in one of her older Instagram posts – an arty photo of Lily in a yellow meadow.

I glance back at the door to check her parents aren't about to walk in. Then I let myself dissolve. I drop to the floor and crawl over to the chair, reaching up to pull the top slithering down towards me. It's so delicate in my hands. I get up on my knees. Then I crush it into my face. Breathing it in. I can see only red. I can smell only her.

46

Ruth

12 June

I WAKE UP DESPERATE to go back to sleep. Light peeks out from behind the blinds. Slowly, the dream comes back to me.

Like all dreams, this one had started in the middle. But I knew automatically that we were playing a game. She's a child when I dream – six or seven – and last night I was chasing her through a forest. She was giggling hysterically with excitement. Only she was running too fast and I couldn't keep up. 'Slow down,' I called. But she couldn't hear me over the sound of her own laughter. I yelled at her to stop. But she only ran faster, darting over tree roots with the ease of a woodland creature while my muscles screamed with exertion.

I woke up just before I lost sight of her completely.

*

A photograph of Lily is stuck to the whiteboard in the briefing room as Max and I sit going over the results from the post-mortem. On his laptop, Max clicks through the photographs with his hand over his mouth. I don't want to look at them again. I don't need to. The images are seared into my brain.

Eventually he looks up. 'The ripped clothing,' he says, grimacing.

'It could indicate a sexual motivation,' I reply. 'There was no concrete evidence of a sexual assault. But then there sometimes isn't.'

Max nods. 'Might just be a struggle. They reach out to grab her. She tries to run. They hold on. The top breaks.'

'Because of the water damage, it's difficult to say exactly when she was killed. But it looks like a brief attack based on these injuries. And I don't know how the killer could have hidden her somewhere all this time and then disposed of the body in the loch a couple of days ago. Not with this manhunt going on. So chances are this all happened on the same day. The 2nd of June.'

Max gets up and approaches the whiteboard, where a map of the Devil's Hand is pinned up beside Lily's photograph. 'So do we think she was killed at the loch? Or moved there?'

'I don't see how someone could have moved her during the day. I think someone killed her at the loch. SOCOs found her backpack in the bushes nearby. There was no phone. They must have taken it.'

'The text Georgia received. You think the killer sent it? To make it look like a suicide?'

'I'm certain now that I think about it.'

Max looks back at the map. 'Those videos she filmed in the forestry… that wasn't her. The killer was trying to throw us off.'

I suppress a shudder. 'Which means she was almost certainly dead before 11 o'clock. They killed her that morning. Maybe not long after she started walking.'

Max stares at the map with his arms crossed. 'All of this suggests they knew her, doesn't it?'

'They knew posting a story on Instagram was the sort of thing she'd do. They knew Georgia was her best friend here. Plus they must have known the passcode to her phone.'

'Then again, they might have used her fingerprint to open it.'

'True,' I reply. 'Remind me what else was in the backpack again?' We've sent the bag off for DNA testing. But given the killer left it behind, I'm not feeling hopeful.

Max consults the relevant photos from the file. 'Water bottle. Snacks. The remains of an extremely old sandwich. Pencils. And a receipt—'

'What?'

He locks eyes with me. 'A receipt from a place called Maggie's Arts and Crafts. In Hobkirk. Dated the 31st of May. When Stuart went there.'

47

'IT'S TRUE, ISN'T IT?' Stuart stares at me with haunted eyes from across the table in Interview Room Two. 'It's her. The human remains they found.'

I nod.

'Why do they have to say that? Human remains. It makes it so much worse.'

'You said you last saw Lily on the 26th of May. You lied to me, Stuart.'

Stuart goes very still. But he doesn't try to deny it.

'You saw her after that. So tell me what happened.'

He scratches the back of his neck, looking around the room. A long moment passes in silence before he says: 'Okay. I saw her on the 2nd of June.'

My skin goes cold. Next to me, Max is repeatedly tapping his knee with his index finger.

'It's not what you think,' says Stuart. 'I was driving to my mum's when I saw her coming out of the Spar and I just… wanted to say hi. So I pulled over.'

'How long did you talk to her for?'

'Not long. I swear. Maybe twenty minutes.'

'What did you talk about?'

'I said I was missing her,' he replies. 'I said I'd thought about what she'd said, how I should explore what made me cheat. I said she'd really helped me work through some personal stuff.

That I thought she was an amazing person.'

I resist the urge to vomit. 'And what did she say to that?'

'She said she had a nice time with me. But she stood by what she'd told me before about not wanting to get involved with a married man. I—' His eyes dart nervously to mine. 'I don't know what my plan was, honestly. I think I just wanted to end things on a good note.'

'That was it?'

'That was it.'

'You didn't, I don't know, give her a present?' asks Max.

Stuart's face reddens. He looks down at his lap.

'Lily was carrying a receipt from Maggie's Arts and Crafts, Stuart,' I say. 'And we know you went to Hobkirk on the 31st of May. The date and time on the receipt matches up.'

Stuart bites his lip.

'Why would she have that,' I continue, 'unless you gave her something?'

'Okay,' he says. 'I bought her a sketchbook. You know, for her art. I wanted to show her how much our time together meant to me. So I kept it in the car in case I ever saw her. And yeah, during that conversation, I gave it to her. At first she wouldn't accept it. But I said she should think of it as a parting gift.'

'And she took it?' says Max.

'Yeah. Put it in her backpack.'

'The problem with that,' I say, 'is we found her backpack. And it isn't there.'

Stuart frowns. 'What? But it would be.' His face fills with bitterness. 'Well, unless she chucked it.'

'Or,' says Max, 'unless you took it.'

'What?'

'She had used pencils in the backpack. Maybe by the time you found her later, she'd done a sketch or too up near the Devil's Hand. Maybe you wanted to keep it. For old time's sake.'

Stuart looks at me imploringly. 'Ruth, I swear. I didn't take it.'

'Did she tell you where she was going?'

'Yes,' he says.

'Maybe you went after her.'

'I didn't. I swear. That was the last time I saw her.'

'Your problem, Stuart, is only your mum can vouch for you being with her on the 2nd of June. There's no security footage confirming that. Nothing.'

'Well, that's where I was.' He sits back in his chair, looking defeated. After a moment, he says: 'Claire's kicked me out.'

'I heard.'

'Have you?' He laughs bitterly. 'Word travels fast in a small town, doesn't it?'

Probably should've realised that before you started shagging around, I think. 'Where are you staying?'

'With my mum,' he says, crossing his arms over his chest. 'Barely anyone will speak to me. Craig's reached out. He's a nice guy. But that's it from Braeside. The whole internet hates me.'

'We have a unit dedicated to taking down inappropriate posts about this case. You can report anything to us.'

He scoffs. 'Because your lot will have so much sympathy for me, I'm sure.'

'I'm serious. Interview terminated.' I press the 'stop' button on the recorder.

I'd expected Stuart to leap to his feet. But he stays where he is, gnawing his lower lip.

Finally, he says: 'How did she die?'

'I can't say yet. It will be a while before the post-mortem results are released.'

'But was it…' he swallows. 'Quick?'

I say nothing.

'Oh, God.' He rubs his eyes. 'I can't imagine someone wanting to do that to her. I just can't.'

48

AS WE HEAD BACK into the office, Max taps his folder against his open palm in agitation. 'We need to find this sketchbook,' he says.

'Surely the killer's got rid of it now,' I reply.

'But then why take it in the first place? I think they wanted to keep it. As a memento.'

My phone buzzes in my pocket. It's a message from Kirsty. Reading it, I let out a groan. 'I told her not to do this.'

'What?'

'Georgia Reid's given an interview.'

We stop in the corridor and watch it on my phone. Georgia is sitting on a park bench being interviewed by a journalist. At first she speaks tearfully about Lily's murder and appeals for information. But soon the conversation moves on to that text Lily sent her.

'Kirsty says it's gone viral,' I say.

Max opens TikTok on his phone and searches Georgia's name. Endless videos appear with clips or snapshots from the interview. It's strange seeing Georgia's face replicated over and over again, looking washed-out in the camera crew's unflattering lighting. Max chooses one clip of a tattooed man in his bedroom, speaking quickly into a small microphone: 'I'm a body language expert and I'm going to tell you the three key signs that Lily's friend lied in her interview.'

'What the fuck?' I can't help muttering.

'Studies show that people who are lying tend to fidget excessively. Now watch what Georgia does when she's asked how close she was to Lily.'

The video cuts to Georgia mid-interview, squeezing her fingers self-consciously as she listens to the next question.

I burst out: 'She's fidgeting because she's on national TV and she's nervous. Do people actually believe this crap?'

Max silences the TikTok with a swipe of his finger. 'Unfortunately yes.'

He selects another video. My breathing speeds up.

It's her. Looking freakishly beautiful with a doll-like complexion. The lighting is dim but the cream walls and sheepskin rug tell me she filmed this from Vanessa's second bedroom.

Mia says: 'In one part of the interview, Georgia seems to suggest Lily is one of her best friends. But in another, she admits Lily hadn't come up to Scotland for a couple of years. And in fact she hadn't even seen Lily for two weeks by the time she disappeared. That doesn't sound like they were best friends to me. Did they fall out? What is it that Georgia isn't telling us?'

Anger pulses through me. 'This idiot. Of course Georgia had nothing to do with Lily's disappearance. If Mia had spent longer than fifteen minutes with her she'd know that.'

Max shakes his head and pockets his phone. 'Look, whatever. It's not serious. We've got to ignore this noise. If people want to speculate on the internet, let them.'

49
Harris

12 June

HARRIS LEAVES HIS HOUSE after dinner, just like they agreed. He walks out of town and follows the path up the hill, past a farmer's field. Scraps of sheep's wool caught on the fence tremble in the wind. The evening sky is eggshell-white, fringed with orange where it meets the coast.

Georgia is already there, waiting. There is no one else around and yet she looks like she is trying to shrink into the environment, shoulders bunched up, hands in her pockets. As he steps closer, he sees her eyes are wild with panic.

'Everyone's looking at us now,' she says.

'I know.'

'I shouldn't have done it,' she says, raking her fingers through her hair. 'I looked so suspicious. Why did I do that?'

'You just looked stressed. It's fine.'

But he's not sure it is fine. His friends keep texting to ask if he and Georgia are okay. All day he's been glued to his phone, scrolling obsessively through clips of Georgia's interview and photographs of himself that people have lifted from Instagram. He's not sure why he keeps looking. Maybe he's hoping that eventually someone will come out and defend them. But he can't seem to stop. It is horrifying yet compulsive at the same time. Like watching a car crash in slow motion.

All these years he's been waiting for a hand to scoop down and rescue him from his irrelevant young life. For someone to notice. Now his face is all over social media, and he can't bear it.

But seeing Georgia this upset forces him to steel himself. She has always been a nervous person – hyperventilating ahead of exams, overthinking every party she's ever been invited to – and in these moments he has learned to take on the role of big brother.

'It'll blow over,' he says. 'Everyone's a suspect right now. You wait. Tomorrow they'll have forgotten all about it.'

Georgia swallows. 'What if someone—'

It feels like a hard lump has formed in his chest. 'They won't.'

'What if they start looking into it? What if they work it out?'

'They won't, Georgia.'

This to him is unthinkable. He can't even entertain the possibility.

Georgia rocks back and forth on the dusty path, looking back at the town. 'I can't believe she's gone.'

He swallows.

'Do you remember when we camped on Lily's beach?'

He nods. 'We wanted to stargaze.'

'Except it was really cloudy.'

'And we couldn't see fuck all,' he says.

'You thought you saw that shooting star,' she reminds him.

He shakes his head. 'Looking back, I think that was just a fly caught in my torchlight.'

'And then there was the time by the loch. With the midges.'

'When we wanted to eat lunch but every time we sat down the midges would swarm.'

'Lily hated them,' says Georgia.

They both fall into an uneasy silence. He bites the inside of his mouth, not knowing what to say.

'I keep thinking about those times,' she says. 'The memories come to me out of nowhere.'

Georgia looks so desperately sad that he feels there is nothing else he can do except pull her in for a hug. As she rests against his chest, he feels a painful surge of nostalgia. The truth is, he thinks about this stuff all the time. The three of them used to have the most amazing summers. They cycled everywhere, stole booze from the Howards' drinks cabinet, drank it on their private beach, went swimming at night. It was perfect.

It all feels so long ago now.

He places his chin on Georgia's head.

'It'll be fine. No one will work it out.'

50
Mia

13 June

VANESSA'S MOODS HAVE BEEN difficult to predict since they found Lily. Sometimes she's manic, calling the police for updates while she paces the kitchen in her dressing gown. Other times she is inconsolable. Earlier today I found her curled up on Lily's bed with her head in her hands, like she was ill. But this evening, all she wants to do is talk. To me, about Lily, on the Howards' balcony overlooking the bay, with a breeze in our hair and a cold bottle of sauvignon blanc on the table, its contents steadily draining as she revisits the past.

'She was so creative. I don't know where she got it from. Even when she was small, she'd pick up pebbles on the beach and arrange them into these pretty designs. Leave her alone for five minutes and she'd make something.'

The breeze is cold this evening and she has a silk scarf over her shoulders. The light from the house turns her cheeks amber. You can hardly see the sea this late but you can hear it; the slow and steady beating of the waves against the shore.

'Perhaps I left her alone too much. She seemed so self-reliant at such a young age. And by the time she was a teenager that self-reliance had turned into this… overconfidence. Like she couldn't see risks. You know, no, you can't go backpacking in Asia all by yourself. Yes, you do need to wear a seatbelt. No, you can't just walk from that friend's house back to ours late at night, call a taxi.'

Her head is sinking closer to the table, her hand over her forehead. Her eyes meet mine.

'Are all young people like that? Were you like that?'

'No. I was very shy. I had a night light until I was fourteen.'

Vanessa smiles softly and reaches out to squeeze my arm. 'Sometimes I wish Lily had been more like that. Shy. Cautious.' Her eyes glaze over. 'I should have told her more about the world. About men. If there's one thing I know about, it's men.'

I don't know what to say. I often don't when Vanessa opens up to me like this. Part of me feels honoured she's this comfortable with me now. But it can be overwhelming. Like we're staring down a long dark tunnel together.

This is what I need to do, though. I need to put the time in. Because this is how I win Vanessa's trust.

The light across her face shifts.

We both turn around to see Martyn watching us from the open balcony doors. A bag of groceries dangles from one hand. He looks tired.

Vanessa dabs the moisture from her eyes. 'Did you just get back?'

'It's getting cold. Don't stay out here all night. You'll make yourself sick.'

'I'm fine.'

His eyes drift from Vanessa to the bottle of wine and finally to me. He frowns. But he says nothing and stalks inside. As we retreat back into the house I hear him filling up the fridge with his purchases.

'I wish our last week together could have been… happier,' says Vanessa, carrying our empty wine glasses. 'I wish I could have seen that she was struggling. There was one time a few days before she left when we were looking at old family photos. Just a bit of fun. And she seemed to be enjoying herself at first. But it was as if something upset her. She went completely quiet and took herself off to bed. I wish I'd gone after her. Found out what was bothering her.'

Blood is roaring in my ears.

'Could I see these photos?'

51
Ruth

13 June

I WAIT AT THE top of the high street, clutching my wrist in agitation. The sky is blue but the town is empty, still in a strange state of mourning. I check my phone. He's six minutes late. I wish we could just get this over with.

I'm glad I suggested we meet here before walking down to the pub together. I'm nervous enough without Declan bounding up to me and saying something gleeful like: 'Who you meeting? A fella?'

Finally I see him walking up the street towards me. I make a point of looking everywhere except at him until he's right in front of me.

'Hi.'

'Hi.'

He's going in for a hug. I didn't expect this. His familiar scent rushes through me.

'The Nag's Head good with you?'

'Not like there's many options. Pleased it's still going.'

As we walk to the pub, I think to myself: this was a terrible decision. This was the worst decision I've made in a long time. A woman has been murdered and I'm wasting precious time poking around in the darkest parts of my personal life.

'I'm so sorry to hear about Lily,' he says.

'It's awful,' I reply.

Before we head in, he takes out a bottle and squirts water into the palm of his hand before rubbing it over the back of his neck. I still can't work out his intentions. Why this? Why now?

'Lager?' he says.

'Yes please.'

As he passes, he touches the small of my back, so fleetingly it could have been an accident, and I feel a tug underneath my ribcage.

I'd forgotten how quickly Connor gets through his first pint. He always slows down after that, but he knocks back the first one like he's drinking water. Soon he's back at the bar for a second round, leaving me alone in the garden for a few minutes. Trying to match his pace has made me tipsy. It's golden hour and there's a bubbly quality to everything.

He is wearing shorts and his well-muscled legs are tanned from all the sun we've been having. As we're talking, he moves loosely, sometimes swaying his body within inches of mine. Every time he does, electricity spreads over my skin. I can see him thinking about it. He doesn't know there's no way I'm sleeping with him. Once we start, we won't stop. And that would only make things worse.

'You said you couldn't imagine coming back here,' he says.

'I didn't say that.'

'You did. You said you wanted to retire in the city.'

I realise with surprise that he's right. I can half-remember telling him this once at the kitchen table. A love of Glasgow I haven't felt in years comes back to me. It takes my breath away for a moment. How could I have forgotten something that seemed so important at the time?

Connor is staring at me. I realise he's watched these thoughts play out on my face. Heat rushes up my neck. He can read me as well as I can read him.

He tilts his head back. Golden light passes between us. Braeside looks particularly beautiful this evening.

'It was perfect, wasn't it?' he says. 'Sometimes I wonder if it seems better in hindsight. But I knew it at the time.'

I nod. 'It was perfect.' I can't hold in the question any longer. 'Why did you come here?'

He places his almost-empty pint on the windowsill.

'I saw her.'

My heart beats faster. 'Where?'

'In a café in Glasgow. With Reece. I was driving past when I saw them. I parked and got out as soon as I could but by the time I reached the café, they'd gone.'

He rubs his neck.

'I want everything back,' he says quietly, almost to himself. 'I want everything back as it should be.'

Maybe I'm supposed to say something now. But I don't know what to do with this information.

'What do we do?' he asks.

'Have you done anything?'

'No.'

'Well, what are you suggesting we do?'

'Talk to businesses on that street. See if anyone has security footage. A car registration number. Anything that will help us find them.'

'In order to do what?'

He turns around to face the pub, looking lost. 'I don't know.' He puts his hands on the windowsill and leans there, stretching out his body, head bowed, mumbling: 'I don't know. Kill him. Maybe kill him.'

He lets out a breath of dark laughter through his nose.

I scan the pub garden to check that no one heard that. I'd forgotten what it felt like. To be together like this. Two mad grieving people.

'Nothing,' I murmur. 'We shouldn't do anything.'

Something in his eyes changes. In an instant this exciting version of Connor is gone. The old resentments are back.

'You don't mean that,' he says, straightening up and crossing his arms over his chest. 'What is it? What's wrong?'

I swallow, preparing myself for what's coming.

'I see him.'

Connor's eyes are fixed on mine. A muscle in his jaw moves. 'What do you mean, you see him?'

'After I moved here, I started messaging him on Facebook. Asking if I could see her. He said she didn't want to. I said, well, if she doesn't want to see me, can I give her birthday presents?'

Connor is staring at me dumbfounded, with his mouth slightly open.

I go on: 'And he said that would be okay. As long as I gave them to him on the side of a road. Without me coming to the house. Or seeing her.'

Connor looks stunned. In a daze, he turns around and slowly leans back against the wall of the pub, like he needs the support. He stares out into the garden.

'How long have you been doing that?'

'For the last four years. Every Christmas and birthday.'

'Do you get him a birthday present as well?' he snaps. 'I mean, why not, right? Welcome him into the family.'

'I need to have some kind of connection with her,' I say. 'I don't care what that is.'

'That's not a connection. That's like… a vote of confidence in him. A way of legitimising his behaviour.'

'No, it isn't.'

'You would never have done that before,' he says, shaking his head. 'Not in a million years. You would never have done that before.'

It feels like something has snagged on my heart. I clench my teeth.

'Well, a lot's changed since then,' I reply.

I knew this was a bad idea. I should never have agreed to come.

He narrows his eyes, studying me. 'What's happened to you? I don't understand how you can… be here.'

I scoff. 'What does me being in Braeside have to do with this?'

'Everything,' he hisses. 'You're hiding. Do you know what I do? Sometimes I block out the weekends and I drive. I drive everywhere the police ever spotted her. Searching. Because that's all I can think of doing. And you. You just… send her presents? Like she's on holiday or something?'

'She'll only come back if we don't go looking for her.'

Connor looks as if I've slapped him. 'What?'

I don't say anything.

'Do you really believe that?'

'She chose to leave. And now she needs to choose to come back.'

'You want to pretend that we've drifted apart and she's somewhere starting a nice little family, happy. Safe. That's a lie. Someone dangerous took her away from us. She could be locked up in a room all her life. She could be blocked from contacting us even if she wanted to. She could be getting beaten up every day—'

'I tried everything to get her to leave him. Everything. And I see now that that was the stupidest thing I could have done. Because I gave him ammunition. He could say, "Look how controlling your mum is. Look how much she hates us, look how much she hates you." That's what he said. I'm sure of it. That's what made her leave. You always underestimated how clever he was. How coercive. And you never understood just how much she loved him. As incomprehensible as that is to us.'

'It's my fault, is it?'

'That's not what I said.' I shake my head. 'The best thing I can do is show her that I'm here, whether she wants to leave him or not. If she wanted me to play best friends with him, I'd do it. I don't care, I'd do it.'

Connor looks disgusted.

'There is nothing else we can do. Except wait. And hope that one day she comes back.'

'I can't do that,' he says.

'I know you can't do that. Why do you think it ended? I would do anything. That's the difference between you and me.'

There is a wild look in his eyes that reminds me of Vanessa. Of how I felt for years. It reminds me of thinking: *if I feel this way for the rest of my life, it's going to kill me.*

'You think you can just show up here and everything will be back to normal?' I say. 'It's gone. We lost it, we lost her, and it's gone.'

52

Six Years Ago

I KNEW WHAT WOULD happen. I had seen it a thousand times before on the job. I knew one day he would slip up so badly there'd be no coming back for him. And when that moment came, I would be ready.

One night in October, I arrived home at 9 o'clock after a long shift. For once, I had the place to myself. Connor was out for a friend's birthday and she was – as usual, much to my distress – at Reece's. Sweaty, I kicked off my heavy boots, flexing my toes on the warm wooden floor, before traipsing upstairs for a much-needed shower. Already I was playing through the day's events in my head, choosing what I would recount to Connor, when I sensed movement on the landing.

How she didn't hear the front door open and close or the sound of my footsteps on the stairs is still unclear to me. I can only assume she was lost in her own thoughts, wandering out of the bathroom in a trance. But somehow she didn't notice me until I was three steps away from the landing. I watched Molly look down at me in horror from over the top banister, her blonde hair hanging around her misshapen face.

One eye was almost fully closed, narrowed to a slit by a shiny pink skin swelling. Her forehead was bruised and her lower lip bulged out.

Involuntarily, I screamed. The sound made Molly flinch away.

'Oh my God,' I said.

She backed away.

'I fell over,' she said desperately.

'What's he done?'

'I fell over, Mum.'

I lurched up the stairs, needing to hold her, to feel that she was okay. She let me touch her face as I took in the damage. I felt like my heart had been knocked out of me.

'We're going to the hospital. Get your shoes on.'

She blinked at me with one watery eye. Then, to my surprise, she nodded and slipped past me down the staircase, heading for the shoe rack.

The moment her back was turned I made the call.

'It's DI Lindsey. I'm calling to report a domestic assault.'

Molly whipped around with such speed she almost tumbled down the flight of stairs.

'Mum!' she screamed.

I braced myself against the wall as she charged towards me. Throwing one arm up to act as a barricade between us, I gritted my teeth against her blows, surprised by the strength in her small body.

She was shrieking at the top of her lungs and I had to shout down the phone just to be heard: 'That's my daughter you can hear. We're fine. She doesn't want me to make this call. She's just been assaulted by her boyfriend.'

I rattled off Reece's name and address while she writhed and kicked against my side. Her nails caught my face as she clawed for the phone. But it was too late. The call was over. I let my arm fall to my side with the phone still clutched in my hand and Molly still pummelling me in the side. But her blows were getting weaker and weaker. All her energy was going into her tears.

'He lost his temper!' she choked out. 'He's not like this, Mum. He just – has a problem—'

I had heard it all before, all of it, from the women I saw every other night. Defending the indefensible. Blaming themselves. Describing a kind of split personality disorder.

I could feel her getting tired. After a few moments she started melting to her knees. I crumpled onto the steps so she could collapse in a heap on top of me. We stayed like that with her whole body trembling, her nose wet against my collarbone. It was the longest I'd held her in years.

I rested my chin on her head and stroked her smooth hair. 'It doesn't have to be like this. It won't be like this with someone else.'

She sniffed. In a small voice, she said: 'I think I need help, Mum.'

I had been waiting for this for two years. Permission. I squeezed her tighter.

'It won't ever be like this again, all right?' I said.

A square of light stretched like a UFO along the dark hallway before disappearing. I lifted my head. The raindrops that had collected on the diamond-shaped window in the front door glowed yellow as someone's headlights flooded the front lawn.

Connor hadn't taken the car.

And I hadn't told the police to come here.

'Wait here,' I said.

I crept down the remainder of the stairs. A column of light appeared on the wall as someone triggered the motion-sensor light. I opened the front door.

Reece was hovering at the edge of the front step with his arms straight by his sides, wearing a grey hoodie. In the light he struck a ghostly figure, with his pale hair glowing bright white. I knew Reece wasn't a drug user but he looked as though he'd taken something. He was jittery and his pupils were the size of pinpricks.

'I thought you were working,' he said.

'Not anymore.'

This wasn't a part of his plan. To take the risk and show up here, he must have been desperate.

He said: 'I need to speak with her. It's not what you think it is. It wasn't me.'

Even now, he spoke in a controlled manner, with no trace of stress in his voice.

'You're a fucking idiot for coming here,' I said.

To my surprise he didn't run. Instead he did as I said and slowly lowered himself into a seating position on the front step. I kept a constant eye on him as I called the police again to update them on his location. Reece sat with his head bowed. At one point, he glanced back inside the house.

Molly was still sat on the stairs, her hands covering her face.

When the car arrived, its headlights engulfing us, I felt a sense of relief unlike anything I've experienced before or since.

53

INSTEAD OF HEADING HOME I go to Kirsty's. I could do with some comfort. Everything Connor said is still spinning around my head.

I find her in her back garden deadheading roses. She's wearing a thick pair of gardening gloves and there's a wheelbarrow beside her that is filling up with faded, crumpled flowers.

I stand at the top of the small set of steps leading down into the garden.

Kirsty squints up into the evening sun at me. 'How did it go?'

'Terribly,' I reply.

'I'm sorry, Ruth. Do you want to talk about it?'

'Not particularly.'

'You know, why don't you come for a drink with me and Craig tonight?'

I rub my forehead. 'I've just been to the pub.'

'Yeah, but what you just did wasn't exactly relaxing, was it? You need a break. It'll be good for you.'

It is tempting, to be honest. I feel like I need to be around friends. Forget about Connor for a bit.

'Did you see Georgia's interview?' she asks.

'I did, unfortunately.'

She shakes her head. 'It's awful. The way she's getting ripped apart online. Declan's told her to stop working at the pub for a bit.'

I grit my teeth at the thought of Georgia suffering because of Mia's actions. 'I've been wanting to get your thoughts on something. Don't laugh.'

She drops a couple of clippings into the wheelbarrow. 'Go for it.'

I climb down the steps. 'Do you think she could be behind this?'

'What? Who?'

'Mia. She could have… orchestrated this, couldn't she?' I feel restless, the two pints still jumping around inside me. 'She's got a motive. A murder means more clicks for her. More money. And Lily always has seemed like the perfect victim. Beautiful. With a large social media following. What if Mia chose her?'

Kirsty continues pruning with her back to me. Eventually she says: 'Do you not think that would be sort of insane?'

She deadheads one rose with a satisfying snip of her secateurs.

'I'm not saying she did it by herself,' I reply quickly. 'Maybe she got help.'

She throws the chopped rose in with the others and turns to look at me. 'That's even more insane, isn't it? Someone agreeing to help her kidnap someone for likes on social media?'

'Maybe she paid someone on the dark web. Who knows?'

Kirsty's face is now filled with concern, which makes me dig my nails into my palms.

'You haven't met her, Kirsty. If you had you'd see why I'm saying this. There's something… not right about her. The way she talks, like it's not her own voice. The way she moves. Like it's a performance.'

Kirsty puts a hand on her hip. Then wipes her nose on the back of her gardening glove, thinking.

'I told you not to laugh at my idea,' I say.

'Do I look like I'm laughing?' Kirsty frowns at me. 'I just think, you know, forget about her. I don't like what she's doing around here either. But it's just… noise, isn't it? Forget about it.'

The distress in her voice surprises me. We look at the freshly pruned rose bush in silence. The sun is just about to go down over her fence.

'Do you want to put these in the compost for me?' she asks. 'Stay for dinner. Then we can head.'

54

'WHEN DID WE STOP doing this?' asks Craig, with a blissful drag on his cigarette.

'Since most of us need to be in bed by ten,' I reply.

After dinner I returned to the Nag's Head with Kirsty and Craig. Before long, we were the only ones in. Declan closed up for the night but joined us for a drink. Now I've lost track of how many drinks I've had. Craig has magicked up a pack of cigarettes from nowhere and we're standing in the pub garden talking loudly and sloshing our pints. The argument with Connor feels like it happened years ago.

'You don't bring your wife with you enough, that's the issue,' says Declan, pointing at Kirsty. 'She's way more fun than you.'

'You two have a little boys' club going on,' says Kirsty. 'I feel bad interrupting.'

'Please interrupt,' says Declan. 'Please save me from all his whining about the Howards.'

'Ah come on, can I go one night without hearing that name?' I say, taking a sip of my pint.

'I think the most shocking thing about all of this,' says Declan, 'is that Stuart managed to not only convince a woman to marry him but also convince another, totally different woman to have an affair with him.'

'Agreed. That has been a surprising development,' says Craig, slurring his words slightly.

'I think Stuart's pretty good-looking,' says Kirsty.

Craig squeezes her middle. 'Do you now?'

Kirsty frowns, reconsidering. 'Well, less so after all this,' she admits.

Declan shakes his head. 'He's an idiot. Always has been. I bet after a couple of dates Lily saw right through him. Is that what happened, Ruth?'

I roll my eyes. 'Don't think just because you've got a couple of pints down me that I'm going to start talking about the case,' I say, taking another sip.

'God, she's inscrutable,' says Declan.

There's nothing I want to do less right now than discuss the investigation. I didn't realise how much I needed this. A few hours talking nonsense with friends. I'm more drunk than I've been in a long time and the investigation feels like it could be happening on the other side of the earth.

We head back inside and I go to the toilet for a wee. I can hear the others laughing in the other room as I wash my hands in the tiny sink.

Suddenly a voice carries through the pub.

'Can you keep it down please?'

The laughter dies down.

I recognise that voice.

Hands dried, I step out of the ladies to find Max at the bottom of the stairs in his pyjamas, slippers on, hair dishevelled, channelling rage at the group gathered around the table.

He turns to look at me.

'Cute PJs,' I say, glancing down at his Christmas-themed pyjama bottoms.

I'm not too drunk to feel my cheeks redden as he glares at me with searing disapproval.

'See you bright and early,' he mutters, before skulking back upstairs.

God, he's annoying. Re-entering the bar, I pass the front door and notice most of us have been too drunk to properly wipe the mud from our shoes. There's a cluster of footprints around the doormat. I slow down, studying each footprint. One of them looks familiar.

My heart stops. I take out my phone. Bleary-eyed, I manage to navigate back to the photo I took all those months ago when I found the footprint outside the Howards' house. It's the same. I recognise the manufacturer's logo in the heel of the shoeprint. Whoever killed the hare – they're right here.

But who?

I stare down at the muddied chaos on the flagstones. The footprints of the hare-killer are turned towards me. They run beneath my feet, in the direction of the toilets. My mind whirs. Who was it who just went to the toilet? I can almost picture someone heading in ahead of me. Almost, but not quite. Why did I have to drink so much? This was a stupid idea. I use my phone to take a quick photo.

'Ruth! What are you doing?'

Who was it? I grit my teeth, trying to summon the memory. The back of someone's neck. A hand holding the squeaky door open for me. The sleeve of a fleece. What colour was the fleece? Green. It was green.

I look up.

Declan is laughing loudly at something Craig said, wearing a green fleece.

55

THE THREE OF THEM watch as I return to the table. I don't even try to force a smile.

'Oh no,' says Declan, with a glance at the stairs. 'Are you in trouble, Ruth?'

'Should we have invited him?' asks Kirsty anxiously.

'No, not him, he's a snob,' says Craig.

I'm barely registering anything they're saying. I sit down and they keep talking but I feel adrift in the conversation. Unable to latch onto anything. Declan smiles at me. In the low lighting, the shadows make him look ghoulish. I break eye contact and disappear into my drink, then realise with a nauseous twist in the stomach that I've had too much and place my glass back down on the sticky table while everyone continues laughing.

What's happening to me? I feel like I looked away for one second and when I looked back, everything had changed.

I get to my feet.

Declan snaps up, pointing at me. 'No. You are not going anywhere.'

'I'm heading home,' I mumble, pushing my chair under the table.

'Oh no, you don't. It's Craig's round next—'

'I'm going.'

'Maybe we should head as well,' Kirsty says to Craig. 'I feel bad knowing we're keeping someone awake.'

Craig, who's pink in the face, eyes half-closed, nods absent-mindedly. It looks like Kirsty might have to carry him home.

'When did you all get so boring?' says Declan. 'All right, let's call it a night.'

He gathers up a couple of glasses between his thumb and fingers and heads off to the bar.

'Coming, Ruth?' asks Kirsty, picking up her handbag.

Beside her, Craig sways from side to side.

Suddenly it's clear to me what I should do. 'You go ahead,' I reply. 'I think I lost my keys.'

'Really? Want us to help look?'

'That's fine. They should be here somewhere. Thanks though.'

I watch them leave the pub – Craig requiring some guidance through the door – and then I'm alone with Declan.

'What's up, you?' he asks, heading over with a handcloth and wiping the spilled beer off our table. 'Did I embarrass you in front of your colleague, is that it?'

I watch the back of his neck. The words leave me before I can help it: 'Your footprint. It's the same footprint we found at the Howards. Next to one of the hares.'

He continues wiping the table, but in slow, languid strokes, as he works out what to do. The backs of his ears turn pink.

Straightening up, he says. 'Okay. Okay, obviously we need to talk.'

He walks back to the bar and tosses the handcloth in the sink. Then he takes out a couple of short glasses and pours whisky inside. The floorboards creak as he carries the glasses back to our table, placing them on the dark, glossy wood.

He sits himself down, slow and steady, like we're settling in for the night.

'You're scaring the shit out of me,' I say.

'You know how much I love this place, Ruth. Did you know it was actually my dad's idea?' He takes a sip of his drink. 'Except he didn't want the Nag's Head. He had a vision for a restaurant overlooking the bay. It was going to have local venison, fresh fish, all of that stuff. He thought this place would have a tourism boom in a matter of years. Well, so did I, for a long time – but we're still waiting, aren't we?

'Anyway, do you remember when the Howards first bought their place up here? Around that time, they came in here for a drink. Can you imagine? Yeah, it was about the only time. They sat over there—' He points to one of the tables in the corner. 'Vanessa wincing as she drank her chardonnay. Didn't even have the manners to keep their voices down. "It's very dingy, isn't it?" But I thought, I want to show them this place has stuff going on, so I went over and made a point of chatting to them, telling them all about the great walks and local businesses. And eventually I started talking to them about my dad's idea for a restaurant. I thought, if I can ever get it off the ground, then these guys would be exactly the sort of customers who'd drop a couple hundred quid on a meal without batting an eyelid. And they lit up when I was talking about the restaurant. I thought, great, there's some future customers locked in. Except—'

'The Lighthouse,' I say.

'You may think I'm being paranoid. Maybe they had an idea for a restaurant up here before I said anything. But guess what? I told them exactly where my dad wanted that restaurant, and that's exactly where they built The Lighthouse. I actually put an offer in for that plot as well, when it went up for sale. But they outbid me.

'We do all right, but you know as well as I do it's not as busy as it used to be. All the tourists are losing their minds over a cocktail with a seaside view. And most of the year, the Howards aren't even here. I'm breaking my back trying to run a pub, and they just cruise in, "oh very good, very good".' He put on a pronounced English accent and mimed a polite, regal clap. 'And they're the ones raking it in. Can't even pay their own workers properly.' He shakes his head. 'It was my dream. And they took it away from me.

'I wasn't planning to do it. I was driving home one evening in December, Christmas presents for Georgia in the back. The last month had been dead quiet, and I passed The Lighthouse. It was all lit up, beautiful, full of people. My blood was boiling. I thought, if there's just one thing I can do to show they're not welcome here, I'll do it. And that's when I hit it. The hare.'

He cocks an eyebrow and a familiar mischievous light returns to his eyes.

'You've got to admit it's funny. I really wanted to hang about and see Vanessa's reaction for myself.'

I stare back at him, unamused.

'I know. It is a shame. They're pretty animals. But I liked the symbolism of the hare. I hoped they might think the ghost of William Wallace was haunting them, telling them to go back across the border.'

'It's a protected species.'

'I only killed them in the open season, Ruth. Come on.'

'You know we're still going to have to investigate you for threatening behaviour. And I need to tell the Howards, so they can stop worrying about it.'

'I'm really sorry, Ruth,' he says.

Heat rises into my face. 'You should have told me this earlier. Do you realise how much time we've wasted looking into this?'

'I'm sorry. I really am. I didn't know that.'

I should feel relieved. But instead I just feel hollow.

'We're worried about you,' he says. 'Kirsty tells me the sleuth girl is getting to you.'

Internally, I wince. Kirsty. I didn't think she spoke to Declan about me like that.

'Just take care of yourself,' he adds.

I walk home in the darkness, taking a shortcut through a field.

I pass slumbering sheep and trees twisted into monstrous shapes. The mountain in the distance is a pitch-black heap, blocking out the starlight, the only thing darker than the sky. I think of Declan in the pub, red-faced and bitter. He had seemed so far away. I'd felt like I was eavesdropping on a stranger, rather than talking to a friend. I think to myself: when did it all change? Days ago? Or years ago, and had I been too desperate for this place and all the comfort it brought me to notice the ugliness, lurking like mould in a room, and slowly but steadily spreading?

56
Mia

14 June

After breakfast, I make a cup of green tea and take it up to my room before looking through the album Vanessa has shared with me. Every photo was taken in Braeside. Some are very old. One shows Toby and Lily as young children building sandcastles on the beach on an overcast day. Others are far more recent, including a number of professionally taken photos from a party a few years ago. I frown. So many memories here. How am I supposed to work out which one disturbed Lily?

I go through my spreadsheet of notes about Lily's social media – who she was with, where and when, who commented.

That's when I see something I haven't noticed before. It's so obvious. I can't believe I missed it.

I rush downstairs and find Vanessa in the kitchen, washing the dishes.

'Do you remember much about this party?' I ask, showing her my phone.

The opening of the Howards' restaurant is memorialised on Lily's Instagram. I hadn't realised before. But until recently, it was the last time she'd posted about Scotland.

Congratulations mum and dad! Officially restaurant owners, she wrote underneath a reel of photos taken around the Shorehouse. It looks more vibrant than ever. Raucous teenagers and glamorous parents, plates of canapés on the kitchen table, champagne cocktails.

'Oh yes,' Vanessa replies, rubbing her forehead with a gloved hand. As she takes in the image, her eyes turn misty with nostalgia. 'Oh that was lovely. All the family together. All Lily and Toby's friends as well.'

'When was it?'

'It was the 31st of May 2022. The day we opened the restaurant.'

'Did you have anyone from the town over as well?'

'Only Georgia and Harris since they were Lily's friends. We didn't really know anyone in Braeside, after all.'

Not much has changed there, I think to myself.

'It looks like Lily had a good time,' I say.

'Yes,' she says softly.

Vanessa turns over a plate in the soapy water and continues scrubbing.

'You mentioned Lily didn't come to Scotland for a couple of years. Was this the last time she came up here?'

'It might have been. I'm not sure. Perhaps it was.'

'Do you remember if anything happened at this party?'

Vanessa stops scrubbing. Soap bubbles slide down the plate.

'Why?'

'I just wondered if there could be any connection. Her coming back here.'

Vanessa looks anxious. 'I don't think so,' she replies, panic rising in her voice. 'Most of the people at that party were our friends and family. And the vast majority weren't even here when she went missing.'

She tips out the washing-up bowl. The dirty water tumbles out in a cascade.

57
Ruth

14 June

'WELL, CONGRATULATIONS,' SAYS MAX after I've told him.

'Sorry to steal your thunder,' I reply. 'I know you wanted to solve the mystery of the Howards' hares.'

I knock back a couple of paracetamol with a glug of water as I sit recovering at my desk. I've given up trying to count the number of drinks I had last night because the tally is too depressing. What an idiot. Why did I have to push it so far on a work night? I'm usually more careful than this.

Max looks similarly rough this morning, his eyes puffy and bloodshot.

'Sorry about last night,' I say.

'Thanks for the invite,' he mumbles resentfully.

'You wouldn't have gone.'

'Yeah, but I'd rather be kept awake by an event I decided not to attend than one I wasn't invited to, thanks very much.'

I resist the urge to roll my eyes. 'Anyway, at least that's one less thing to worry about. We can forget about these hares now. We'll see what the Procurator Fiscal says but there was no other intimidating behaviour from Declan so I doubt he'll get more than a warning or a fine.'

'What do you think about him? This sort of gives him a motive now.'

I arch an eyebrow. 'You think Declan killed the Howards' daughter out of revenge after they stole his idea for a restaurant? He's petty but he's not that petty. Besides, he has an alibi. He was opening the pub, remember? Craig was there too.'

I look up BlackBird's channel on my computer. She hasn't posted so far today. Her video about Georgia's interview is still racking up views. It makes me feel sick.

I look over at Max, who's moodily typing on his keyboard.

'I wanted to run a theory past you,' I say.

He stops typing and glances over.

I lower my voice. 'Do you think that Mia Chaplin might have arranged for someone to kill Lily Howard?'

Max blinks slowly. 'No.'

'You haven't even heard my reasoning.'

'I don't need to. That's ridiculous.'

'It was just an idea. We're supposed to share ideas.'

Max goes back to his computer in silence. But I can tell he's barely looking at the screen.

'What?' I ask.

'Nothing.'

'What?'

To my surprise, he pulls at the roots of his hair. I can tell he's gathering himself. Suddenly he releases his hands – and explodes.

'You're *obsessed* with her,' he says.

For a moment the room rushes past.

'I'm not obsessed with her,' I snap. 'If anything, *she's* obsessed with *me*. Filming me. I mean, what the fuck? Could you get more personal?'

I say all this so quickly that I'm almost out of breath by the time I'm finished. Embarrassment crawls up my neck. I look around to see if anyone else heard that and catch eyes with Giblin, who blushes and ducks down behind his monitor.

Max rolls his chair forward and returns to his computer. Like he wants to move on. But I'm not going to drop it, not after that.

'What's your problem?' I hiss.

'My problem is you're more concerned with investigating some TikTok influencer than you are with finding a killer.'

'How dare you? Finding Lily's killer is the most important thing to me right now.'

'Are you sure? Because you seem to be spending a lot of time on Mia's social media. Have you ever thought about how many views you're giving her? How much do you think she's making in ad revenue from your clicks?'

'Of course I need to look at what she posts. You should be looking at it too. She's disrupting the investigation.'

'What does it even matter? It's not our job. Why has this person got under your skin so much anyway? She's practically a child.'

'Acts like one anyway,' I mutter.

Max raises his eyebrows at me, looking unimpressed.

'Look, you're not from here,' I say. 'You don't see what it's doing to this community.'

'I can see that perfectly fine, thanks. But from my perspective, the sooner we find who killed Lily, the sooner Mia stops.'

'Great suggestion. Who are they then? Go on, don't be shy.'

'You know what I think? I think you're scared that some random influencer's going to find out what happened before you do.'

'That's not what this is about.'

'Really? So you wouldn't feel embarrassed at all if she solved this one? You can't even stand having a partner on this case.'

'You know, this whole thing is going to be a lot more painful if we don't go for a drink together sometimes.'

'You don't want to go for a drink with me. You made that pretty clear last night.'

'Is that what this is about? Look, I'm sorry we didn't invite you.'

'Oh my God.' Max covers his face with his hands for a few moments. Then he looks out the window. 'This is a terrible place. I'm trying to think why I would come here willingly. Maybe to die? Yeah, I think maybe this would be a good place to die. The sea breeze. Very quiet.'

I scoff with disgust.

'The Howards have the right idea,' he says. 'Turn up here for two weeks a year and then fuck off.'

This is going nowhere. I should go make a cup of tea, get away from him.

Then something clicks.

'The Howards,' I say.

'What?'

A memory has surfaced from last night. 'Declan said something about the Howards not paying the people who work for them.'

Max narrows his eyes. 'So?'

My heart plunges into my stomach. 'Craig.'

58

Craig opens the door slightly out of breath, in a t-shirt flecked with paint. He looks pale and worn out after last night.

'How's the head?' I ask.

'I almost painted the wall with my tea, so I've been better. You?'

'Surviving. Is Kirsty around?'

'No, actually. She's working at the café with Archie. D'you want to come back later?'

'Actually it's you I was hoping to talk to.'

Craig gives me a concerned look before replying, 'Sure.' He lets me in.

He's midway through repainting the windowsills in the living room. Newspapers lie flat on the carpet and the furniture is gathered up on the opposite side of the room.

'Go on then,' he says, hands on his hips. 'Ask me what you want to ask me.'

I fold my hands over my chest. 'The Howards haven't paid you everything, have they?'

Head down, Craig digs his toe into the carpet, and suddenly I see the resemblance to his moody teenage son.

'Did Declan tell you?' he asks.

I make a face and he swears under his breath.

'How much is it they owe you?'

'Ten grand,' he says reluctantly.

I suck in air through my teeth.

'But somehow they can still offer a fifty grand reward,' he adds with resentment.

'You're working on The Lighthouse now, right? Why, if they haven't paid you?'

'They keep promising they will. But the situation's getting insane. The other week I saw Martyn in the street. I confronted him about it but he just got in the car and drove away.'

'Does Kirsty know?'

He closes his eyes and shakes his head. 'I don't want her to worry,' he says.

'How've you even managed that? Ten grand? Jesus, Craig, she needs to know. It's not your fault.'

'It is my fault, Ruth. That job, it was good money. But I really talked it up. We started spending it before I even got paid. And now…' He searches for the words, overwhelmed. 'Now there's a lot to pay off. But I'll pay it off.'

'Did you ever bring this up with Lily?'

He sighs and rubs his face.

'When I asked Archie about her coming over, he looked a little… concerned,' I say. The memory came back to me as I was driving over here. Archie had reacted strangely that day when I spoke to him about Lily's disappearance.

Craig says: 'You noticed that? The second-last time she came over, I confronted her about it. And I think Archie must have overheard. I said to her, "Look, your dad hasn't paid me, he's not returning my calls, can you talk to him about it?" I can't say it was a nice conversation, and maybe I was a bit emotional, but I wasn't aggressive. Anyway, when she next came over…'

Suddenly it clicks. 'The four grand in cash,' I say.

He nods.

'But that wasn't their money, it was her inheritance.'

'What difference does it make?' Craig snaps, his face turning red. 'What are you suggesting I do, pay them back?'

I shake my head, appalled. 'Were you angry she didn't get you the full ten grand?'

'Of course not, no. She explained it was her money, not her parents'. I felt awful but to be honest… to be honest, I really needed it, I wasn't thinking straight. It seemed fair taking it at the time.'

'Is there someone else who can back up what you're saying?'

He looks at the floor. 'I haven't spoken to anyone about this.'

'It's just… a woman giving you four thousand pounds the day before she went missing. It doesn't look good, Craig.'

He clasps his hands together, pleading. 'Everything I've told you is the truth. I'm sorry I didn't own up to it before.'

'Did you put her under any kind of duress to pay you that? Did you threaten her?'

'Ruth. Come on. You know me. I wouldn't lay a finger on her.'

I hold his gaze. 'Kirsty would want to know if she was spending Lily Howard's money.'

He crosses his arms over his chest, lets out a heavy breath. 'I know. I'll tell her. I promise.'

59
Mia

14 June

I WATCH DI LINDSEY say goodbye to Craig Moffatt in the doorway of his home. I know of him – he's friends with Stuart Marsh and helps with renovations at The Lighthouse. *Strange*, I think. Are they friends? Or is he a suspect in the case?

I step under the awning of a rundown shop but luckily DI Lindsey doesn't see me – she's driving in the opposite direction. I breathe a sigh of relief. I haven't come to Braeside for her. I've come to get some space from the Howards, think over the photos Vanessa shared with me. And get a bite to eat.

It's lunchtime and the café is busy. I glance at the menu. I would do anything for a matcha latte. But a standard latte will have to do. As I wait to be served, the queue falls silent. Up ahead, a man in his sixties with a blotchy complexion looks over his shoulder and shoots me a look of total disdain. I'm in a cold sweat by the time I reach the front of the line.

Kirsty Moffatt is at the till wearing a blue apron. She has a lovely maternal smile. But it disappears the moment she sees me.

'I can't serve you, I'm afraid.'

'Can't?'

I wish I hadn't come in here. The sweet smell of pastry wafting over the display counter is making me feel nauseous.

Kirsty narrows her eyes at me. 'Do you have any idea how much you're hurting people around here?'

I tighten my grip on my purse, but it's slippery under my sweat-covered palm.

'Are you serious?' I ask quietly, embarrassed that people in the queue are listening in.

'If you could go, please, I'll serve the next customer.'

I turn and leave, stumbling out into the blinding sunlight. As I walk down the pavement, I swear I hear someone in the café make a noise of approval, followed by a smattering of applause.

God. What was that about? My heart clattering around in my chest, I look at the white-painted houses with their colourful doors. Maybe I could take a picture of something aesthetic and upload it to Instagram. Maybe I could crawl under a car and die.

That wasn't about the post I did about Georgia Reid, was it? Huge overreaction if so. I open my phone and try to soothe myself by scrolling through TikTok videos of women making nutrient-dense breakfasts.

Don't these people see I'm trying to help? None of us had to be here. We *chose* to come all this way and search for Lily, then her killer. This whole case will probably get solved a lot quicker thanks to us.

A thin woman brandishes a smoothie bowl and spoons some performatively into her mouth. Maybe cutting a few calories today will make me feel better. I could cut out a glass of wine or two with Vanessa. Those are definitely empty calories.

As I walk in the heat, my distress turns to anger. I hate the parked cars, hate this town, hate the café owner and all her snobby customers. I try to think of a reason why she would act this aggressively towards me.

And then it hits me.

Of course, there is one explanation. She doesn't want me looking into the case. Posting about it online. What does she have to hide?

I open the Notes app on my phone and write down *Kirsty Moffatt*.

60
Kirsty

15 June

KIRSTY MOOCHES DOWN THE supermarket aisle, adding milk and dishwasher tablets to the trolley. She's grateful to be out of the house. She doesn't want to speak to Craig right now. Not after what he told her about Lily. How could he have accepted her money? It wasn't his to take. Now she has to find a way of paying Vanessa back. She bites back tears. Why hadn't he told her about any of this?

She shakes herself and tries to focus on the task at hand. What else had she meant to get? Unable to remember, she roots around in her purse for her phone, where she'd typed out a shopping list into the 'Notes' app.

What appears on the locked screen brings her to a stop in the middle of the aisle.

Five new messages. One missed call. Eleven notifications.

Immediately her heart leaps into her throat at the thought of her elderly dad. It's a fall. Or a car crash. She knew he should have stopped driving years ago. Shakily she unlocks her phone and scrolls through her messages.

She reads the ones from her family first. Her blind panic starts to fade once she realises that no one is in hospital.

But the feeling of relief doesn't last long.

The gist of the messages is largely the same.

Have you seen this? Hope you're okay.

Followed by a link.

Some of the messages are from random people in the town, which makes her feel horribly exposed.

She clicks on the link. Her hands turn cold and clammy. Her mind goes blank. She can't believe what she's reading so she closes the phone and opens it again. She tries refreshing the page. But there's no mistake.

It's her son. Pictured in one of BlackBird's videos.

'Does anyone else think it's strange that the police aren't looking into Archie Moffat, the local boy Lily was tutoring? Even though she saw him the day before she disappeared?

'And does anyone else think it's concerning that his mum just so happens to be the best friend of DI Ruth Lindsey, the lead detective on this case?'

61

Ruth

16 June

THE PAVEMENT OUTSIDE KIRSTY's house is overflowing with people. I swerve to avoid them as I park up. Even before I open the door, I can hear what they're shouting at the front door.

'Admit what you did to Lily!'

'Killer!'

My jaw tightens. I climb out of the car, Giblin and Hughes right behind me, and shoulder my way into the crowd. Some leap away the moment they see us. But others press closer. Shouting louder. Encircling us as we reach the door. The urge to punch one of these idiots in the face is almost overwhelming.

'You're protecting him!' one of them yells. 'We know you're friends!'

I've never seen these people before. Who are they? But I know already. Mia's followers.

The front door bursts open, revealing Craig. 'Get away from my house!' he yells. 'He's a kid! He's done nothing wrong.'

As the officers start pushing the crowd back, I slip inside after Craig.

'Are you all right?' I ask.

He slams the door shut behind him. 'Fucking arseholes. It's been like this all morning.'

Kirsty is coming down the stairs towards me, her face puffy with lack of sleep. I pull her in for a tight embrace. It scares me how weak she feels. Like she can barely summon the strength to hug me back.

'Where's Archie?' I ask.

'Upstairs. He won't leave his room.' She releases a shaky breath and hugs her stomach. 'I don't know what to do.'

I squeeze her shoulder. 'It's going to be okay. Can I speak with him?'

Archie is sitting at the end of the bed. As I come into the room, he removes a huge pair of noise-cancelling headphones. He looks dishevelled, like he's just woken up. On the bed I notice there is a dip marking where he's laid down on top of the covers. I imagine he has been lying there all day, listening to music, audiobooks, anything to block out the sound.

'This started yesterday, is that right, Archie?'

He nods. 'I was playing on the Xbox when my friend sent me the video. I froze. I didn't know what to do.

'And then all of these other messages started coming in. Some of them were texts from unknown numbers. But most of them were messages on social media or comments under the video.'

'What sorts of messages?'

'People saying I deserve to die. Saying they're going to come to my house and kill me.'

Even though I knew this was coming, hearing him say it out loud sends cold shivers running down my neck.

'Can you show me?'

He opens his phone, revealing screenshots of the messages he's received online. I read them with my nails digging into my arm. He sits there, not saying anything. I can sense how hard he's trying to hide his fear from me. I clench my jaw, wishing I could plunge my hand into the screen, grab every single one of these vile people by the neck and haul them into reality.

'They won't stop,' he says. 'Even at night I was getting messages.'

I look him in the eye. 'Anything threatening you've received, send us screenshots. If you don't have those, then send us details. We need to know the username or phone number, the time it was sent and on what platform, and the details of what they said. Can you do that?'

He nods.

'Once we've got those details, we can work out who's behind these accounts and we can find them and arrest them.'

I want to comfort him. But there is still a lost look in his eyes as he stares at the bookcase.

'People I go to school with think I did it. I can see them talking about it on social media.'

I place a hand on his narrow shoulder and squeeze.

'I didn't do anything to Lily,' he says.

'It's going to be all right,' I say. 'Your family's here for you. Your friends. And we're here for you as well. We'll do everything we can to make you feel safe.'

As I exit the room and close the door behind me, a wave of guilt hits me. Even leaving him alone right now feels like a betrayal.

Heading down the hallway, I notice the curtains in the front room are closed. A constellation of dust circles in a shaft of sunlight escaping through the gap.

We can't hear the shouting anymore. Hopefully the officers have moved the crowd along.

'Do you have any friends you could stay with outside of Braeside?' I ask.

Kirsty squints at me with a strange look, as if I've spoken another language.

'Why would we do that?' says Craig.

I continue: 'Just for the time being. Until this dies down.'

'Well, how long is this going to go on for?' asks Kirsty, her voice filled with panic.

'I don't know. No one knows. It could be just a few days. It could be… longer.'

I feel nauseous even saying this.

Horror fills Kirsty's eyes. 'So it's on us, is it?'

'He hasn't done anything,' snaps Craig. 'Why should we have to change our lives because of this?'

'I just want you to be safe. If you don't want to leave, then I'll come round every day. We can have an officer stay with you all day if that's what you think you need. But you need some kind of protection.'

Part of me thinks: what if this never ends? Even if we find who really did it, what if some of these conspiracy theorists don't believe it's them? Would they keep hounding him online forever?

'Is he a suspect?' asks Kirsty.

'No. There's no evidence pointing to Archie.'

'Say it then. Tell that to the press.' Kirsty swings one arm out, pointing through the wall, as if various newspaper editors are stood right outside.

'Do you think we haven't already done that? Kirsty, it was the first thing we did.'

'There must be more you can do!'

I don't feel like Kirsty's friend right now. I feel like an officer talking to a victim, which I guess is what I am. There's a knot in my stomach.

I've never seen Kirsty this distressed. Her breath is coming out in short sharp hiccups as she fights back tears.

'It's going to be all right. I promise. It will pass.'

'Please just help us, Ruth. Make them stop. They can't do this.'

She's right. This time I can't let Mia get away with it.

62

Mia glares at me from across the table in Interview Room Two.

I clench and unclench my fists, trying to calm myself down before speaking. 'So a few days ago it was Georgia Reid, now it's Archie Moffat. You move on fast, don't you?'

Mia says nothing.

'Why Archie?' I ask.

'All I did,' she says, 'was point out that Lily tutors him. That's all.'

'Everyone knows what you were implying,' I snarl. 'He's fourteen. He's a child. And he is not a suspect in this case.'

'In your case, you mean.'

Her childish tone makes the blood rush to my head.

'Do you understand what you've done? Do you know what that family is going through because of you?'

'I didn't incite violence. I didn't say he was a suspect. I've done nothing wrong.'

'There are people outside their house. People posting on the internet that he's a rapist and a killer. Making death threats. Have you ever experienced that? Can you imagine what that's like?'

'That must be very upsetting for them. But I can't control people's actions.'

Her nonchalant tone of voice baffles me. I don't understand how none of this seems to shake her. Talking to her leaves me feeling empty, like a vacuum has just opened up in my chest.

I narrow my eyes. 'Why are you doing this?'

'I'm just trying to solve this case.'

'No, it doesn't make sense. There's something else. There must be. Why would you do any of this?'

I feel for the first time in this case something approaching clarity. She must have a reason for being here. For doing this. A personal reason. Skin in the game.

'You're hiding something. And I'm going to find out what.' I sit back. 'We're letting you go pending a charging decision, but with a warning and on three conditions.'

Mia's face falls.

'First, you delete the post about Archie. Second, you never ever contact him or his family. And third, you stop posting about the case. If you break these conditions, you're straight back here. Do you understand?'

Mia stares at me in shock. 'You can't do that. What about freedom of speech?'

'Those are the conditions. Or would you rather we kept you here?'

'It's my income,' she blurts out.

I hit 'stop' on the recorder before placing my hands flat on the table and leaning in close.

'I knew you would take it too far. Didn't I already tell you how this was going to end?'

63
Mia

ONLY ONCE I'M BACK in my room at the Shorehouse can I let out my anger. Biting my lip to suppress a scream of frustration, I throw my phone onto the bed. But it skids off the duvet and clatters to the floor. Now I really do scream, launching myself across the room. Within seconds I'm kneeling on the plush carpet, inspecting the handset. Thank God. It's unscathed.

I squeeze the phone for comfort as the detective's words play in my mind, no matter how hard I try to block them out:

'You're hiding something. And I'm going to find out what.'

I close my eyes and purse my lips together and breathe in one, two, three, out one, two, three.

My inner reality creates my outer reality. My inner reality. My inner reality.

Then it hits me.

My eyes snap open. I leap up onto the desk chair and turn on my laptop before typing two words into the search engine:

Ruth Lindsey.

So she's going to dig up dirt on me?

Two of us can play that game.

Until now I've been sleeping very well in the Shorehouse. It's so quiet here compared to my flat in London. No hovering cars, no loud music, no late-night arguments floating up from the street. But tonight I'm restless. As I lie awake in the darkness, I start to pick up on the tiniest of sounds. I hear the creaking groans of the Shorehouse and the whisper of waves along the beach.

Then my phone buzzes on the bedside table.

Wide awake, I turn onto my side and open it. My bleary eyes adjust to the brightness of the screen.

Unknown number

What are you doing in Braeside you piece of shit are you investigating that case

My chest tightens. I close the phone and roll onto my back, staring at the lamp on the ceiling. They must have seen my posts. I pull my duvet up to my nose and squeeze my eyes shut.

The house now feels still and safe and more real than anything else.

64
Ruth

17 June

I'M NOT SURE WHAT I'd expected Mia's family home to look like, but certainly not this.

I'm standing outside a semi-detached house in Croydon with a front garden and a garage. It's taken me all day to get here and the drive has exhausted me. But I don't care. I had to see it for myself.

I ring the doorbell, and a dead woman answers the door.

'Mrs Chaplin?' I ask.

'Yes,' she replies.

Her round blue eyes – Mia's eyes – widen with alarm when I show her the badge.

'Is your daughter Mia Chaplin?'

'Oh God, is she all right?'

'She's fine,' I say quickly. 'We're looking into her social media posts under the name BlackBird. Is it all right if I come in?'

She leads me into the sitting room. A black cat is curled up on the sofa.

'Mia's not in trouble, is she?' asks Mrs Chaplin.

'She's okay, we just need to ask a couple of questions about her investigation. Do you watch Mia's videos?'

'I don't use social media,' she says. 'Oh no, she is in trouble, isn't she? Has one of her posts upset someone?'

'Has that happened in the past?'

'Not that I know of. But it seems only a matter of time, to be honest, if you're going to be rooting around in other people's lives like that. I wish she'd get started with a proper career. But I think the job market's so awful for young people now.'

I nod silently, not knowing what to say.

'Tea?'

She disappears off into the kitchen before I can protest.

Left alone, I look around the room. It's serene and cosy, with family photos covering the walls. In one picture, pride of place above the fireplace, Mia crouches underneath the tree on Christmas morning, basking in the attention afforded to an only child.

Mrs Chaplin returns, presenting a mug of tea and a plate filled with more biscuits than I could possibly eat in one sitting.

'You know she's in Scotland at the moment, investigating Lily Howard's disappearance?' I say.

'Is she? She never tells me anything. Although, I should've known she would want to investigate that.'

I frown. 'Why?'

She blinks at me in confusion. 'Oh, she hasn't mentioned?'

We stare at each other blankly.

'One moment,' she says. 'I'll just fetch something.'

She crosses the room and unhooks one of the photos from the wall, then comes back and hands it to me. I'm looking at a group of teenage girls in someone's garden, their arms looped around each other. Mia must be about 14. She peeks out self-consciously from behind a curtain of straight glossy black hair.

One of the girls posing with her is taller, older and less camera-shy. I almost drop my mug of tea.

It's Lily.

65
Mia

I GREW UP IN Croydon. I don't remember much about my teenage years apart from long drawn-out summers. I would lie on my bedroom floor listening to the drone of a lawnmower in next door's garden and the chatter of reality TV downstairs, thinking I must be destined for more than this. The girls at school thought I was weird. The boys kept their distance, afraid to join me in my social quarantine. I craved and yet feared attention, posting provocative selfies and deleting them the next day. I auditioned for school plays and cried when I didn't get the part. I was like a revving car stuck in neutral. There seemed no end to my dreary existence.

Lily was different. A shot of Hollywood glamour in black-and-white suburbia. I knew her through Gabriella, one of my few school friends, as Lily was close with her older sister. That meant there was sometimes a crossover. Us both round theirs at the same time. In the winter she wore heeled boots everywhere and the sound of her walking up the garden path to Gabriella's house used to fill me with excitement.

I don't remember much about the party. I hadn't seen Gabriella in so long I was surprised I got an invite. All I remember is retreating outside after I received that text – *you are the most vile person on earth* – and breathing hard in the garden trying to ward off a panic attack. That was when I heard the familiar sound of her heels clacking across the kitchen floor.

'Mia?'

I spun round. There she was, hanging out the door in a vintage Afghan coat. Her hair spilled out in a beautiful red mane.

'I didn't see it was you! It's been so long. Getting some air?' She clip-clopped down onto the patio beside me. 'Is it just me or are Gabriella's uni friends the worst men you've ever met? One of them just explained to me that feminism's redundant in the twenty-first century. Now he's hogging the speakers dancing to Soulja Boy with his friends.'

I laughed. I didn't like them either but I had thought I was the only one.

She pulled a bag of tobacco from her pocket and placed a filter between her lips. 'Do you want one?'

I had sworn I would never smoke in my life. But I found myself nodding. I watched Lily roll up, her nails gleaming with clear polish. I took a drag and tried to hide how much my eyes were watering as the smoke clawed at the back of my throat.

She talked like a river. Surging forward, darting this way and that. I found myself having to focus very hard to catch hold of something she'd said before she'd changed the subject. I could have spent all night lost in the tumble of her conversation.

The cigarette had hit me like an espresso and my heart was beating fast. Fairy lights glittered around the garden fence. I prayed no one would come outside and join us. She had beautiful cheekbones accentuated with blusher. Her skin looked very soft and I liked the way her full lips moved around words.

'Seriously, though, are you all right? Out here by yourself.'

'I don't know if you heard about that girl who was killed? Hayley Pieterson?'

'Oh my God, that was you, wasn't it? Who solved the case. Mia, I'm so sorry. I forgot. That's incredible.'

My chest glowed. 'Thank you. It's just, it was quite high profile and sometimes I get…' I gesture with my phone. 'Trolls.'

'Really?'

I nodded.

'That's awful. What the fuck is wrong with people?'

'That's what happens when you get involved with these cases, I guess.'

'Oh, babe.' She hugged me. She was being overly affectionate without embracing me like a friend. I hoped she would never let go.

The air was cold and there was something earthy between us. I'm convinced that that was the moment. If I had kissed her then, she would have kissed me back. I would have woven my fingers into the hair at the back of her neck and her lips would have felt smooth and pillowy against mine.

I was always meant to find her.

It was supposed to be me.

66
Ruth

18 June

I PACE IN FRONT of the memorial, listening to the dial tone ring out while the trees at the bottom of the hill shake their leaves in the wind. I'd spent the night in a cheap hotel on the outskirts of London and driven back this morning. I'm exhausted but I can't go home just yet. I need to talk to her.

The dial tone rings out three times before her voice cuts in.

'This is Mia speaking.'

'I notice you've stopped posting. That's good to see.'

Down the other end of the phone it's completely silent. For a moment I wonder if she's hung up. But a quick glance at the screen tells me the call's still going.

The wind blows a strand of loose hair into my mouth. I tuck it behind my ear and say into the phone: 'I want to talk, Mia. Just us two.'

My mind is racing. A seagull gliding above me tilts, caught off guard by a forceful gust of wind, and dips mid-air before righting itself.

'All right,' she replies. 'Where?'

*

'I said I was going to do some digging into you,' I say.

Gorse bushes surround us. She has agreed to meet me at this stretch of coastal path which is only a ten minute walk from the

Howards' property. A windswept hawthorn leans over the field behind Mia like an outstretched hand. In the distance, long waves roll in across the grey sea.

Mia stares at me as the wind sweeps her black hair to one side.

'Your parents aren't dead. They live in a four-bedroom terrace in Croydon. Your mum is a care worker. Your dad works as an accountant.'

I see Mia's eyes flicker as she processes this, trying to work out if she can fib her way out of this. But she knows she can't.

'Why did you lie?' I ask.

Mia shrugs.

'I know why. Because your story's not interesting enough for you, is it? You want darkness. I bet you can't stand it that your personal life is so ordinary.'

'Dead, alive, what does it matter?' snaps Mia. 'They don't have anything to do with this.'

'But that's not the only thing you've left out, is it?' I step closer. 'Your mum told me everything. You knew Lily through an old school friend called Gabriella. Lily was friends with her older sister. You met at their house a few times. You were at the same parties.'

Now Mia is glancing up and down the bay, like she's looking for an escape route.

'You going to deny it?' I raise my voice. 'Or are you going to tell me why you've covered up your connection to a murder victim?'

Mia reaches up to scoop her hair behind her ear and I'm pleased to see that she's shaking.

Finally, she says: 'You're right. I knew her. That's why I wanted to help when I saw she was missing. I thought it was a weird detail my followers didn't need to know. So what?'

'Did you know her family?'

'No. I'd never met them before I came here. Why do you care? Don't you think this is a pretty big waste of police time?'

'Maybe you take a different approach, but in my job, when people leave something out, you have to ask why.'

I don't like the small silence that follows.

Mia smiles incredulously. 'You think *I* killed Lily?' she says.

'You've benefitted from her death, haven't you?'

'I've never been here before and you know it. I didn't get here until days after she went missing. You can check everything. I wasn't here.'

'Plenty of others were. People pass through all the time in summer.'

Mia steps back, running her hands through her hair. 'This is insane. You're actually insane.' Her tongue darts out to wet her lips. 'I decided to investigate this because I *care*. Lily was an amazing person. I liked her. And I care that she's gone. More than you do, I bet.'

Maybe it's true. For possibly the first time, there's real emotion in Mia's voice. Empathy.

'Does Vanessa know?' I ask.

Mia takes too long to react. Delight surges through me.

'She doesn't, does she? You don't think that would make her pretty uncomfortable? Finding out that all this time, you've known her daughter – and decided not to mention it?' I bare my teeth. 'I know why you didn't mention it. Because you were worried Vanessa would see for what you really are. A hanger-on. A leech. I know people like you. You cling. You suck the life out of others.'

Mia is staring at me with fury. Her hair flares out in the wind. 'I can investigate you too, you know.'

'Oh yeah?' I open up my arms. 'Go for it. I don't have anything to hide.'

'That's not what your daughter thought.'

The wind surges, hitting me in the middle.

Mia keeps her face very still. But her eyes light up with glee.

Cold hatred seeps into my stomach. 'She wouldn't speak to you.'

Mia unlocks her phone and brandishes the screen, showing a conversation on Facebook Messenger. I squint. I recognise that photo. That social media profile. I've clicked on it almost every day for the past four years. I've opened a conversation just like this. Waiting, praying I'd see the blue speech bubbles appear on the other side of the chat.

'I don't know, she seems pretty happy to talk.'

Molly. Replying. Conversing. With this thing, this parasite.

I curl one hand into a fist. 'You don't go anywhere near her,' I say, 'all right?'

Mia chews her bottom lip playfully, looking like she might burst from excitement.

'You know what she says about you? She says you're toxic. That she's had no choice but to cut you off.'

The air feels thin. 'I'm being serious. She has an abusive partner,' I say breathlessly. 'He reads all her messages. That's probably who you're talking to. Not her. If – if he thinks she's contacted you – an investigator—'

Mia brings her phone close to her chest and starts typing frantically. 'I'll message her now, shall I? See what she has—'

I lunge forward but Mia steps back.

'You stay the fuck away from her,' I snarl.

Mia stares at me, still clutching the phone but no longer typing. She's got the reaction she wanted.

'You can investigate me as much as you want,' she says. 'Charge me for whatever you like. You can't stop me. You can't stop people finding the truth.'

She pushes past me and I watch the waves roll in like tiny white sails.

67

19 June

My hands tremble on the steering wheel as I drive to the station. I was so worried about Molly that I barely slept last night. What if Reece does think she contacted an investigator? What if he hurts her? What if he reacts by cutting her off from the world even more than he already has?

I'm approaching the gate of the station when a figure blocks out my car window.

'Why did you silence BlackBird?'

A red-headed man in his early twenties is walking quickly alongside the vehicle, phone out, filming me through the glass. He's not a reporter. This is too amateurish. It's another one of them. As the gates open, I keep my gaze trained on the car park ahead, trying my best not to engage even though my face is flushing with anger.

'People want to hear what she has to say,' he shouts. 'Do you have a problem with sleuths aiding your investigation?'

I drive through. In the rear mirror, I see him filming through the gates as they close in front of him.

'Is there something about your friend you don't want anyone to find out?' he yells after my car.

The receptionist Laura looks up in concern at the sight of me rushing through the door, frazzled and out-of-breath.

'Everything okay, Ruth?' she asks.

'Nothing threatening. Just another weirdo.'

'Plenty of those around lately,' she remarks. 'I don't know if you heard but there's going to be a protest in Braeside tomorrow. Anti-police. They're sending a couple of officers in case it gets out of hand.' She shakes her head. 'Do these people realise they aren't helping anybody?'

I head into the station with my heart still racing. How did he know Mia had been told not to post online about the case anymore? I'd known she might breach her bail conditions, but has she really done it so soon? Or did she tell him? I clench and unclench my fists. As soon as I'm in an empty corridor, out of sight of the receptionist, I pull out my phone and search Mia's name. She hasn't posted a video recently. But she has written a long, self-pitying Substack about her 'terrifying' arrest and subsequent 'gagging order', as she calls it.

I skim through it, knowing if I read it in too much detail it will just make me even angrier.

'Fuck me,' I mutter. A passing cleaner looks back at me in alarm. I've barely registered them pushing a trolley through the corridor. I try and almost certainly fail to reassure them with an awkward smile before plunging back into the online world.

Has this spread far? I click 'back' and select a recommended video called 'Police cancel BlackBird: my reaction'. The thumbnail is a sultry image of Mia with cartoon duct tape covering her mouth.

The YouTuber talks at a million miles an hour. He is American. I will never understand how people on the other side of the world have become so engrossed in this case.

'We already know that DI Ruth Lindsey, the chief investigating officer, is a close friend of Archie's family. Now, as soon as BlackBird goes after Archie, the police tell her to stop posting? Seems like a pretty big coincidence. You've got to ask, did the police shut her down because she was getting close to the truth?'

I put my phone away, not wanting to hear anymore. Pain twinges in my left temple. I put my back against the wall and let my head drop back, looking up at the harsh office lighting.

I thought banning Mia from posting would diminish her influence. Somehow I've given her a bigger platform than ever.

68

I FIND MAX ALONE in one of the meeting rooms, with boxes of evidence on the table in front of him.

'Where have you been?' he demands.

'Croydon,' I say reluctantly, closing the door behind me.

'*Croydon*? You want to tell me what this has to do with Lily Howard's murder?

'Mia knew Lily.'

'What are you talking about?'

'Mia was friends with her friend's sister. They knew each other. Went to the same parties at school.'

'You went to Croydon to look into Mia?'

'Are you seriously telling me that doesn't concern you? An internet sleuth who's been investigating into this case and living with the family not disclosing they knew the victim this whole time?'

'That checks out to me. She's obsessive. What are you suggesting? That Mia killed Lily? Are you still entertaining that idea?'

I hold my head in my hands and drag my nails through my hair. 'I don't know. Maybe. We don't know for certain when Lily was killed. It could have been after Mia came up here.'

'Does Mia even drive?'

'Or maybe she – paid someone to do it.'

'Paid someone to kill her? Can you hear yourself, Ruth? Look,

I know she's hurt your friend. But we need to focus on the real suspects here.'

Embarrassed, I look at the floor. My eyes are scratchy. My head is whirring. I don't think I can think straight anymore.

Max lowers his voice. 'We have three men here with a possible motive. Stuart, Declan and Craig. They're who we need to be looking at. Not Mia. If you're not prepared to investigate them, then we need to talk to the superintendent about—'

'It's fine, Max,' I snap.

Max looks away from me, going red. My heart is racing. My partner suggesting I take myself off the case. I really am losing control here. I should have told him. We can't investigate independently of each other like this. We have to do it together.

I nod at the boxes. 'What are you doing here?'

Grateful for the change of subject, he pulls on a pair of disposable gloves and drags one box towards him. 'I've been thinking about Lily's missing sketchbook. Why did the killer take it? Maybe it wasn't nostalgia. Maybe they were worried Lily had drawn something or written something down. So I went through her other sketchbooks and notebooks, to see if she'd done that kind of thing before.'

'And had she?'

He retrieves a notebook and places it on the table in front of us. 'See for yourself.'

I pull on a pair of gloves and flick through the pages. She had left some pages untouched and covered others with half-formed plans and unfinished sketches. There was a drawing of a songbird. A few lines from a poem. A list of potential jobs, ranging wildly in sector and location:

conservation officer (Blairgowrie)
gallery assistant (London)

She had also drawn local wildflowers in exceptional detail. I'm amazed how easily she captured stalky pink flowers that bloom along the roadside at this time of year. I keep thumbing through the pages.

Then I see something that brings me to a stop.

Near the end of the notebook, scrawled in the corner of one page, are the words *Tell Georgia and Harris. Make them understand.*

69

GEORGIA AND HARRIS STARE at me, wide-eyed.

'I don't know why she would write that,' Georgia says.

I've asked them both to meet me at Harris's parents' house. Harris sits on one end of the sofa, in shorts, his legs badly sunburned. Georgia sits on the other end, hunched over.

'Can you have a guess?' I ask.

'That could mean anything,' says Harris. 'Maybe she meant Stuart. Yeah, maybe she meant she wanted to tell us she'd started seeing someone.'

'This wasn't written on her to-do list. It was scribbled in the corner of a page, like she was in a panic.'

'We don't know what it means,' Georgia blurts out, her voice rising. 'Maybe she got killed before she could tell us.'

I rub my temples. 'There's something that isn't adding up here, guys. It sounds like everything was fine between the three of you. You were meeting up regularly for a couple of drinks or whatever. And then suddenly, about two weeks before she went missing, you stopped meeting up. Instead, she called you. According to her call records, she rang each of you from time to time for conversations lasting about ten minutes, sometimes even longer.'

'Like I said, we just spoke about her mental health. Family issues,' says Georgia.

'Is that true, Harris?'

Harris nods. 'Yeah. That's true.'

‘And why couldn’t she talk to you about that in person?’

They exchange a fearful glance, each waiting for the other to speak first.

‘She retreated into herself when she was feeling that way,’ says Georgia finally.

‘Is that right? Are you sure you two didn’t fall out with her over something? Over something she told you?’

They shake their heads quickly.

‘Right.’ I squeeze the bridge of my nose, pissed off. ‘I have the feeling you two are hiding something from me. And I hope I’m wrong. But if I’m not, you better tell me sooner rather than later.’

A clamour of rooks fly overhead as I walk through Braeside. Georgia and Harris loved Lily. I can’t imagine them having anything to do with her murder. But Max’s words are still playing on my mind. He’s right. I need to stop writing off the people I know and care about. Any one of them could have done it.

My phone buzzes. Giblin is ringing me.

‘Someone’s called in, Ruth. I think you and Max might want to talk to them.’

70

20 June

I ARRIVE AT THE flat on the outskirts of Glasgow at about 1 o'clock. The woman told me on the phone to turn up on her lunch break while she worked from home and her husband was in the office. Max has decided to wait in the car. It's better to leave this sort of thing to me.

Her name is Leila. She is pretty and well-put-together, with long nails and whitened teeth. I can tell from the large amount of beige and baby pink in the flat that her husband leaves her in charge of the interior decoration and, after the long, sticky drive, I appreciate the comfortable, well-ventilated living room.

We sit down on her plush sofa and she starts to tell me what she told the call handler. Like most women in her position, she immediately comes across as embarrassed and overly apologetic.

'This was ages ago so I don't know if it's relevant,' she says, gesturing a lot with her long nails. 'But after someone told me about Lily Howard's murder, I just thought, "I have to say something."'

'You did the right thing.'

'So, last year I was in the area for a friend's wedding. Me and a bunch of the bridesmaids and their partners were staying in an Airbnb on the coast. The day before the wedding, me and some of the girls thought we'd explore the area so we went for a walk near Tod Fell. And… I can show you the route we did, I'm not very good at describing them, but in this forested area, someone flashed me.'

'Can you describe exactly what he did?'

'I was at the back of the group, walking along the forest path. I think I must have seen movement out of the corner of my eye or something because I looked to my right and through the trees there was this man, fully clothed, but holding his, you know, his penis and looking at me. And he was—'

'Was he masturbating?'

'I don't think so, but I don't know, to be honest. But even though he was far away, I could tell he was, you know, properly looking at me—'

It's like a wave of revulsion has just hit her – she reels back and places her hand flat on her chest. 'Sorry, just – urgh – don't usually…'

'Are you okay? Do you need a glass of water?'

'I'm fine, I'm fine,' she says, nursing the spot around her breastbone. 'Sorry, I haven't thought about this for ages.'

'Can you remember anything else about this man?'

'He was wearing jeans and a black jacket and a beanie hat. To be honest, I was so shocked, I didn't really get a good look at his face. I turned around to call out to one of the girls and when I looked back he was gone.'

'Hair colour?'

'I couldn't tell under the hat.'

'Can you say how old he might have been?'

'Honestly no. Definitely an adult, not a teenager. But that's all I can remember.' She shakes her head. 'Sorry, I always knew I should have called the police. I knew it. But there was so much going on in my life. And you start to doubt yourself, you know. Like, did I actually see what I saw? But I know I did.'

'Did you and your friends ever visit Braeside?'

She nods. 'We parked there and got a coffee before the walk. We were only there for maybe half an hour.'

On the drive home, the sun is beating through the windscreen, turning my car into a hot tin can. Max lowers the window slightly to let in some air.

The incident has troubled me. It might have nothing to do with Lily's murder. But there have been so few sexual offences like this in Braeside that any one of them could be significant. Maybe it was an opportunistic walker, who visited the area once and never again.

Or maybe it was someone who saw the women in town – and followed them. Someone local.

'She said he was definitely an adult,' I say. 'I think that rules out Harris. He looks younger than he is.'

'I agree,' Max replies. 'But it could have been Stuart. Or Declan. Or Craig.'

My stomach clenches with anxiety at the thought. 'It was a year ago, I doubt there'll be any CCTV footage. We'll be lucky if we find a way of identifying this guy.'

Max lets out a sigh of frustration and looks out the window.

I stay silent, knotted with guilt. I've spent so long looking at Mia. I've potentially lost sight of the real danger that Lily was in.

71

WE DRIVE PAST THE park on our way into Braeside. I notice three teenage boys gathered around the swings, their long shadows stretching across the grass in the evening light. As we drive closer, one of the taller figures shunts a smaller boy into the metal frame of the swings.

Max has spotted it too. 'Shall we break this up?' he says.

I'm parking up on the roadside when the other tall boy takes a swing. My heart jolts in my chest. I recognise the smaller boy falling to the ground.

'Archie.'

Hastily I unclip my seatbelt and get out of the car. The two boys are kicking him now while he curls up, trying to protect his face and stomach. Max and I launch ourselves across the park, shouting. The two boys stop kicking and whip round. The second they see us, they fly in the other direction, heading for two bikes that lie abandoned on the grassy bank. Max takes off after them but it's too late. They're already pedalling down the road, right past our car.

One of them stands up on his pedals and yells something over his shoulder before he zooms away. I hear Max shout something unintelligible back, but I'm still running towards Archie, who's rooting around for something that's fallen into the grass. After a few moments he holds up a pair of glasses. I sprint the remaining distance, ignoring the pain in my lungs. By the time I reach him,

I'm out of breath. I hold out my hands but he gets shakily to his feet without my help and puts on his glasses. His lip is pink and distended.

'Oh my God,' I say, grabbing his shoulder. 'Are you all right?'

He avoids my eyes. Breathing heavily, he stares at the ground. I can see blood gathering between his teeth where he's bitten the inside of his mouth.

'Let us drive you to your mum's.'

'I can walk.'

'Don't walk, Archie, it'll be quicker with us. Who were those boys?'

'It doesn't matter,' he says, sniffing.

'Archie, you need to tell us who they are—'

'It doesn't matter!' he shouts. 'You can't help me.'

His voice trembles with rage. I've never heard Archie raise his voice. Before I can say anything, he turns and powers up the hill, his hands balled into fists. Looking at his slight figure under his baggy t-shirt, I can feel my heart breaking. I've failed him. Failed Kirsty.

I hear Max jogging up. Panting, he comes to a stop beside me and stares after Archie.

'There's a security camera over there,' he says. 'We've probably got the whole thing on CCTV. We can get them.'

I watch Archie push up the hill with difficulty.

'What did that boy say?' I ask Max.

'He said, "That's for Lily".'

72
Mia

20 June

I FOLLOW THE ROAD into Braeside with my earphones in, drum and bass playing, volume up. The police's ban on my content has left me feeling cut off from the case. And I'm not making much progress at the Shorehouse. I've looked at the photos of the party again and again and still can't work out what upset Lily. So I feel like my best shout now is to talk to someone in Braeside and find out more about Archie Moffat. I'd seen an anti-police protest advertised online so maybe this could be the moment.

I hear shouting up ahead. The memorial rears into view. People swarm around it holding posters above their heads. I squint. *Stop the police cover-up*, reads one. *Justice for Lily*, reads another. I draw closer. My music is so loud I can't hear the shouting very clearly. But I can practically feel the heat emanating off the crowd. Wow. I never expected this kind of reaction.

I sense a vibration in the air and freeze. Something has changed. It's barely noticeable, like a shadow creeping across the floor as the sun changes position, but something about the crowds ahead has shifted, putting my inner animal on full alert. It's the same feeling as when I was on the mountainside and I turned around to meet eyes with the detective. The buzz in your brain as you realise you're being watched.

I scan the faces of the crowd until eventually I see the head and shoulders of a woman standing in the middle.

It isn't the detective.

It's her. She's here.

She looks like a tear in a painting. Unreal and out-of-place. She's the only person in the crowd with their gaze fixed on me. Every part of my body screams at me to run but the pain in her watery eyes, underneath her dark fringe, streaked with white, keeps me rooted to the spot.

Everything happens in slow motion. She opens her mouth to shout at me. But whatever she says is drowned out by the noise from the crowd and the drum and bass pounding in my ears. Then she advances, pushing through the crowd. The sight wrenches me out of my trance. I turn and run, clutching the strap of my handbag. I dive down the first side-street available, mapping out the fastest route back to the Shorehouse. Already I have a stitch. But I have to keep going.

The music in my ears stops. My ringtone kicks in.

She's calling me.

I keep running. Ignore the ringing. Repeat to myself:

My inner reality creates my outer reality. My inner reality creates my outer reality.

I burst through the door. 'There's someone here.'

Vanessa looks up from the sofa. 'Who?'

'She's followed me. I never thought she would do that.'

'Who's followed you?'

I need to show her. It's the only way.

I hand over my phone. The white screen glows in Vanessa's wide eyes as she takes in the abusive text messages I've screenshotted over the months.

'I try blocking her. But she just texts from another phone.'

I still don't know how she does it. Either she has a wide circle of friends lending her their phones or that woman is spending a fortune on Sim cards.

I continue: 'She's been harassing me. Stalking me.'

'Did she find you online?'

I nod, relieved Vanessa has arrived at this conclusion.

'Have you reported it to the police?'

'I have,' I lie. 'But they're useless. I've never heard anything back.'

Vanessa reaches out and grabs me, pinching my shoulder. 'Oh my God. You poor thing. And she's here?'

'I just saw her. Staring right at me from across the street. She's going to try and come here and talk to me. Is it okay if you don't let her in? Or talk to her?'

'Of course we won't! Please don't worry. Of all the houses for you to stay in, this is the absolute safest. What does she look like?'

'In her early fifties. Dark hair, a fringe.'

'What's her name?'

I pause. 'Louise,' I lie.

'Well, if she ever comes here I'll deal with her. But I do think you should call the police if you feel threatened.'

Damn. I thought I'd put her off the police.

'I will.'

73

So it looks like I'm stuck here. I can't bear the thought of going outside and running into her again. So I'll spend the afternoon looking around the Shorehouse for anything that could help me decipher the photos. I open the bureau, revealing Martyn's papers organised into different compartments. Starting on the left side, I begin slowly working my way through the documents.

Seeing as this is only a holiday home, most of the Howards' paperwork must be back in London. But here I find bank statements and marketing plans for the restaurant stashed in one compartment. I sort through them but nothing there strikes me as unusual.

Another compartment contains instruction manuals for the various pieces of electronic equipment around the house. I force myself to flick through guides to the speakers, TV and the outdoor sprinkler system. I'm about to put the rest away when one of them stops me cold.

I glance around the room, half-expecting to see a lens glinting in the far corner of the room.

In front of me is a guide for home security cameras.

But I thought the Howards didn't have cameras in this house.

I ask the question over dinner, when I'm alone with Vanessa.

As I eat my pasta, she stands at the kitchen counter with her back to me and her blonde hair in a loose bun which bounces gently as she chops pecans for homemade granola bars.

The other day I overheard Martyn telling her to spend less time in bed. Since then, cooking has become a way for her to distract herself. But there is too much food for any of us to eat. And she seems to have no appetite at the moment. Yesterday I saw her slide almost an entire tart she'd made into the bin. Flies buzzed happily around the sticky apricot juice that gleamed on the leftover plate.

'Do you have security cameras here?' I ask.

Vanessa uses the back of the blade to scrape the chopped pecans into a glass bowl, which she places on the side.

'No, we don't,' she says. 'I know it would be useful if we did.'

'Have you ever had cameras here?'

Vanessa is silent for a moment.

'No,' she says finally. 'I don't think we have.'

The heat has been inescapable today. Like you could choke in it.

The air is cooler down here. An ocean breeze stretches up the beach and blows the hair off my shoulders.

Hearing my footsteps on the pebbles, Toby turns around. A bottle of red wine lies half-empty beside him.

'Oh. It's you.'

His tone of voice is difficult to read. At first I wonder if he wants me gone. Then he waves at the empty space next to him in an uncoordinated gesture. I take this to be an invitation so I sit down beside him.

The water gently slaps against the hull of the Howards' boat, which I haven't seen them use all summer. Everything is dark blue. The clouds are wild. Any day now and the heatwave will break.

He knocks back some of the wine and holds it out for me.

Tentatively, I sip from the bottle. The thick, jammy liquid coats my tongue.

He hasn't been around much lately. Even after Lily was found dead, he kept walking the hills. Like he was still looking for her.

His skin looks sticky with sweat and suncream and grit blown in from the sea.

'The last thing I said to her—'

His eyes narrow. His breath has that same sourness it had the first night I met him.

'The night before she disappeared, we argued. It was the worst argument we'd ever had. I told her to fuck off.'

'I – I—'

As I'm formulating a response, he cuts in: 'I can't get over it. I keep trying to forgive myself. But I don't know if I ever will.'

He looks out to sea then takes another, bigger swig from the bottle.

'What were you arguing about?'

'Doesn't matter,' he says, before lowering his head between his knees and rocking from side to side.

Cautiously, I place a hand on his back, which is rising and falling with each unsteady breath.

'You didn't know. It's not your fault,' I say.

Slowly I start to stroke up and down. My heart is in my throat. After a few moments, his back stops moving. Then he raises his head and sits up straight.

'You don't need to do that,' he says, looking at me.

I stop stroking.

He sways, his eyes drifting around my face.

His mouth tastes dark, like blackberries.

74

21 June

I WAKE UP WITH a weight across my chest. Morning light escapes through the shutters, revealing the contours of Toby's bedroom. It takes me a moment to realise the weight is his arm. He is face down beside me, fast asleep.

I glance at the clock. Eight o'clock. Time to go. Vanessa can't know I was here.

I carefully lift up his arm and place it on the mattress, then shuffle sideways, slowly extracting myself until I'm perched on the edge of the bed. Toby inhales deeply. I glance back to see if I've woken him up. But he just pulls the sheets closer and continues sleeping.

My eyes are adjusting to the partial darkness. It looks like Toby started drinking here last night. A desk faces the window and there is a glass on it that is stained with wine.

Then I see something else.

Something I've been hoping to find.

I get up, walking as slowly and carefully as possible to avoid making any noise. At one point there's a rustle behind me and I freeze, looking back over my shoulder. But it's only Toby rolling over in bed. He's facing the opposite way, his hair a mess of darkness on the pillow. I can tell from his long, dragging breaths that he's still asleep.

I creep forward until I'm standing at his desk, where his phone is. Last night he left it here, on the side, presumably too drunk to plug it in.

There's a crack in the screen where he's dropped it. I pick up the device and type in the passcode. I memorised it last night, having craned my neck to watch him open his phone and drunkenly read a friend's WhatsApp message.

It works. Heart racing, I swipe through the apps on his phone.

I find the one I'm looking for and open it.

I feel like the curtains have been flung open, engulfing me in blinding light.

Here it is.

Here's what I've been looking for. The key to this case.

I click 'download' and email the file to myself. Then I delete the email.

75

I DIVE OUT OF Toby's room and scurry across the hallway. The moment I cross the threshold into my own bedroom, I let out a sigh of relief. No one saw me. There's no reason for Vanessa to work out anything happened with her son. And there's no way Toby will say a word.

I pull on my dressing gown and gather up a towel, looking forward to a cool, refreshing shower. Then I freeze.

The upbeat chime of the doorbell is ringing through the house.

Listening out, I detect the sound of someone shuffling across the tiled living room floor on their way to answer it.

I tug the chord of my dressing gown tight and fly downstairs.

'I'll get it!' I call out as my feet pummel the stairs.

I'm barely halfway down when I see Vanessa in the middle of the living room hunched over her phone.

I slow down as I approach her, trying to see what she's looking at. It's a video of the blue sky with a figure looming in the foreground. She's watching the livestream through the doorbell camera.

'I think it's her!' she shrieks.

My stomach drops. I manage to swerve past her, heading straight for the door.

'I can go and talk to her,' I shout over my shoulder.

It might not be too late. The doorbell is at the security gate. If I can just make it there first—

My hand is closing over the brass doorknob when a tinny voice pierces the air.

'Vanessa Howard? Please, I need to speak with you.'

I turn around to find Vanessa holding the phone near her chin.

She's talking through the intercom system and Vanessa has her on speaker.

Cold sweat gathers between my shoulder blades, sticking to my dressing gown.

It's like a seance. A voice from the past arriving in the room.

Vanessa says loudly into the phone: 'This is Vanessa Howard. Listen, I know who you are. You're not welcome here!'

The voice replies: 'Whatever she's said, it's not true. I just want to help you. There's something you need to know about Mia.'

For one moment confusion flashes in Vanessa's eyes. Then she says firmly: 'You're not welcome here. Please leave.'

She ends the call.

I let out a deep breath, feeling my whole chest deflate.

Vanessa is studying the floor.

'I'm so sorry about all this,' I say.

'No, no, don't be silly, it's not your fault at all.'

But her voice is faint and she hasn't once looked at me.

I say: 'She was just trying to mess with you there. That's what she does. She manipulates people.'

Vanessa seems to shake herself. 'What a horrible person,' she says.

I wince because for one panicked moment I think she's directing this at me. But no, of course not.

I'm aching for Vanessa to say something else, something to show that she believes me and not that strange woman outside. I've grown fond of Vanessa. I care what she thinks of me. But instead she retreats into the kitchen in silence, leaving me with my heart beating fast in my chest, staring at a painting on the wall. The dark eyes of a bloodhound watch me hungrily from the foot of his master's armchair.

76

Ruth

21 June

I WAKE UP TO a text from Kirsty that makes my blood run cold. I rush out of the house and down the high street to the café. A spiderweb of cracks spread out from a dent in the corner of the shopfront window. The glass door, on the other hand, has completely shattered. I step closer and peer inside. There are shards all over the floor around the door. The wall behind the till looks different and I realise they've smashed up the stuff there as well – the teacups and glasses that Kirsty had carefully arranged on shelves and dangled from hooks. The paintings on the right have been knocked off the wall. In their place are scrawled the words, 'rapist killer'.

I step back, trembling. I know how much this place means to Kirsty. Every penny spent on it has been diligently saved over years and years, every piece of crockery lovingly selected.

I look at Kirsty, sat in the back of the police car facing out. It scares me how tired and defeated she looks right now.

'It's just stuff,' she says.

'We'll find out who did it.'

'The officers will look into it. You're too busy.'

She says this in a flat tone that's unusual for her. Perhaps she's lost faith in the force's ability to help her with any of this. Or perhaps what she's saying is she needs me to stop being a detective right now. She needs me to be her friend instead.

'Craig will be pleased,' she says. 'They smashed up that china model of the cuddling cats that he hated.'

I glance back into the café. 'They left the plate with the dancing mice on it though.'

'That's because even vandals appreciate true art when they see it.'

'Shit, that was my moment, wasn't it? I should've knocked it off the wall before you noticed.'

I hold out my hand. She squeezes it and leans against my side. She gives me a small, almost sleepy smile but I can feel her rocking slightly from side to side.

My radio beeps. An officer says: 'Ruth, someone's turned up at the station. She says she's got information relating to the Lily Howard case.'

77

THE WOMAN TAKES A seat opposite me in Interview Room Three. She's in her fifties. She wears baggy clothes, including a jacket that comes down to her thumbs, and her dark fringe is threaded with silvery grey.

I open my notepad, struggling to hide my frustration. So far I've succeeded at palming off time-wasters on the officers. But now it's finally my turn. Hopefully I can get this over with quickly.

'What's your name please?'

'Jackie Pieterson.'

'So you say you have some information about Lily Howard's murder. And what is that?'

'It's not about Lily's murder as such,' she says.

Here we go. I tighten my grip on my pen, bracing myself for the rant that's coming.

'But it is relevant. It's about Mia Chaplin.'

The name snaps through me. Suddenly my mind is completely clear, as though I've dunked myself in the sea midwinter.

She continues: 'Online she's called BlackBird.'

'I know who Mia is. What information do you have on her?'

'Well, I know she's staying with Lily's mum now. Vanessa? And I was hoping you could tell Vanessa for me that she needs to get Mia out. She shouldn't stay with her.'

My heart is pounding in my chest.

'Why?'

'It's not safe. She could do it again.'

'Do what?'

'Get someone killed.'

78

'SHE'S DONE THIS BEFORE,' says Jackie. 'This is what she does. A pretty young woman dies or goes missing. She worms her way into the family. Pretends she's investigating those around them. When really she's investigating them.

'I had a daughter called Hayley. I'll get a picture for you.'

She rummages around in her handbag for her phone and opens the screen. The wallpaper is of a girl with a wide, toothy smile and brown eyes.

'One day, five years ago, she didn't come home from school. They found her the next day, in a field. She was just seventeen.'

I swallow a painful lump in my throat.

'Two years went by with no suspects. The police interviewed witnesses, made a few arrests, but it seemed like everyone had an alibi for the evening she died. We were getting nowhere.

'So we decided to raise the profile of the case through the media. There'd been loads of interest in that first month but it had fizzled out when there were no obvious leads.

'We spoke to some journalists and a few articles were published. More people started coming forward after that. Speaking to the police. And to us as well.

'And that's when Mia got in touch.

'I still remember her first message. It was very nice and professional. "I'm so sorry for your loss. I'm an investigator who uses mainly online tools to solve cases. I've been trying to find your daughter's killer and I would really appreciate the chance to talk to you about what I've found so far. This is all pro bono, just to let you know."

'At first I was suspicious. There's a lot of weirdos online. And she was so young, not much older than Hayley had been. But no one else had offered to help us like that before. I thought, how much harm can it do? So I arranged to meet her in a café. Have you met her before?'

I nod.

'Then you'll know she's very charismatic.'

I'm not sure she's ever turned on the charm for me, I almost say, but I keep my mouth shut.

'She'd spotted a few things the police hadn't. I liked her. I see now it was a sales pitch. This was just a teaser and the implication was, if I wanted her to do more digging, I had to cooperate with her.

'So she started coming round more and more. Some of the questions were intrusive, but I was fine with that. It was nice to feel like someone was giving the case the attention it deserved. That Hayley deserved.

'I can't believe I let her in so easily. I think on some level I was – you know, I was lonely. I was shutting myself away in my room. Not talking to friends. It sounds awful to say, because they were so good, my friends. But they still had their kids. They were still living their normal lives. For a long time, I found it hard to be near them without being constantly reminded of what I'd lost.'

I nod. I know the feeling myself.

She continues: 'I can see now she was just getting information from me. In her eyes, I was as much a suspect as anyone.

'I can't believe I did this, but I admitted to her that my husband Sean lied about his alibi. He struggled with drug addiction for a long time. He told the police he was at home when she was killed, but really he was out buying drugs. I kick myself for telling her. I don't know, I just – I trusted her. I thought she should know everything that happened and she would understand why we didn't want that coming out. But about a month after we met, she posted a video on YouTube. Saying Sean had given the police a false alibi. She'd found a picture on social media where he was in the background, sitting on a park bench, proving he wasn't at home.

'That video changed everything. The police interviewed Sean again and concluded he had nothing to do with Hayley's death. They sent him on a drug awareness course. But we started getting trolled online. Death threats. I had to shut down my social media accounts. Someone graffitied "murderers" on the front of our house. But we didn't want to move. Our friends were nearby. And I felt like if she'd died here, how could we just leave, without even knowing who did it?

'The police never did anything. Never found who it really was, never came out and said it wasn't us, never identified anyone who'd sent the threats.

'One night, my husband, Sean, was at the local pub with his friends. I never wanted to go out after Hayley died but he was the opposite. He wanted to get out, take his mind off things. He and his friend were heading home when a group of lads came stumbling after them. They'd spotted him in the pub. They started shouting: "You! You killed your own daughter!" His mate was telling him to leave it but Sean stopped and started shouting back. And then they hit him. His head hit the pavement.

'They pleaded manslaughter in court, and the jury believed them. The maximum one of them got was seven years. The judge said the attack was clearly motivated by their belief he'd killed Hayley. They didn't even know her.

'It was never like that before. I just keep thinking, if she hadn't come into our lives, would he still be—'

Her voice starts to break. She looks up at the ceiling as she rubs away the tears.

'That was last year. I thought, "There you go, he's dead now, you got what you wanted." I thought everyone would see he was innocent. But it was the opposite. Like now he could no longer defend himself, it was definitely true.

'And she cashed in on it. Big time. That original video she posted has almost a million views. Look her up and she's known as the woman that solved the case.'

'Did she communicate with you after she posted that video?'

'Not once. After that post, she disappeared out of our lives. I still have her number. I text her all the time. Call her names. Ask her how she can live with herself. I know that's bad. I shouldn't. But I can't help it. She doesn't get to do that to me and just vanish. She haunts me, so I'm going to haunt her too.

'I still check her social media. Just to see if she tries posting about me again. A few days ago, I saw she'd got involved in the Lily Howard case. And I knew then, I knew she was going to do the exact same thing to this family that she did to me. I had to warn them: don't speak to her. All she's doing is trying to get as many views, as many likes as possible. She wants a circus.'

79

As I rush up to the security gates of the Shorehouse, I see Vanessa walking around the lawn in her Hunter boots, head down, deep in thought. I call her name and she comes over to let me in.

I realise it must be the first time I've seen her outdoors in weeks. Ever since Mia came into her life, she's been barricading herself in that house.

'How are you? I ask as we walk around the grounds.

She looks at the sea. I'm not sure if she heard my question.

'I spend a lot of time out here when I want some time to myself,' she says.

By that, I wonder if she means she wants to escape Mia, living rent-free in their house.

She continues: 'Or up on the cliff. But only very early in the morning though. I'm worried if someone sees me, then word will spread and people will be there waiting for me. Taking pictures.'

She sounds different. The usually haughty tone is gone from her voice. She speaks with the softness of someone who's just woken up. 'You know, Lily used to talk about the restorative power of walking in nature. I never got into it myself. But now I do see.'

I chew the inside of my mouth. Maybe now isn't the best time, but I have to tell her.

'There's a woman who wants to speak to you, Vanessa. She said she came round here. But you wouldn't let her in.'

She purses her lips in disdain. Tightens her arms round her body. 'I know all about her already. Mia's stalker. Louise.'

'She's not called Louise. She's called Jackie. Jackie Pieterson.'

Vanessa blinks in confusion.

'Did Mia tell you she was harassing her?' I go on.

'She *showed* me. I saw the texts.'

'Did she also tell you that woman is the mother of Hayley Pieterson? The girl from Croydon who was killed five years ago? Whose case Mia solved?'

Vanessa frowns. 'That's not true.'

But there's panic in her eyes.

'Mia's taking advantage of you. She's not your friend.'

'How do you know this woman isn't lying?' she says tearfully. 'Or in denial? Have *you* investigated that case?'

'She went through the exact thing you did. Mia contacted the family, built a relationship with them. And then one day she posted a video that destroyed their lives. Mia's posted about every major connection Lily had in the town. Except you. I don't know for sure. But I'd bet that your family is next, Vanessa.

'Has she asked you questions about where you were that night? Has she asked to see old photos, diaries?'

'But they think it's us. The people who live here. They're the ones who think I could have killed my own daughter. Not Mia.'

'I don't know if that's true, Vanessa,' I reply carefully. 'I think a lot of people in Braeside want to help you. I don't know if Mia does.'

Vanessa looks at the sea again. The wind blows a strand of hair across her face. 'Was your daughter taken? Or did she run away?'

The question catches me off guard. I look at my boots. After a moment, I say: 'It was both, in a sense. Someone got in her head. A parasite.'

'I never knew. I'm so sorry.'

I swallow down my emotions. 'Let me help you, Vanessa.'

She hesitates. She glances back at the house. I imagine Mia up there in her room, scrolling through social media, searching for clues.

Then she says: 'There's something Mia's been focusing on. We had a big party the last time Lily was in Scotland, back in 2022. I was looking over family photos with Lily and something seemed to upset her. I've no idea what. But Mia seems to think it was something to do with that party. I could send the photos to you? See if you notice anything?'

'Yes,' I reply. 'Please do.'

I look at the photos as soon as I'm back in the car. The photographer must have used a drone because some are taken from an aerial perspective. The house looks huge, impressively underlit just for this shot. The guests' cars are parked in a horseshoe in the car park at the front of the house. There's so many of them it could be a wedding.

I scan the photograph again and my vision blurs. Blood roars in my ears.

And I realise. I realise someone is lying.

80

THE LIGHT IS FADING as I walk down the high street. The white-painted houses glow pale blue in the darkness and the sky looks stormy over the dark smudge of forest. I have no idea if they will be home. But I have to check. I can't sit on this until morning. I need to know now.

I turn off the high street and down one of the roads, passing an older neighbour carrying their shopping home from the Spar. Then I reach a house with a blue-painted door and a well-kept front garden. Someone is home. The curtains are open and a light is on in the kitchen.

I walk up and knock.

When Georgia opens the door and sees me standing there, her expression is one of fear but also acceptance, like she's been waiting for me all this time.

Georgia is home alone while her parents are working at the pub. I tell her to call Harris over and we wait in a long silence until we hear the sound of the door closing and he appears, ragged and out-of-breath, damp from cycling in a brief drizzle. He puts his bicycle helmet on the table.

'Sit down,' I tell him.

He does.

'The Howards' party on the 31st of May 2022. There's another reason that date's so significant. Tell me what happened.'

They look at each other.

'You already know,' says Harris.

'I want to hear you two say it.'

'It was a party to celebrate the launch of The Lighthouse,' he says. 'The Howards had invited a load of friends up from London. We were some of the only locals there. It was really glamorous. Champagne cocktails. Golden balloons. They had a proper photographer and everything.'

'Why did you leave?'

His face darkens.

'There's no point hiding anymore, Harris.'

'Some of Lily and Toby's friends from London were asking if we had any drugs. A couple of them had already taken something, but they were out and they wanted more. They were being really insistent. Pushy.'

'It was only weed, that was all we ever had,' Georgia adds quickly. 'I swear. We never bought anything else.'

'Anyway, I – I said I had some back at mine. I really wanted them to like me for some reason. Everyone was over the limit. But suddenly it was like someone *had* to go. At one point, they were even saying, "we'll go then, what's your address?" Like, "oh yeah, just drive to my house off your face on mandy and sneak in. Say hi to my mum for me." So, before I even really understood what was happening, I was going.'

Georgia says: 'And I'd driven us here. So of course it had to be my car, and if it was my car, then I had to come as well.'

'And Lily?'

'Lily was in this rebellious phase. Didn't care what her parents thought. She wanted her London friends to have a good time. So she came too.'

'The three of you?'

They nodded.

'How much had you had to drink?'

'A couple of cocktails each.'

'The car park in front of the house is so big and everyone was inside, so no one even noticed us leave. We drove back to mine without any trouble. You know how quiet the roads are round here. I knew my parents would be watching TV. Our back door's really quiet, it doesn't squeak at all, so I snuck in, got the weed, came out without them seeing or hearing me. They were none the wiser.'

'It was…' Georgia swallows, 'exciting.'

'We felt invincible. So on the way back, we turned up the tunes. We were all singing along. And then one of us screamed.'

'It might have been me. I don't know,' says Georgia.

'We saw the car too late. Coming out of a side road. Smashed into it.'

'My whole body jolted forward. I thought my spine had snapped in two.'

'The noise was immense. Just metal on metal. So loud I thought it was the sound of the car coming through the windscreen. The sound of death. I must have closed my eyes because when I next opened them, we'd skidded to the far left of the road. I remember thinking, "Oh my God, I'm okay. I'm alive." And I looked up and Lily and Georgia were okay too. I couldn't believe it. And then—'

'And then I saw them. The tail lights. Glowing out of the ditch on the side of the road.'

'I got out. I was shaking like a leaf. I ran to the car. Called out to the driver. Started clambering down in the ditch. But then I could see – I could see the bonnet had hit a tree. And the driver. His head was down on the steering wheel. There was so much blood. I – I just knew.'

It feels like all of the air has been sucked out of the room. Georgia and Harris sit there in silence, their heads bowed in shame.

'You didn't check on him?' I ask. I still can't believe what I'm hearing.

'His head was smashed, Ruth. There was no way.'

I bite the inside of my mouth so hard I almost draw blood. 'I was on that case. I remember the post-mortem. And you're right, Harris, he died instantly. But do you know how many times they don't? How many of them could have been saved, if they got help just that little bit sooner?'

Harris is grey in the face. Frantically, I run through what they've just told me in my head, committing it to memory, and I notice there's one crucial detail they've left out.

'Who was driving the car?' I ask.

They look at each other, then back at me.

'We're not going to say that,' says Harris.

'Who decided not to call the police?'

'We're all in this together. We're all to blame.'

Presumably, Lily isn't the one chiefly responsible here, otherwise they'd admit that. One of these two was behind the wheel that night.

'Well, go on then. What happened after the crash?'

'We drove back. It was so dark. Lily was almost sick. I was worried about her leaving her DNA on the side of the road so I told her to hold it in until we got back. You were crying,' he says to Georgia, whose eyes are welling with tears. 'And I was just… numb. Totally numb. In shock, I think. We got back. Unbelievably, we hadn't even been gone for an hour. It had all happened so quickly, barely anyone had noticed we were gone. We tried to act normal, rejoin the party. Give Lily's friends the weed. They said we looked really rough. I think they thought we were terrified about getting caught. I always worried they'd work it out. But I don't think they ever did. They all got the train home the next day. None of them would have passed the scene of the accident. And why would they have checked the local news anyway?'

'Did no one notice the damage to your car? There must have been some.'

'The front was bashed up,' says Georgia. 'I had to leave early anyway to help my dad at the pub. So no one at the party ever saw. My dad was obviously furious when he saw the damage. I said I'd crashed into the Howards' gate on the way out but none of their property was damaged and they'd said to forget about it. I was crying so much I think he decided to drop it. He took it to a mechanic and paid for it to get fixed.

'The next day, we were having breakfast together and the radio was on. You were speaking.' She looks at me. 'Telling anyone who knew anything about the crash to come forward. And I was looking at dad with my heart in my throat. Thinking, "Is he gonna work it out?" But he just took a bite out of his toast and said, "Such a cowardly thing to do. Hope they catch him." And kept munching his toast. You'd think I'd be relieved. But instead that was one of the worst moments for me. Because…' Her voice thickens. 'Because he believed me. Even with all the signs in front of him, he couldn't believe his own daughter was a bad person.'

'How did you work it out?' asks Harris.

'The photographer took a couple of aerial pictures with a drone that evening,' I reply. 'Some when it was still light outside and the rest after it got dark. They show the whole house, including the car park. In the earlier shots, your car is there. But in the later ones, it's missing. Yet you guys are all drinking in the photos. So I thought: "Who was driving?" And that's when I remembered the hit and run.'

They both wince at the phrase.

'James McTavish,' I say. 'That was his name. I'd forgotten it until I read the news story again. He was fifty-four-years-old.'

Harris buries his face in his hands. 'Don't,' he mumbles.

'I'm sorry, is this painful for you to hear? He had a wife. Two kids. Who've never known why their dad was killed.'

'It was an accident,' says Harris meekly.

I look at them both – sat around the dinner table hunched over and wide-eyed like a couple of wounded animals – and feel a surge of parental anger so painful it almost knocks the air out of me.

I let my head drop forwards. 'You idiots. You bloody idiots,' I say.

I think about that ridiculous teenage trio prancing about on the beach. I can't believe where they've all ended up.

'This is why Lily didn't come back here for years,' I say.

Georgia nods. 'After that, she just associated this place with the crash. We grew apart. Until this summer.' She looks out the window. 'I think she really did just want a break from things. And maybe she was old enough to see the practicalities of living rent-free in an empty five-bedroom house. But then…'

'But then, two weeks before she went missing, we were having dinner at hers, just the three of us. And she said she wanted to talk about it.'

The message in the notebook, I think. *Tell Georgia and Harris.*

'We hadn't spoken about it in years,' says Georgia.

'No. And basically… well, basically Lily said she wanted to tell the police. Not admit who was behind the wheel. But all of us come forward and admit we caused the fatality.' He shakes his head as he relives the memory. 'And I was like, "are you out of your fucking mind?" But she said she couldn't get over it. She said she felt like she needed to do time in order to forgive herself.'

'She was a good person,' says Georgia quietly.

'We were like, "absolutely not, no fucking way". But she made us promise to think about it. Which we did. Like, every day.

'We didn't see each other after that. But Lily would call us. Ask us if we'd made a decision yet.'

I remember Lily's phone records. 'The calls,' I say.

Georgia nods. 'You asked me why she didn't talk about her dates to me. That was why. Because we were barely even talking. And when we were, it was just the same thing. The last conversation we had on the phone was a full-blown argument. She was saying we needed to do it.'

There's a long, horrible silence.

'It wasn't us who killed her,' says Harris. 'Honest to God, it wasn't us.'

'We never would have done it.'

'Forgive me for not really knowing what to think of you two now. Even with your friend dead,' I say, 'even with her murderer still out there, you two didn't have the balls to admit what you did?'

The lower part of Georgia's face wobbles. 'I'm sorry,' she says. 'I know it means you've had to waste time looking into this. But it's not like this has anything to do with her being killed. If we thought it was, we'd have said sooner. I swear.'

'I'm sorry,' says Harris. 'I'm sorry for everything. We were scared of going to prison.'

'I think you two should come to the police station and say what you just told me. Is that all right?'

They look at each other. Georgia rubs tears from her eyes. They nod.

My ringtone cuts through the silence. 'One minute,' I say, heading out into the garden.

I check my phone. It's Max.

Picking up, I say: 'You're not going to believe the day I'm having, Max—'

'Ruth. You need to come quickly. It's the Moffats.'

81

Max makes it into Kirsty's house first, ducking under the police tape.

The hallway is dark but upstairs the lights are on. I follow Max up to the landing where another police officer is waiting. The bathroom door is wide open and bright, almost surgical light floods out of the room. Two paramedics crouch on the tiled floor inside.

A metallic taste in the air hits me in the back of the throat.

The world slows down as Max pushes past the officer and reaches the bathroom. The moment he steps inside, a vibration runs up through his body. He looks like a man on top of a mountain. Like he's caught himself before stepping over the edge and out into the void.

He half-stumbles back out of the bathroom. The crouching paramedic gets up to talk to him, revealing more of the tiles. Against the white, the blood is unbelievably red. Max grabs a hold of the doorframe to steady himself.

I force myself to step forward until the bath comes into view.

I only see a part of it. But it's the worst thing I've ever seen.

And then I hear Kirsty screaming outside. It is an inhuman sound. But I know it's Kirsty because it can only be her.

I run downstairs and through the house. The back door is open, revealing Craig and Kirsty locked together on the lawn. Craig has his back to me. He's gripping Kirsty's arms. She is thrashing around, screaming, her hair flying in her face. Craig throws his arms around her, trying to embrace her. But she resists, pushing back, inconsolable, shrieking words I can barely make out.

Then, Kirsty sees me over her husband's shoulder. She pulls herself free of his embrace and runs towards me with the desperation of a person fleeing a burning building.

'Tell them to save him, Ruth, tell them to save him.'

She falls onto me. I throw my arms around her.

'My baby. My baby.'

'It's too late,' I say. I know. I know from what I just saw that it's already too late.

Kirsty collapses, pulling us both down. My knees hit the lawn.

She's grabbing fistfuls of my jacket and shouting, 'I told you to do something. I told you to help him, Ruth.'

Her voice is shrill with hatred. As my eyes well with hot tears, I pull her closer and hold her as close as I can. But I know she is further away from me than she has ever been.

I barely make it through my front door before my legs start shaking. My legs first, and soon after, my hands. I manage to shut the door before the trembling becomes too much and I slump to the floor. Curling up against the door, feeling the draft creep in from underneath, I close my eyes and for the first time in years, I let myself cry.

82

22 June

I MEET GEORGIA ON the steps of the police station first thing the next day.

'You're doing the right thing,' I say. 'Just tell them everything you told me.'

She gives me a nervous nod and swallows before heading inside for her interview.

Declan has driven her here. He stares after her from the bottom of the steps as if he's worried she might never walk out of there. Then he turns to me, his eyes wild with distress.

'She doesn't have to go to prison, does she? Not for this?' he says, his chest rising and falling quickly.

'She hasn't been charged for anything yet.'

'But if she is, she could just do community service? Couldn't she?'

'I don't have any influence on sentencing.'

He's not listening. He spills out: 'She doesn't deserve to do time, Ruth. She was only young when it happened, for God's sake.'

'A judge will take her age into account. But this is a serious crime, Declan.'

'It wasn't her behind the wheel, Ruth. I know it. But she won't say it was Harris. Can't you make her say, Ruth?'

'We'll try and get the truth. I promise.'

He runs a hand over his hairless head. 'I keep saying to her, "please. Just say who it was." But she won't. She says they promised. What does that mean?'

He stares at me in despair. I have no idea what to say.

'And Archie as well—' He rubs his face. 'What the fuck's happening to us all, Ruth?'

I log into the interview from my computer and watch Georgia give her statement to one of the sergeants. I wish I could be in the room with her, holding her hand. I wish I could turn back the clock and prevent this terrible accident from ever happening.

I see the superintendent approaching me in the reflection of my computer screen. I take out my earphones.

Thompson studies the footage on screen. 'Do you believe they could have done it?'

'Honestly,' I reply. 'No. But it's possible. They were scared Lily would tell someone.'

His gaze drifts to me. 'Are you okay being in today?'

'It's fine.'

I don't want to be sent home. Sometimes – after a day like that – working in the office is better than being stuck in a room, alone with your thoughts.

'It wasn't your fault, Ruth,' he says. 'You know that?'

I clench my jaw.

He continues: 'Archie Moffatt was a vulnerable kid. Maybe more vulnerable than anyone realised. And all that stuff online… There was only so much we could control. You know that.'

I watch the footage of Georgia nervously squeezing her own arm as she answers the sergeant's questions. Declan's right. What the fuck is happening to all of us?

'I don't know if I can tell myself that,' I say.

I don't believe Thompson. It is our fault. But mostly, it's mine.

83

I NEED SOME AIR. Before Georgia's interview has ended, I head downstairs to the car park outside the custody suite. Looking around at the empty patrol vehicles and police vans, I lean against the brick wall of the station, taking deep breaths.

I sense someone nearby. A man in a white shirt is a couple of metres away doing the exact same thing as me – leaning against the same wall with his head bowed, taking a moment to himself. Suddenly he seems to realise I'm there and lifts his head, looking at me with red eyes. It's Max. Embarrassment floods his face. He pushes away from the wall.

'I was just – going back in—'

'No, don't,' I tell him, walking over to stand beside him.

He relaxes back onto the wall. 'Sorry, I—' He sniffs, wiping his nose on his sleeve.

'Do you want to go home?'

'No, no, I'm fine. I want to be here.'

'You sure?'

'Yeah. Thank you.' He stares across the car park. 'This is so embarrassing. It was your friend's son. It should be me looking after you. Not the other way round.'

'It was a really hard day for everyone.'

He goes quiet for a moment. Then hopelessness fills his eyes. 'I don't know if I can do this job.'

'What are you talking about?'

'I've seen that once before. A man who killed himself. But never a kid.' He shakes his head. 'I just don't know, if I had to see that again, on another job, or with someone younger… I don't know if I could handle that.'

His voice is trembling. He breathes in sharply.

I try to think back to the first thing I ever saw that really hit me, that sank into my bones and stayed there. I try to think of what I wish someone had said to me then.

'There are always things that haunt you in this job. You never get over them. But that's why we have each other. Everyone here knows what it feels like. So never feel embarrassed about talking about it. I know we don't know each other that well, but I'm always here to talk about that stuff with you.'

He nods.

'Yeah. Yeah, you're right. Thanks.' Then, after a moment, he says, 'Your daughter. Can I ask what happened to her?'

I always hoped he wouldn't ask me this. But now the moment's here, I feel strangely calm.

'I lost her,' I say, 'to an evil person. An abusive partner. She doesn't speak to me anymore.'

'When did you last see her?'

I close my eyes. For the first time in a long time, I let the memory in.

*

There was no natural light inside the courtroom. Members of the jury were looking woozy. But throughout the proceedings I'd been completely alert, soaking in every piece of information.

I was sitting in the public gallery. I had been staring at the back of Reece's head so intently that I had memorised the placement of a dark mole beneath his hairline, a small red spot to the right of his neck. It brought me great satisfaction to see him standing in the dock. I had been trying to gauge his emotional reactions to the prosecution's case through tiny signs. The reddening of the tips of his ears. Twitches of the head. I wished I was facing him. So I could see him squirm.

Molly stepped up to the witness box, her head bowed. The moment he saw her, Reece went totally still, his attention hyperfocused on her. But not once did she even glance in his direction.

Connor squeezed my hand in my lap. I took a deep breath and squeezed back, wishing I could send her all my strength and his in a beam of light.

The judge asked Molly to confirm her name and swear the oath.

'I swear by Almighty God that I will tell the truth, the whole truth and nothing but the truth,' she said softly.

And then it began.

'Can you describe for me the assault that took place in October?'

It felt like there was no one else in the room. Just Molly in the box under a shaft of light.

'No.'

Gasps scattered around the courtroom. I still remember the prosecutor's reaction. He had been facing the court, studying the notes in his hand. But after Molly spoke, he lifted his head, confusion entering his eyes, and turned to look directly at her.

Connor's hand tightened painfully around mine.

She's distressed, I thought. Confused. She's misunderstood the question.

'You do acknowledge the assault that took place on the fourteenth of October?'

'No.'

Ice-cold water flooded my insides.

When Molly's voice reached me, it sounded faint, as though she were standing very far away.

'I fell.'

Mist and clouds swam around me. I looked at Reece. The edge of his cheekbone was glowing red. I could sense his elation, as clearly as if he were whooping for joy from the dock.

No, I thought. No, this can't be happening.

I stared at her in that box, willing her to look up, convinced that a moment of eye contact with me would compel her to change her statement.

But deep down I knew she'd already looked at me for the last time.

*

'I'm sorry,' says Max. 'I didn't know.'

'Well, I didn't tell you, did I?'

'You shouldn't blame yourself,' he says. 'I've seen it myself on jobs. Those relationships, where one person's so powerful… sometimes there's nothing you can say to the victim that will convince them.'

I rest my head against the wall. 'I don't know. See how you feel about it if you ever have kids. You're always going to blame yourself. He took her. But I pushed her away.'

'But you could get her back, right? She was so young when it happened. As she gets older, she might see what he is. She might leave, right?'

'Yeah,' I reply. 'But could she if she wanted to?' I stare at the wall. 'For a long time I thought I could wait it out. But I'm starting to think I'm done waiting.'

84

THERE'S A KNOCK AT the door. I breathe out, readying myself. I don't feel like I have the energy for anything right now. Rubbing my eyes, I head down the hallway and open the front door.

It feels like a dream – Connor stood there on the doorstep with the night rolling out behind him.

'What are you doing here?'

'I saw a friend nearby and I thought – I heard—'

He takes a long look at me. My tiredness fades and I feel a stab of self-consciousness. My hair is pulled off my face into a tight ponytail. The temperature has dropped since the sun went down and my figure is swamped underneath a baggy sweatshirt.

'I can go if you want me to,' he says.

'No, come in.'

I return to the living room and wait for him. I watch through the doorway as he takes off his jacket, retrieves something from its inside pocket and then carefully hangs it up on the coat hook. I look at the back of his neck. I used to adore that part of him. The space from the bottom of his shoulder blades all the way up to his hairline. The moment he enters the room, I look away, burning.

He walks over with an envelope in one hand, which he holds out to me.

'I wrote them a note,' he says. 'I don't know if that's what they'd want. But I thought I would leave it with you.'

I take it from him. *Kirsty and Craig*, is written on the front in his simple cursive.

'I don't know if Kirsty wants to hear from me right now,' I say. I'm out of energy and my voice comes out completely flat.

'I'm sure she would. Even if it doesn't feel like it. You're her best friend.'

I sit down on the sofa, placing the envelope on the side table. To my surprise, rather than taking the other sofa, Connor sits down beside me. Pinpricks rush over my skin at the sensation of his weight shifting the cushions under me.

'No, I've fucked it,' I say.

I feel brittle – my emotions all over the place. Why did I let him in? Is this really what he wants to talk about? Do I want to talk about it?

He clasps his hands together in front of his knees. 'They're such good people. Everything online, it was unbelievable. They didn't deserve it. I wish I'd reached out to them earlier.'

This doesn't feel right. They're my friends. Not his. They haven't been his friends for years.

I pinch my nose in frustration. When he looks round, I lower my hands and hold them out, palms open, inviting an explanation.

'Why do you keep doing this?' I ask.

Confusion flickers in his eyes. 'What?'

'Using these moments as an excuse to show up out of nowhere.'

'An excuse?' he repeats.

His voice is filled with uncertainty and I feel a surge of guilt but it's like my mind is racing ahead of me and I can't stop myself from blurting out: 'The worst things happen and here you are.'

Connor blinks rapidly, taking this in. *Here we go*, I think. *Well done, Ruth, another argument. Is that what you wanted?*

'I'm sorry. Maybe I shouldn't have turned up out of the blue like this. It's just, I care about you. I know how something like this – and Lily's murder – I know how it makes you feel. And I want to make sure you're looking after yourself because I know you and sometimes you don't.' He grimaces painfully, looking around the room. 'I hate to think of you just… hiding yourself away here. Suffering.'

Normally this is when I would leap to Braeside's defence. But I'm done with that. He's right. This was my exile. My hideaway. My way of saying goodbye to the world.

Connor shakes his head. 'Listen, I've been wanting to say… I should have looked after you more after she left.'

'You did,' I say quietly.

'Not enough. My head was in pieces.'

'You were angry with me.'

'I shouldn't have been. First I couldn't protect her. And then I couldn't protect you.' His jaw is clenched with shame.

'It wasn't your fault,' I tell him.

Knowing Connor as a husband and father, it makes sense that he would see this as a failing. But it's also absurd. Protect us how? Lock Molly away before she ever met Reece?

'It wasn't yours either,' he says.

He's looking at me and I can't bear the intensity of his blue gaze so I focus on an upturned corner of the rug below us.

'I wasn't a good mum, I don't think.'

I've never said this out loud before. But I realise as soon as I do that I've believed this for a long time. I was too absent. Too harsh. Too quick to anger. Molly deserved better. If she'd had better, maybe none of this would have happened.

Connor replies quickly and firmly: 'That's not true. You were a brilliant mum.'

The corner of my mouth twitches. Hearing him say this is like listening to a beautiful note in a song. But even now, I'm not sure I believe him.

Perhaps he's forgotten. So maybe I should remind him.

'What I said to her—' I manage, my throat closing up, voice thickening, 'that day. Before she left—'

Connor is very still now. But he must be distressed because somehow I can feel his strong heartbeat vibrating through the air between us.

And it flashes through my mind, as vividly as the day it happened.

*

I waited outside the court until Molly emerged. Her long straight hair hid her face as she picked her way sheepishly down the steps, hand-in-hand with Reece.

I called her name. But they kept walking away from me, as though they hadn't heard. And all the exhaustion of the past year, all the pain of the case, rose up within me and exploded out.

'Go, then!' I shouted after them. 'Just fucking go!'

I swear I saw Molly flick her head involuntarily. But they kept walking, disappearing towards the taxis. Air rushed past me. And that was when Connor went charging down the steps after them.

*

My chest tightens.

'That's the last thing she heard me say,' I gasp out.

'You didn't mean it.'

'She doesn't know that.'

'It's all right,' he says. 'You were angry. You didn't mean it.'

He places his hand on top of mine and a door within me opens. I sink into his chest. It feels like it always has felt as he holds me, saying, 'It's no one's fault. It's no one's fault but his.'

I inhale deeply, breathing in his familiar smell.

'It doesn't have to be this hard,' he says. 'It could be easier than this. I want to make it easier.'

Afterwards, lying in my room, I press my nose against his chest while he strokes my hair. It could be any time at all.

85

Mia

23 June

My phone vibrates. I slide open the screen. **Teenage boy, 14, found dead in Braeside.** An electric current shoots from my fingertips up my arms. My surroundings fade to a blur. It's him. Archie Moffatt.

Frantically, I read the story, scouring the page for an explanation. Again? Has it happened again? But then a sentence leaps out at me. *Police are not treating the death as suspicious.* But that doesn't make sense. Could it be health-related? He always seemed perfectly healthy to me so that seems unlikely.

I head for the front door. I need to find out exactly what's happened. There must be someone in Braeside who'll talk to me. My hand has just closed around the doorknob when Vanessa calls out.

'Mia. Stay.'

I turn around. Somehow I've moved through the room without noticing Vanessa and Martyn sat on the sofa. The cloud is low today and the light from the window turns Vanessa's hair into a silvery crown. Somewhere a window is open, letting in the foamy sound of the waves.

Vanessa's hands are folded in her lap. There's a book underneath them.

It feels like my legs are dissolving.

My notebook. Where I've been keeping some of my research. My thoughts on the case.

Her hand slides across the cover. Slowly she opens it. Already I know the page she'll land on.

She reads out: 'Potential suspects. The Howards.'

My grip on the doorknob loosens and my arm falls to my side. 'Those are just – notes—' I mumble.

Vanessa ignores me. Getting to her feet, she turns a page and continues reading.

'Night of 31 May 2022.'

Martyn gets up and comes over to stand between me and the door, blocking my way. He's so close I can see the spidery red veins in the whites of his eyes.

Vanessa's voice reaches me again. 'Argument with Toby. The night before Lily went missing.'

She gets up and starts walking towards me. I back away, something prodding me in the spine. Flinching away, I realise it's the corner of a side table and now it dawns on me that I'm backing into the wall, with Martyn and Vanessa on either side of me, drawing in like wolves.

Vanessa snaps the notebook shut. 'We welcome you into our lives, and you think we would kill our own daughter?'

My heart feels like it could explode out of my chest. I'm certain now. How did they do it? Did they smash her head on the tiles beneath my feet? Suffocate her with a cushion? I look at the heavy lamp on the coffee table and think how easily it could crack someone's skull.

Vanessa is trembling. 'That woman who keeps coming after you. The one you told me to avoid. She's Hayley Pieterson's mum, isn't she?'

I don't say anything. I'm not sure I can. My throat has closed up.

'You lied to me. Because you didn't want me to know the truth about what you did to that family, isn't that right?'

The light from the windows grows brighter. Vanessa and Martyn are fading into shadows.

'Do you even realise you're the reason her husband is dead?'

My hands and face go numb. I feel like I'm falling down a long, dark tunnel.

I read the news story once. Once and never again. I had almost forgotten the brutal description of his death. The words come back to me now, along with the image of him tending the flowerbeds on the window sills. *Sean Pieterson died of his injuries in hospital two days later.* I don't know why that image has stayed with me, crystal clear. Perhaps it was the look of meditative concentration on his face. The first truly peaceful moment I'd seen since I'd met that family. His daughter had died but he wanted – needed – to keep on gardening.

My inner reality becomes my outer reality. My inner reality.

I repeat what I sometimes say in therapy: 'I've processed what happened and I've forgiven myself.'

They stare at me in horror and confusion, like I've just cursed them in an ancient language.

'What the fuck?' says Martyn.

He moves forward and automatically I take a step to the side.

'Is there nothing in you? You know what you are? You're a vulture. A leech.'

My spine stiffens. My breathing is shallow. Is this what it was like for Lily?

Without thinking, I say: 'I know it was one of you.'

I regret the words as soon as they leave my mouth. I imagine Vanessa's thin hands pinning my wrists to the tiled flooring. Martyn's spittle in my face as he raises the lamp above his head, ready to bring it crashing down over mine.

Vanessa lashes out, pointing at the door.

'Get out. Get out before I call the police.'

'I – my stuff—'

'Take your thing and go.'

I swerve past the couple, moving so fast that my feet skid across the tiles. Then I run up the stairs and down the hallway to my room, the place that has become my home for the last few weeks. The window is open, the thin curtain drifting in the breeze. I pack frantically, gathering up my few clothes and belongings scattered around the room. Where will I go? The hostel? What if they don't have any rooms left?

I drag my wheelie case down the front steps. The sky looks grey and foreboding. The trees on the distant hills shudder in the wind. The rain will be here soon.

The sound of my suitcase wheels clattering over the gravel path hides the sound of his footsteps.

I let out an involuntary yelp at the feeling of a hand closing around my upper arm and pulling me back.

I turn around to face Toby, whose eyes are glittering with rage.

'You,' he hisses.

I jerk forward, tugging my suitcase, but his grip is too tight.

'Let me go.'

The wind thrashes around in our hair, blowing mine into my eyes.

Toby bares his teeth at me. 'This whole time you've been spying on us.'

'Calm down.'

'What the fuck's wrong with you? Why did you come here? That boy is dead, you know that? Archie! That boy is dead because of you.'

Ice-cold blood floods my insides.

'That's not true,' I murmur.

'Killed himself,' Toby yells. 'Killed himself because everyone thought it was him!'

I sway on the spot.

'Then it's your fault!' I launch back. 'Because it's you. It's always been you.'

'What are you talking about?'

'The cameras. Your family had cameras around the house.'

His mouth hangs open, lower teeth sticking out.

'They would have shown who came and left on the day Lily disappeared. But someone took them down before the police could arrive. They never knew the cameras existed.'

His grip starts to slacken.

'Who else could do that except one of you? Why else would you do it unless you had something to hide?'

Now I can feel Toby's palm is hot and slippery with sweat. 'If you post anything about my family, I'll – I'll—'

'You'll what? You'll do what? Kill me too?'

Fear flashes in his eyes. Slowly, his grip loosens.

'I would never – I would never have hurt her.'

But his lips hardly seem to move, his voice faint under the sound of the wind.

I look into his pale eyes once before turning away, pulling the suitcase with me past the security gates.

86
Ruth

23 June

A KNOCK ON THE door disturbs me. Connor has already left for work. My heart lifts at the thought that it is Kirsty, coming over for support. But I know it won't be. I know it will be Max with an update on the case, or someone from town in need of help. I check my face in the mirror, smoothing out my hair. Then I go downstairs to face reality.

When I open the door, my heart stops. Mia is standing on my doorstep, looking timid, with a suitcase next to her.

'Can I come in?'

I manage a nod. She lifts the suitcase over the threshold and leaves it in the hallway before following me into the living room. She looks different. Her usually sleek hair is unbrushed, her skin looks tired and she is wearing a waterproof jacket in case it rains.

'I came here to give you this.'

She extends her arm. She's holding out a USB stick.

'There's something on it you should see.'

'What is it?'

'It will show you who the killer is.'

I stare at her in disbelief. 'You've got some nerve. You really do.'

Her eyelashes flutter but she says nothing.

'My friend's son is dead. Because of you. He was fourteen.'

'I didn't tell anyone to do anything,' she says. 'I didn't know he was going to—'

I slap her hand, knocking the USB, which pings off the wall and disappears somewhere into the room.

'You're nothing. There's nothing inside you, you hear me? *Nothing.*'

Mia is trembling. 'I didn't mean to—'

'Just get out. Get out.'

She whips past me and vanishes. I hear the door slam shut and watch through the window as her slight figure hurries past the house and into the green, pulling her suitcase behind her.

I shake my shoulders, trying to dismiss the encounter from my mind.

What a creep. What an absolute fucking creep.

Then I see the USB glinting by the fireplace.

It will show you who the killer is.

Does this mean she's targeting someone else? At the thought, a rush of adrenaline surges through me. Scrambling, I pull my phone out of my pocket and quickly load up BlackBird's YouTube channel, expecting to see a new post. But there isn't one. In fact, there's fewer than there were before. She's deleted some.

I frown. Confused, I walk over to the fireplace, squat down and pick up the USB.

I'd better see what's on this, then.

I carry it through to the kitchen, where my laptop is sat on the table. I turn it on before boiling a kettle, thinking a cup of tea might help to settle me. While I'm waiting for the hot water, I plug in the USB. There are five folders on it, named CAMERA 1, CAMERA 2 and so on.

I scrunch up my nose. Is this CCTV footage? How did Mia get hold of this?

I click on one at random. There are dozens of files on it. Each one labelled with a different date, in chronological order. I select one and find three mp4 files inside. I click MOTIONEVENT09.23.

I blink in surprise as the footage plays. I'm watching Vanessa drive her Range Rover out of the Howards' main gate.

This is from their security cameras. But they didn't have security cameras. We'd searched every inch of that place.

Suddenly a cold chill runs down my spine as I realise why Mia gave this to me.

I click 'back' and then I select '2 June'.

The day Lily went missing.

87
Max

23 June

'Come on, Harris. Just tell me who was behind the wheel.'

Max tries hard to keep the impatience he's feeling out of his voice. He's 40 minutes into his interview with Harris. Whereas Georgia had opened up without much nudging – like she was desperate to talk about that night – Harris has been much harder to pin down on specifics. Max finds himself getting annoyed at Ruth for not having recorded their earlier confession. Now that Harris is in a police station, it's all feeling too real and the young man is retreating into himself.

And that makes Max suspicious.

'Georgia seems like a sensible person. I'm struggling to picture her getting into the driver's seat.'

Harris doesn't reply.

He continues: 'It was her car, sure. But it was your idea to go to your house, wasn't it? It makes sense that it would've been you driving.'

Harris looks down at the table.

'I understand you want to look after each other,' says Max. 'But I need you to be fully honest with me about what happened. If it was you, then your friend may be about to spend years of her life in prison because of something that was your fault.'

Harris's face crumbles.

'Come on, Harris. If there's something you need to tell us, now's the time to say.'

Harris lets his head fall into his hands and knots his fingers in his hair.

'We were all in it together. That's what Lily said,' he mumbles.

'I'm sorry, Harris, I'm going to need you to speak up for the microphones.'

'Lily said we were all in it together,' he says, more loudly, without looking up. 'After she went missing, we – we wanted to do right by her.'

'You wanted to do what your friend would have wanted,' says Max. 'Out of respect for her.'

Harris nods. One tear lands on his forearm.

'Lily wanted us to protect him,' he says.

'What?'

Harris looks up, his dark eyes filled with tears. 'Toby. It was Toby driving the car.'

88
Mia

I MAKE MY WAY down the lane from DI Lindsey's house. The road is badly maintained. Tufts of grass emerge from cracks in the tarmac and I have to manoeuvre to avoid welts that are filled with water. My jeans are still damp from the earlier rainfall. If I was staying with Vanessa, she would tell me to take off my socks and sit in front of the fire, propping my feet up on a footstool to warm up. I have been trying to avoid thinking of Vanessa and this unexpected mental image makes my chest hurt. I used to think of our evenings indoors together as relationship-building necessary for the case, or a chance to pick her brains about her daughter. Now I see how much comfort they brought me.

I feel daunted by the prospect of the long train journey back to London. Maybe I should see my parents when I get back. I could buy Mum a present. Some flowers maybe. I think she would like that.

The road widens and the trees become taller as I walk back to Braeside, where I will wait to catch the last bus of the day. Detecting the sound of an approaching car behind me, I move closer to the edge of the road. But the car never passes and soon the sound fades.

There is an explosion among the vegetation as my movement disturbs a bird lurking in the hedgeway; I hear its wings beating as it flies away. Sunlight emerges from behind the clouds and glows in the trees. It looks beautiful.

Something slams into my back. Suddenly a pair of strong arms are locked around my middle, holding me in place. I can't move. Everything slows down. I try to pull their arms away but the person behind me has an iron grip.

I scream, but then another hand slaps across my face, covering my mouth. A muffled noise leaves me. The smell of their sweat fills my nostrils. Someone grabs my arm and wrenches me down. I don't understand. How many of them are there? My knees hit the road. The canopy spins above me. They've pulled my arms behind my back and they're wrapping something around them. I try to get up but can't. Close to my ear I hear the sound of fabric rustling. Then I feel a scratchy covering being pulled over my head. I scream until it feels like my lungs could burst.

The last thing I see is the sunlight creating a dappled effect on the tarmac, like a splatter of silver-gold.

89
Ruth

TOBY GLARES AT ME and Max from across the table in Interview Room Three. He has instructed a local solicitor who is wearing a gaudy tie that if you ask me is obnoxiously cheerful for his line of work.

'You told me you were at home on the day your sister went missing. But that's not true, is it?'

'No.'

'Where were you?' asks Max.

'I was driving,' Toby replies. The smell of old sweat rolls off of him.

'Were there security cameras around the house?'

'Yes.'

'Why weren't they there when our officers searched the premises?

'Because I removed them.'

'When?'

'As soon as Mum told me the police were going to turn up.'

'Why did you remove them?'

'Because they would show I was lying.'

'We've been sent the video footage.'

'Three guesses who sent you that,' he mutters resentfully.

'Do you want to explain what really happened that day, or do you need us to remind you?'

'I got up before my parents. Saw Lily's note. I got in the car to go and find her. I never did. I got back home around lunchtime.'

'Two o'clock, to be exact. So you'd have had enough time to kill her and dump her body in the loch.'

'I told you. I was looking for her but I never found her.'

'Why were you looking for Lily that morning?'

'I was just… worried about her. She hadn't been doing well the last few days.'

'That isn't all the footage shows. The camera near the garage shows you and Lily arguing outside the day before she went missing. Do you remember that argument?'

'No comment.'

'What were you arguing about?'

'No comment.'

'I want to ask you another question. Where were you on the 31st of May 2022, the night of your parents' party, celebrating the launch of their new restaurant?'

Toby keeps his face very still.

'I don't know what you mean,' he manages.

I'm certain now. I wasn't before but the flicker of emotion in Toby's eyes has confirmed it for me.

'Harris told us you were in the car that night,' says Max.

He doesn't look away from me. Next to him, his solicitor is staring at us in silent horror as he realises his client hasn't told him the whole story.

I continue: 'I should've listened more carefully. It wasn't just Lily's friends who wanted drugs. It was yours as well. You were there with them. It was you. You were behind the wheel.'

The solicitor splays his hand on the table. 'I think we should take a break now,' he says, turning his squeaky chair towards Toby. 'I need a minute to talk to my client.'

But Toby shakes his head, eyes still focused on me, as if there's no one else in the room.

'Georgia and Harris kept you out of it,' I say. 'They were protecting you because they know it's what Lily would have wanted. She wanted you to come forward as a group of four, or not at all. She didn't want you, her brother, the driver, getting all the blame.'

Finally, Toby breaks eye contact. He lowers his head, defeated, and brings his hands together in the centre of his forehead.

'This is not what you think,' he tells the table.

But I keep going. 'She didn't just have to convince her friends. She had to convince you as well. That's what the argument was about. And that's why you went out to find her on the day she left the house. Because you thought maybe this was the end. After the argument, you thought she was going to the police. Isn't that right?'

Toby's broad shoulders are rising and falling with each shaky breath.

'You know, people haven't had a lot to say about you in interviews, Toby. But there's one thing the locals here have noticed. You like a drink. Perhaps too much. Have done ever since you were a teenager. Or maybe since that party.'

Toby slams his hands down on the table, making his solicitor flinch. 'Shut the fuck up,' he snarls. 'You don't know a thing about me.'

His solicitor raises a hand to steady his client. 'Easy.'

Perhaps this registers with Toby because he draws in a deep breath and holds it in for a few painful moments, his face reddening. Finally he gasps out: 'I wasn't as brave as her. I wasn't ready yet.'

The air seems to shimmer. Every muscle in my body is taut. I'm worried even a tiny movement from me will distract his attention away from this memory he's about to share.

'You're right. She wanted us all to confess. And I didn't. She was obsessed with it from the moment I got to Braeside. One night, we fought about it. She said we needed to do the right thing. She said she'd do it without us if she had to. I barely slept all night. The next morning, when I saw she was gone, I thought… I thought she was going to do it. Or that she wanted time alone to decide. I thought I had to talk to her, so I went after her.'

'What were you planning to do when you found her?'

'Just talk to her. Make her see she couldn't just throw my life away. She's… she was my little sister. I was never going to hurt her. I didn't. I never found her. I swear.'

'Your parents didn't tell us about these cameras either. Why?'

'Because I told them it would look as though I had done it.'

'Do they know about the crash?'

'No. My parents don't know anything. I swear. They just didn't want any trouble for me. I swear I never found her.' He's crying now, tears glistening on his face. He rubs his eyes. 'You don't understand. It wasn't me. Please.'

It feels like a hand is squeezing my heart, cutting off the blood flow. I want so much to believe him. But I don't.

He pushes away from the table. One hand covering his eyes, he sobs.

'I loved her so much. I didn't know how much. Until she was gone.'

90
Mia

I WAKE UP TO cold stone pressing into my cheek. I'm lying on my side on a hard floor. I try to move but my hands and ankles are tied up. My heart starts to race in my chest. Sweat running between my shoulder blades. I can't see anything. There's something scratchy over my face and my lips are sealed shut by a strip of tape.

I try to work out where I am. The sound of the whirling wind – and the absence of any voices or cars – suggests I'm somewhere wild and outdoors. But I can only feel a draft over my skin, which tells me I'm not completely exposed to the elements. There's a roof over my head. Somehow it feels like I am both inside and out.

Is this where Lily was taken? Is this what she felt?

Suddenly I hear footsteps coming closer. I try to shuffle back across the floor but I've barely moved an inch before I hear the voice of someone standing above me.

'Do you know how much trouble you've caused?'

I freeze, replaying the voice in my head. Is this him? The killer?

If it is, then it's not Toby. It's not Vanessa or Martyn either. The voice is Scottish. And I can't place it.

But I swear I've heard it somewhere before.

91
Ruth

MAX AND I STEP out of the room, leaving Toby inside with his solicitor. I feel dazed and my heart is still pounding from the intensity of the interview.

'What do we think?' says Max.

'What are the chances he drove off looking for her in a fit of rage the morning she disappeared – knowing where she was going – and didn't find her?'

Max nods. 'And why would his family agree to hide the cameras if he didn't have anything to do with this?'

I shrug. 'I don't think the parents suspected him. I think they just wanted to protect him from scrutiny. But he must have been the one who suggested getting rid of the cameras. Would you really do that if your sister was missing? If you needed all the evidence to try and find her?'

My phone buzzes in my pocket. I look at who's calling. It's Kirsty. My heart jumps. Has something happened?

'Kirsty,' I say. 'Is everything all right?'

'Ruth.' She sounds unlike herself – like she's fighting back tears. 'It's Craig. I think he's done something with Mia.'

92
Craig

23 June

Craig zips up his trousers and looks down into the valley. Then he begins the steep climb back up the mountain. Even on this incline, the grass goes up to his knees and he has to step carefully to get a foothold.

The cloud cover means he can hardly see the silvery sun travelling across the sky. He heads back to the building. It must have been a lodge at one point but it's long since been abandoned. It is far from any walking route, so he knows there's no risk of someone stumbling across them by chance.

Stuart is sitting in a fold-up chair some distance from the building, with a blanket laid over his lap. He takes a sip from a flask of tea.

As Craig approaches, he extends the flask, offering a drink.

'No, thank you,' Craig replies. 'Want something stronger?'

He retrieves his own flask from inside his coat pocket. Stuart grimaces, shaking his head.

Craig unscrews it and knocks back a bitter hit of whisky. A fiery sensation spreads across his chest, sending his worst thoughts to the back of his mind, helping him to ignore the dampness of his socks. The cap squeaks as he screws it back onto the flask.

Stuart glances briefly over his shoulder back at the building, as if to check Mia isn't standing in the doorway, armed and unrestrained.

He shuffles uncomfortably in his chair. 'I had to move away,' he mutters. 'The sound of her crying is fucking horrible.'

'Well, the sound of Kirsty crying is worse, believe me.'

Craig stares at the shadowy figures of the other mountains and hills in the distance. He told Kirsty she should stay with her parents for a few days, to get some space from Braeside, and fortunately she agreed. He doesn't know how long they're going to be up here for. He hadn't planned that far ahead. All he knows is he needs to see Mia experience some of the pain they have as a family, or he'll never sleep again.

'When do we let her go?'

'When she's suffered enough.'

'What if she recognises your voice?'

'She won't.'

'It's just… what if she works it out once we let her go? That's what she does, isn't it? She investigates.'

'Well, you should have thought about that before you agreed to do this. Because trust me, I've thought about it.'

Craig grits his teeth. He is beginning to regret getting Stuart involved. At the time it had seemed like the right thing to do. Two men standing up for their families – protecting their community. Now he feels like he's dragged Stuart into something he isn't prepared for.

The image of Mia lying there doesn't bring him any satisfaction either. If she was a man, this would be much easier. But in these moments of doubt he steels himself, forcing him to picture Archie instead. Things he'd thought he'd forgotten have been hitting him out of nowhere lately. Flashes of Archie's childhood. How, when he was a child, about four, he would get so excited seeing his favourite foods arrive on a plate he would kick wildly under the kitchen table, knife and fork at the ready, swinging his short legs back and forth.

Gone. How can he still be here, and Archie not?

How can she?

He looks at the amber glow of the lamplight through the window, illuminating the grain of the stone walls and the spiderwebs of plant roots growing across them.

Maybe Stuart isn't prepared to do what's necessary. But he is.

Stuart leans forward, staring into the distance.

'Cloud coming our way,' he says.

93

Ruth

THE CLOUD IS LOW this evening. It engulfs the mountain so that I'm unable to see more than six metres in front of me. The engine groans with the effort of the climb. I drive, guided by the cats' eyes on the road appearing through an apocalyptic fog, only noticing a bend in the road when it's moments away and turning to avoid a fatal fall off the road and down the mountain. As the road curves, the cloud lifts temporarily, exposing a rivulet of white water tumbling through the dark rocks.

Craig had suggested Kirsty go and stay with her parents after Archie's death. But she'd forgotten some of her toiletries and driven home to find Craig gone – along with their camping gear and a kitchen knife. We tracked him down on CCTV renting a van and traced the vehicle as far as the Devil's Hand, close to a mountain called Scroof Rig. I know he's somewhere in the hills. But there are many different routes he could take, so we've split up to cover more ground.

Finally, I see it. Out of the mist emerges a white van, parked on the side of the road. My heart races. I park up, scrambling to get out. Already I can see there's no one in the front but I want to check the back. I pull on a pair of disposable gloves, brace myself, and open the back door. Nothing. They've not left a trace.

I walk around the vehicle, scanning the immediate surroundings for any sign of where they could have gone. Eventually I find a narrow route leading off the road into the mountains, where the grass has been trampled down by walkers.

I say into the police radio: 'I've found the van. Send officers. There's a path up here they may have taken. I'm going to follow it and search.'

'All right,' Max replies. 'Be careful.'

The recent showers have left the long grass damp and slippery. My boots sink into the thick, squelchy moss. This is going to take fucking ages.

I begin to climb.

94
Craig

Craig circles behind the building and keeps walking through the bracken. He and Stuart have been taking turns stretching their legs. The section of hillside they climb up and down is like a prison yard.

It has been a long day. The light is just disappearing behind the summit. It will be far more intimidating here once it's dark. He knows it can't go on like this for much longer. This needs to end. But how?

There is rustling up ahead and a lone red deer springs out of the ferns several metres away. He watches the doe bound up the hill with her ears straight up, listening out in case he comes after her.

He can't get locked up for this. He can't abandon Kirsty, not after everything she's been through. But he's not sure he can live with this feeling either.

Has he been careful enough? He rented the van from miles away. He doesn't think this could be linked back to him.

Unless, of course, Mia's put two and two together. Unless they let her go and she identifies them somehow.

He stops and swings his bag off his shoulder, then pulls out the bottle of whisky. Even though there's no way Stuart can hear from this distance, he refills the flask carefully so as not to make any noise. After that, he takes a few swigs from the bottle. It's so strong it feels like it could cut his mouth open.

He'll stop drinking as soon as he's back home. But right now it's crucial. The whisky numbs him, keeping thoughts of Archie at bay and bringing him surges of confidence that tell him this is the right thing to do.

He wakes himself up by splashing water on his face and gargles some before spitting it into the grass, which he hopes will mask the smell. Then he gathers up his things and heads back to the campsite.

Eventually he sees the faint glow from the window of the building, emanating from the single lamp they left inside. Sat in the fold-up chair, swaddled in layers, Stuart looks increasingly like an old man on the worst holiday of his life. It's getting cold and he has jammed a black beanie over his head.

He doesn't think Stuart has noticed how much he's drinking yet. He needs to keep it a secret. He can't afford for Stuart to lose faith in him.

'Stuart,' he says. 'I need you to check something for me.'

'What?'

'I think there's a holiday house nearby.'

'Really?' Stuart sits bolt upright. He looks around wildly, as if the owners might emerge at any moment. 'Then why the fuck did we stop here?'

'Because I've never seen anyone there and I'm almost certain it will be empty. But I think we need to check. Could you go? See if there's a car outside?'

'What if they see me?'

'They won't. It's in the valley so you'll have a much better view of the house than they have of you. Plenty of rocks you can hide behind if needed.'

'You want me to go now?'

Craig nods. 'Before it gets any darker.'

'Fucking hell. Okay. Show me on the map.'

Craig highlights the route for him on the OS map on his phone. Begrudgingly, Stuart packs a few things – his bottle of water, a flapjack, a waterproof – tugs his backpack on and gets up. Craig watches him walk back the way they came, curving through the heather back towards the valley, until finally he drops out of sight behind the curve of the hill.

Already Craig is itching for another sip. He retrieves his flask and necks some back. His face feels puffy in the cold, his vision a little unfocused, and yet his mind is totally clear.

He turns around and looks at the building, with the lamplight glimmering faintly in the window.

He knows what he has to do.

95
Mia

I THINK IT'S EVENING. The temperature has dropped and the world is quieter. It has been hours since I heard a bird's call. Perhaps the sun is going down.

My body feels exhausted and the total darkness has warped all sense of time. I roll my stiff shoulders, trying to shift my weight around, but there's no hope of getting comfortable.

I hear shuffling across the hard stone floor and freeze. Instinctively I know I'm not alone anymore. He's here.

'Can I have some water?' I ask the room.

My lips are cracked, my throat parched. Part of me also hopes that reminding my captor of my physical needs will force him to remember I'm human.

After a moment of silence, I hear plastic scraping across the floor, followed by the sound of footsteps. My shoulder blades pinch together as he comes closer. A large hand grabs my shoulder, making me flinch. They help me up to a seating position. Then I feel the familiar ring of a plastic bottle's neck pressing against my lips. Water begins to flow and I gulp down as much as I can, some of it spilling onto the floor.

It's only when he takes the bottle away that I notice I can hear his breathing. It's loud and unsteady, as if he ran here.

'Why did you do it?' he asks.

'Wh – what?'

'Why did you post those things online?'

The phrase seems so out-of-place it's almost funny. Behind the blindfold, my eyes move rapidly. So this is about my investigation. Does this mean I got something right? Is this someone I called out? Who?

My mind whirs as I try and work out the right thing to say. 'I was trying to help with the investigation,' is all I can manage.

'Why did you target the people you did?'

His voice sounds broken. Like he might cry. Oh God. I need to calm him down. I'm terrified that in this state he'll lash out.

'I – I didn't target anyone. I was just posting about the evidence I found.'

'Didn't you think about the consequences?'

'I never meant to hurt anyone. I swear.'

'What did you think was going to happen? When you posted that rubbish about a young, vulnerable person? About a boy?'

A wave of cold hits me. Archie. This is about Archie.

I know now who's brought me here. Who I'm speaking to.

My throat is swelling with emotion. 'I'm – I'm so sorry.'

'Tell me what you know about Archie,' says Craig.

'If I'd known – I never would have said anything—'

'You don't know a thing about him, do you? You don't know a fucking thing.'

Craig gasps out, and he's sobbing now. I can't give any sign I know who he is. I have to get out of this. He could kill me if he thinks I've worked it out.

'Well, I'll tell you who he was. He was clever. He was so clever. And a good person. He was so much more than you will ever be. He did more than you ever did in your worthless, pathetic life.'

He's close now. I can smell the whisky souring his breath.

'You know who I am, don't you?'

Something cold touches my neck. The thin blade of a knife.

Adrenaline shoots through me.

'Don't. Please don't. I'm so sorry.'

He takes off the blindfold. Suddenly a pair of bloodshot blue eyes fill my field of vision. This can't be the last thing I ever see.

96
Ruth

NORMALLY, THE VIEWS UP here would be stunning. But all I can see is the cloud, and through it the narrow path of flattened red and yellow grass, leading me up the mountain.

Sweat collects around my hairline and between my shoulder blades. But I don't want to remove my waterproof – not with the wind hammering into me like this, bringing with it a steady and unpleasant drizzle.

I've been climbing for about 40 minutes and the cloud shows no sign of clearing. Soon I'll have to turn back. It's getting late and I don't want to get stuck up here in the dark. I grind my teeth. My calves are burning. My feet ache. Going up here alone, at this hour of day, was a stupid idea. Maybe I should have turned back when I found the van and arranged to come back the next morning with a team. But no, we're running out of time.

As I climb up the ridge, the cloud to my right finally begins to disperse, revealing the sloping hillside beneath. I freeze. A man in waterproof gear is stood down there with his back to me, peering down into the valley. My heart pounds. What is he looking at? As the cloud drifts, a house appears at the very bottom of the hill. I study his waterproof jacket, his backpack, trying desperately to think where I've seen them before, who in the town owns gear like this, if indeed anyone does.

Appearing satisfied, the man starts walking away from me, away from the house, back along the hillside. He still hasn't noticed I'm here. Ignoring the pain in my legs – and moving as quietly as I can – I follow him.

And that's when the storm breaks.

97

THE RAIN FALLS IN sheets. My waterproof ripples around me in the wind. I lift my arm up to try and shield my face as I follow the dark figure, who is slowly fading into the distance. If I don't keep up, I could easily lose him in the cloud.

Then something emerges. A light in the darkness. Beckoning us through the clouds like the torch of a lighthouse. This is where the man is headed. I continue after him until the outline of a small farm building materialises. It looks like it has been abandoned for a long time and yet a light glows in the window.

Somebody is home.

The man approaches the door. I'm so focused on what's in front of me that I lose my footing. My heart leaps in my chest as I slip forwards in the wet grass – catching myself just moments before I roll an ankle.

When I next look up, the white face of the man is turned towards me. I freeze instinctively. But it's too late. He darts into the building.

Struggling through the grass, I rush after him and throw myself inside. The rain drumming on the thin roof sounds like a hailstorm of bullets. Wind sails in through the broken windows. It's deafening.

I can recognise the man now he's stood right in front of me. It's Stuart. But he's not looking at me. He's staring in horror at the other side of the small cramped space, yelling: 'Craig, don't.'

It would be very dark in here if not for the fiery light of the lamp on the floor, sending a lick of flame up the centre of the room and revealing Craig, dirty, wild-eyed and hunched over. His arm is jammed over Mia's throat, pinning her to his side. Her legs are crumpled on the floor and her face is deathly pale, the whites of her eyes pink in the low light. It takes me a few moments to register the kitchen knife held up against her neck.

'Craig,' I say, holding up my hands. 'Don't do this.'

He bares his teeth. 'Don't try and stop this, Ruth. You know it's the right thing. After everything she's done.'

Mia is frozen. Craig sways on the spot. One wrong move and he could slit her throat just by accident.

'Mate, let her go,' says Stuart. 'This isn't what we wanted. Just let her go.'

Craig ignores him. 'You owe this to me, Ruth!' he shouts over the rain. 'You owe it to Kirsty.'

I shake my head. 'This isn't what Kirsty wants.'

'You don't know that! You don't know what it's like. I can't live with it.'

He starts collapsing into tears. Either he's drunk or he's hysterical with rage.

I manage a cautious step forward. 'I know it seems that way now. But there's people who care about you. People who are going to help you through it.'

'I don't know who I am anymore, Ruth. I don't recognise any of us now. All the pain she's caused, and there's fuck all your lot can do about it. She'll be out in no time if she even gets a prison sentence. This is the only way to make her pay.'

Several things happen at once. Craig ducks down. Stuart shouts. Mia lets out a strangled yelp. I charge forward. And then suddenly everything changes. Mia is lying on her side, hands still bound together. Stuart is on his knees on the floor, weeping, the knife gleaming beside him. And Craig is sprawled on his back, eyes closed.

98

I PUSH PAST STUART and scramble towards Craig, pressing my fingers into his warm, clammy neck.

'Oh my God, is he dead?' gasps Stuart.

'No, there's a pulse,' I reply.

I lower my cheek to his mouth. After a few moments, I feel his breath tingling my skin. I let out a sigh of relief I didn't realise I was holding in.

Bit by bit, the last few moments come back to me. I remember seeing Stuart swoop in front of me and grapple with Craig before hitting him straight across the face. Craig seemed to hover on the spot for a moment before falling flat on his back, his head smacking against the stone floor. I feel underneath his head for blood but miraculously he's avoided cracking it.

I hear footsteps behind me and turn around just in time to see Stuart, hood up, flying out of the door.

'Stuart, get back here!' I yell.

But he's gone, vanished into the storm.

'Untie me,' says Mia desperately.

'I will. I'm just checking he's okay.'

I put Craig into the recovery position then pick up the knife. Slowly and carefully, I cut through the rope until Mia's wrists spring free and she wriggles out from underneath me like an animal freed. Then she too rushes out the door. Swearing, I shoot out after her.

It's like appearing on the deck of a ship in the middle of a storm. I turn my face away from the wind but still rivulets of water pour down my forehead and into my eyes, blurring my vision. I can just make out Mia lurching through the rain, her black hair flattening around her head.

I wade out to her and lock her arms around her middle.

'We have to stay here!' I shout.

She struggles against me. 'I'm not staying here with him! I want to go down. I want to go down!'

She collapses under me like a toddler who doesn't want to be moved.

'You're not going anywhere in this storm. Come on.'

I tighten my grip around her waist and hoist her up.

She screams. 'Don't! That hurts, that fucking hurts.'

'Well, fucking help me then. Put your arm over me.'

Perhaps the rain has become too much because she stops struggling, straightens up and gingerly lifts one arm over my shoulders while I place mine around her side. Together we hobble back to the building, water pouring down my face. Craig's boot is just visible inside, its shadow monstrously huge in the amber lamplight.

Her whole body is shaking. 'What if he attacks me again?'

'If he wakes up, I'll look after you.'

'What about animals? Wolves?'

'You're a few hundred years off.'

The moment we're inside, I let Mia slip out of my grasp. She slumps against a stone wall and slides to the floor. It's no warmer here than it is outside. The wind cuts right through the building.

I use my police radio and ask them to send Mountain Rescue.

'We're on the north slope of Scroof Rig. I can't tell you exactly where but we're in a small abandoned building. There's a light inside.'

'Is anyone hurt?'

'One person. Craig. He's had a blow to the head and he's unconscious.'

'I don't think they're going to be able to send a helicopter in this weather. But a team will find you.'

It's only now that I notice the pangs of hunger in my stomach.

Mia, pulling her knees up to her chest, answers my question for me. 'I think they were camping outside. Their bags are probably there.'

I head back out into the rain where, sure enough, a green two-man tent is pitched around the side of the building. For a second I wonder if one or more of us could sleep in here, as odd as that would be – but no, I need to keep an eye on both of them, and I can't move Craig out here. So I get on my knees and squeeze into the flimsy compartment, where I roll up the sleeping bags and retrieve the backpacks.

Once back inside, I hand Mia a bottle of water, a blanket and a bread roll. She uses the blanket to daub her hair while gulping down water. I leave a sleeping bag at her side and take up my own spot not far from where Craig is lying. I check his vital signs once more before wriggling my cold legs into the sleeping bag.

'You'll – you'll watch him?' she says nervously.

'Yes. Mountain Rescue should be here in a couple of hours, but we can't say exactly when. You get some sleep whenever. I'll stay up.'

She nods. But she looks dazed. I can only imagine what she must have been through.

A crack of thunder rolls above our heads.

I clear my throat. 'Mia… did they do anything?'

She resembles a child right now, small and shuddering, with dirt on her face. But I remind myself who this person is. I'm fully prepared for her to spew all sorts of lies right now.

She says: 'They tied me up and left me here. But they didn't touch me. The only time they threatened me was right before you came in. That was Craig.'

To my surprise, I feel like she's telling the truth.

She unwraps the bread roll from its foil packaging and makes short work of it.

'Did he say anything to you?' I ask.

'He wanted to know why I did it,' she replies, avoiding eye contact.

'Why you posted about Archie?'

She nods.

'Why did you do it?'

Mia squeezes the foil into a ball and clenches her fist. 'I didn't know he was going to do that. Archie,' she murmurs.

I bite back the urge to reply, 'You must have known it would hurt him, though.' Now is probably not the time.

There is no sound apart from the rain drumming against the roof.

After a long silence, I say, 'My daughter is about your age.' I've been thinking this for a while but I've never said it out loud.

She sniffs. 'I saw that,' she replies.

'I'm sorry I said you were nothing. I shouldn't have said that.'

Mia gives me a calm, resentful look out of the corner of her eye. 'Thanks,' she says suspiciously.

'The security camera. That was good thinking. SOCOs should have checked those documents. Maybe they never did. Or maybe they did but they didn't think hard enough about what they meant.' I can't believe I'm saying this. 'Look, you're obviously… bright. Why did you do any of it?' I ask.

She stares into the corner of the room with a lost expression. 'I think all my life all I've wanted,' she says, 'is for people to notice me.'

I shuffle my shoulders against the wall. 'Well, you've certainly achieved that.'

'I think I thought if I found out who killed Lily, then it would make up for what happened with Hayley Pieterson.'

It's the first time I've heard her express anything like remorse. She pulls her knees in close to her chest and hugs them.

'You've got your whole life ahead of you,' I say. 'Just... apply yourself to something else.'

Mia lets her head fall back against the wall.

Then she frowns at me. 'You care about Molly very much.'

I resist the urge to sigh in exasperation. 'Well, obviously. She's my only kid.'

Just when I was starting to warm to Mia, she says something like this that reminds me she's just an alien in human skin.

Mia shakes her head. 'I don't think my mum gives a shit.'

This would explain why she told me her parents were dead. But I probably shouldn't comment on that.

'I'm sure that's not true,' I manage.

'She hasn't texted me this entire time.' Her resentful tone is strange in these circumstances, with both of us stranded in a storm and an unconscious man on the floor. 'I don't know if she cares about me as much as you care about Molly.'

I think back to when I met Mrs Chaplin. She had struck me as surprisingly calm given her daughter was investigating a murder case in Scotland.

Mia looks sideways at me. 'I think you need to help her.' She pauses. 'I just mean...' Her brows knit together. 'I don't think she can be happy with that man.'

'What?'

'Molly.' The look Mia gives me now is serious. 'I get why from your perspective, it must make it easier, imagining that she's happy. But I don't think it's true. I think she's too scared to leave. And I think she's waiting for you to save her.'

I don't know what to say. We fall into silence. As the world rages outside in the pitch-black, I wriggle further into my sleeping bag, my toes tiny blocks of ice, thinking there's no way either of us are getting any sleep tonight. But when I next look over at Mia, she is tucked up in her sleeping bag with her back against the wall and her chin on her chest, fast asleep.

My eyelids are close to shutting when the sound of my ringtone rips through me.

I throw off my blanket and lurch to my feet, answering. 'Hello?'

'Ruth? That you?'

'Raymond.' I feel my heart flood with relief. 'It's good to hear your voice.'

'We think we're close. We're approaching a small building with a light, like the one you described. Can you see us?'

I stumble out of the building and onto the mountain. The rain has stopped. It must be almost sunrise because a pale blue light is creeping over everything. In the distance, I see three pinpricks of light moving through the heather. Torches.

'Yeah, I see you.'

'How are they doing?'

'Craig's still unconscious. He needs a medical check—'

A shriek cuts through the gloom.

I run back inside, where Mia is recoiling in horror as Craig, red in the lamplight, lifts himself out of the recovery position, swaying zombie-like and disoriented into a half-seated position.

I rush over and crouch down beside him. 'Craig, are you all right?'

His eyes are slightly clearer now. But he is still manic as he grabs my wrist and pulls me closer. 'Ruth. I'm sorry. Tell Kirsty I'm sorry.'

'I will.'

'I just want you to know… I didn't have anything to do with Lily's murder. Just because of this. Please. I'm telling the truth.'

'I know that. Don't worry. We've got him. It was her brother.'

But Craig doesn't seem to hear me. He continues: 'It wasn't Stuart either.'

'I know—'

'The sketchbook.'

'What?'

'Stuart told me about the sketchbook. I saw it that day. It wasn't him.'

Something about this doesn't sit right. It's like running my hand over a familiar piece of clothing and finding a stitch has come undone.

'What did you say?' I ask.

But he's already slipped into unconsciousness again.

99

24 June

THE WALK BACK DOWN the mountain is the hardest I've ever done. Up ahead, Raymond cuts through the bracken like a dog, followed by two men carrying Craig in a stretcher. Even Mia is walking faster than me, eager to return to civilisation. But my joints are aching, my feet hurt and no matter how hard I try to calm down, my mind is constantly whirring.

On the drive to town, bumping around in Mountain Rescue's Isuzu, I have to ask people to repeat themselves because every question reaches me as if through a fog. We drive to the hospital, where a couple of officers are waiting to join Craig inside, and then to the police station for Mia to warm up, get some food, and, when she's ready, give an interview.

I should stick around and wait with her. But instead I go upstairs to look at the case files.

*

The Nag's Head isn't serving yet but it's open by the time I get there.

Declan is wiping down the bar. The moment he sees me coming through the door, his eyes go wide. I haven't been home for a shower yet and I watch him take in my sorry state: hair dishevelled, clothes caked in mud, no doubt smelling like a barn.

'Ruth, fucking hell,' he says, abandoning his cloth by the sink. 'Are you all right?'

'I'm fine. Everyone's fine.'

'Take a seat. Water?'

'Yes please.'

I sink into a chair beside the window. It's a beautiful morning and the high street is gleaming after the rainfall. It's strange how everything is as it always was. Yet nothing will ever be the same again.

Declan carries over the glass of water and places it down in front of me before joining me at the table. 'Everyone's saying it was Craig. Was it him?'

I down the water in just a few gulps before nodding.

'After what he's been through, I sort of understand, but… Jesus.'

'Did you notice Craig had a drinking problem?' I ask.

Declan grimaces.

'I suspected. He comes in here pretty early sometimes. If it's a weekday, and there's no one else around. He tells me it's to catch up. But you don't need a pint at midday to catch up with someone.' He looks me up and down. 'If you want one now, no judgement though. After the night you've had, it's on me.'

'When Lily went missing, he was here first thing, wasn't he? At noon.'

'He was, yeah. Couldn't hide that one from Kirsty, had to come clean since you were asking everyone where they were.'

'And he saw the sketchbook.'

'What?'

'The sketchbook.'

Declan's face freezes in a look of confusion. His eyes dart between each of mine. He laughs uncomfortably. Then half-frowns.

'What sketchbook?'

'Stuart gave Lily a sketchbook the morning she was killed. We never found it. But Craig says he saw it. Except Craig didn't see Stuart that day. He didn't see Lily either. He saw you.'

His neck is growing redder by the second. 'Well, just—'

He leans forward, then sits back. He looks away, and back at me, with open-mouthed outrage. 'Ruth, like – what are you—'

'You both said you were here. When the pub opened. At midday. By which time Lily was dead. And you had the sketchbook.'

He shuts his mouth. Covers his face with his hands. When he re-emerges, his cheeks are red.

He leans in close. 'Why are you doing this to me, Ruth?' he says. 'Eh? Why are you doing this?'

His eyes are welling up but I hold his gaze.

His voice drops almost to a whisper. 'You don't think everyone's already hurt enough over this? You gonna hurt my family too?'

I bite the inside of my mouth, almost drawing blood.

He keeps talking, speeding up: 'You gonna put Georgia through this? On top of everything she's going through right now? Can you imagine?'

I block out everything he's saying. I say calmly and quietly, 'Tell me why you did it, Declan. You don't have to say anything. But anything you do say may be given in evidence. And it may harm your defence if you don't mention when questioned something you later rely on in court.'

100

Lily

2 June

As Lily filled up a water bottle, her head was elsewhere. Flashes of last night's argument with Toby kept coming back to her without warning, making her feel raw as she got ready for the day ahead.

She placed the bottle inside her bag, then checked the Mountain Weather Information Service, just in case. *Sunshine strongest in east, often weaker in west due to high level cloud. Excellent visibility*. Perfect.

No one else was up yet. She scrawled a short note on her mum's open notepad. **Going for a walk around the Devil's Hand, back at about 5 p.m.** Then she picked up her bag and headed outside.

With every step, she could feel the stress leaving her body. The argument with Toby had created a charged atmosphere in the house. She needed space, fresh air – nature.

The green mountains gently rose and fell in the distance like an animal's spine. She drank in the sight, imagining her lungs filling with pure mountain air. This summer she'd become much more confident walking by herself for long distances. Some of her friends' parents would be paranoid. But not hers. She could imagine her mum going the entire day without once wondering where she was, only discovering her note when boredom sank in ahead of dinner.

Instead of heading straight for the mountains, she followed the road down to Braeside. There was something she needed to do first.

After stocking up on energy bars at the Spar, she walked to Georgia's house and rang the doorbell. Toby's anger last night had reminded her how much she was asking of all of them. She felt painfully aware of the gulf she'd created between herself, Georgia and Harris.

Declan answered.

'Is Georgia around?'

'She's out with her mum today. Visiting her gran.'

'When will she be back?'

'A couple of hours, I should think.'

Lily nodded, disappointed. She'd been hoping to talk to her face-to-face this morning. But maybe she'd have to wait until she'd finished this walk.

'Would you tell her I stopped by?'

'Of course.' He nodded in the direction of her walking boots. 'Where are you off to then?'

'The Devil's Hand?'

'That's a great walk. I can give you a lift, if you like.'

'That's okay. I'm walking up.'

He looked disorientated for a moment. 'Do you know what? Maybe I'll join you.'

'Oh,' said Lily. 'Really?'

'Not for the whole thing, obviously! I know my limits. But it's a lovely day. Maybe I'll stretch my legs for a bit.'

'Sure.'

Lily turned around. As she walked back to the street with Declan following, she couldn't help noticing an itch of discomfort somewhere in the back of her brain.

Was it just her anxiety playing up, or was Georgia's dad acting strangely?

101
Ruth

'I KNEW ABOUT THE car crash,' says Declan. 'It took me a long time, but eventually I worked out what had happened. When I took the car to the mechanic, there were keys in the backseat. I gave them to Georgia and she said she'd find out which of her friends they belonged to. I asked after them later, out of curiosity, and she said, "Oh yeah, they were Lily's." But I'm thinking, "You didn't drive Lily to her own house party. And you didn't drive her anywhere the next morning – you said you left before anyone else was up. So how did her keys get in your car? Was someone else driving it, uninsured? Or were you driving under the influence that night? Because you sure as hell are hanging out of your arse right now."

'It bothered me, but I wasn't sure what to make of it. Then I heard about the hit and run. I felt sick. I didn't want to believe Georgia had been involved, or that any of her friends would do something like that. I put it out of my mind.

'Until this summer.

'A couple of weeks ago, Georgia was in her room and as I was passing the door, I overheard them talking on the phone. Georgia was crying. Saying, "It wasn't our fault. It was an accident." Anyway, I heard enough to work out they'd been involved. And that Lily now wanted them to come clean.

'So when she turned up at my house on the 2nd of June, looking for Georgia, I knew this was my moment to talk to her. Work out exactly what had happened. I joined her on the way to the Devil's Hand and confronted her.'

'Where?'

'Near the start of the trail up to Tod Fell. I asked her what was going on with Georgia. She wouldn't tell me at first. So I told her I knew about the crash. And then she admitted it. That she wanted them to go to the police. I begged her not to. To leave Georgia out of it. Or tell me who was really driving the car that night. She wouldn't.'

His eyes cloud over as he relives the memory.

'We argued. I lost control of the situation—'

He wipes his face. 'Afterwards, I saw the sketchbook in her bag. I panicked. I thought maybe she'd planned on showing Georgia something. So I took it. Went back to the pub. Showered off. I was so out of it I just left the sketchbook on the bar. Craig noticed it. I lied and said it was Georgia's.

'I only did it to protect my daughter. I didn't want her going to prison. It was self-defence.'

'That's not true, is it? That isn't why you killed her.'

His eyes go wide.

'You always were a good storyteller, Declan. And this is just another story, isn't it? Like the one you told me about the hares. Poor old Declan and his pub getting outshone by the Howards and their fancy restaurant. Bullshit. I should have known then. Who you really are. Why would you follow her all the way to the Devil's Hand? If all you wanted to do was talk to her? Why not just invite her in?'

He shakes his head dismissively. 'I don't know. I wasn't thinking straight.'

'The truth is that wasn't the first time you'd followed a woman to the woods, was it?'

He stares at me, open-mouthed. 'What are you talking about?'

'You flashed a woman in the woods last year. The woman reported it to us after Lily went missing. She couldn't really describe the man. Only remembered that he was wearing a beanie hat, which would have covered your head, stopped us looking exclusively for bald men. I bet you saw her on the high street, didn't you? Who knows how many times you've done it and not got caught? Who knows how many women saw something strange out there but decided not to report it?'

Declan's face is turning purple. 'What the fuck?'

'You enjoy scaring women, don't you?'

'Ruth,' he says, pointing to his chest. 'It's *me*. I wouldn't—'

'The hares started appearing on the Howards' property after the crash. It wasn't jealousy or revenge that made you do it. You'd worked out what had happened and you wanted to show Lily that someone knew. She stopped turning up here. Until this summer she got brave enough to come back.'

Declan is trying his hardest to look confused but I see a flicker of recognition in his eyes.

'Maybe your need to protect Georgia factored in, but only a little. Mainly you wanted to torment her. And the thing about men who want to do that, eventually they want the real thing. They want to see the fear. When you found her in the woods, did you try and blackmail her first? Or did you attack her straight away?'

Declan is shaking. 'Ruth. I didn't do what you're accusing me of.'

'Lily was found with ripped clothing.'

Quickly he says: 'That's nothing to do with me. Nothing to do with me.'

'How thick do you think I am?'

Declan launches himself at me and the next thing I know I'm falling. The ceiling arcs over me. Pain explodes across my back as my chair hits the floor. My brain tells me to roll out of the way but I can't. Declan's heavy body is on top of mine, crushing me. He digs his thumbs into my windpipe. I can't get air in my lungs. I try to free my arms to hit him but I can't. They're trapped underneath his body. My throat burns.

All I can see are his bloodshot eyes popping out of his head, filled with an animal rage I've never seen before.

He's yelling something. Flecks of warm spit hit my face.

'I was your friend, Ruth! We were all your friends! Look what you've fucking done.'

My vision is beginning to blur when I hear a clatter somewhere in the room. Then Declan's grip on my neck loosens. I take in a single deep breath, filling my lungs with air. As I scramble to get away, I feel Declan's weight slowly lifting off me. Before I can work out what's going on, I've flipped onto my front and I'm crawling across the floor to the wall closest to me, where I curl up, spluttering, looking back at where Giblin and Hughes are grappling with Declan on the floor of the pub.

I haul myself up into a seating position, searching my pocket for my phone.

I pull it out and hit 'stop' on the audio recording.

102

I TAKE A SIP of tea, gently squeezing my neck. The muscles still ache when I turn my head too quickly. The officers said I should go to the hospital. But I don't think Declan was gripping for long enough to do any serious damage. And besides, I need to get this done.

The door to the Family Room opens and Georgia steps inside, looking puzzled. We're alone and I gesture to the sofa opposite me.

'Take a seat, Georgia. Do you want a tea?'

'That's okay.'

She takes a seat on the grey sofa, her eyes filled with concern.

'Is this about Toby?' she asks. 'I know Harris told you.' She swallows. 'I'm sorry we didn't say anything. But for what it's worth, I don't think Toby could have killed Lily. I've known him for years. I just can't imagine him doing it.'

I feel sick. I'm worried I might not be able to get the words out.

'It's not about the crash, Georgia,' I say quietly.

She stares at me in confusion. 'Well, then – what—'

'Your dad's in one of the interview rooms. He asked if you could come in here so he could speak to you.'

She frowns. 'Why is he here? What? I don't understand.'

'He says he killed Lily.'

She looks as though I've slapped her. 'That's not true,' she says.

She waits for me to say something else. But I don't. I keep my mouth shut and try to communicate through my gaze that this is real and that I am more sorry than I can ever say.

Her mouth twists into an angry grimace. 'He didn't. He wouldn't. He would never do that.'

'Your dad wasn't at the Nag's Head when he said he was on the day Lily went missing.'

Georgia shakes her head, her eyes filling with tears. 'No. It's not true.'

'He followed her to the Devil's Hand. He's admitted it, Georgia. He killed Lily.'

'It was Toby, wasn't it?' she says desperately. 'It was him, wasn't it? Dad's just – wrong – he's confused—'

As she says this she starts to shake and suddenly she bends double. I think she's going to throw up but instead a sharp cry escapes her. She covers her mouth. My chair legs screech as I get up to wrap my arms around her trembling shoulders. Georgia is crying so much that I feel her tears leaking through my shirt.

103

A shaft of sunlight finds its way down into the station car park, showering Max and I in sunshine as we take a ten-minute break. I lean forward with my hands on my knees, Georgia's face still flashing through my mind. I feel like shit. I still haven't gone home yet and I badly need a shower.

'You'll be heading back to Edinburgh soon then,' I say. 'Job's done.'

'Not quite. I'll stick around until we've got enough on Declan,' he replies.

Is it just me or do I detect a hint of sadness in his voice at this prospect of going home?

'I might need somewhere else to stay for the time being though,' he says.

'You could stay with me if you like,' I offer.

He frowns. 'Nah. It's better to keep work and home separate.'

'You're welcome though,' I say. 'If you ever want to come back here for some walking. Bring a friend if you like. I have the space.'

Max gives me a rare smile. 'Thanks.'

He looks up into the sun, seeming lighter now.

Then he announces: 'We deserve a pint.'

I rub my forehead. 'Sorry, but after that, there is officially nowhere half-decent to get a drink around here.'

'We could go somewhere out of town after work,' he replies chirpily.

I shake my head. 'I think I need some time… away from pubs.'

Max is clearly buzzing. I wish I could be on the same wavelength. But right now all I want to do is sleep for a thousand years.

What would make me feel better? Then something occurs to me.

'Let's go for a swim.'

Max blinks at me. 'Sorry, maybe I wasn't clear,' he says, 'but I was talking about *celebrating* our achievements, rather than punishing ourselves.'

'Come on, the water's warm. We can grab our swimming stuff after work and go.'

'I didn't bring any trunks.'

'We'll buy some.'

104

THERE ARE FEW CARS on the road as I drive to the beach. It is a fresh, clear afternoon and the sight of Sunkhead Bay peeking out from behind the trees fills me with calm.

I change in the car and walk in my flip-flops down to the beach, which is completely empty apart from a lone seagull perched on one of the slimy rocks, and Max, stood with his freckled back to me and his hands on his hips, facing the sea like an old foe. He has procured a pair of swimming shorts so baggy they are practically flapping in the wind. As I trudge through the broken seashells towards him, he looks over his shoulder at me and frowns.

'It looks pretty choppy,' he says.

He's right, admittedly. Waves slosh against the algae-covered rocks.

'That's fine,' I reply.

Max shakes his head dismissively as he surveys the sea. 'There's clearly a strong current. Hazardous rocks. Not a good idea.'

I walk quickly over the broken seashells until the water is lapping at my toes. I wade deeper and then, when it's up to my middle, I take the plunge.

I haven't swum in weeks. And it isn't as warm as I was expecting. The cold blows my eyes wide open, wakes up every part of me, lights up every nerve ending across my skin. I swim until my body adjusts to the temperature. Then I feel myself start to merge with the water. My pale limbs move in a soft blur underneath the surface, through the murky grey-brown. Salt sticks to my nostrils.

I hear a yelp and look back to see Max swimming towards me, stretching his neck above the waves, desperate to keep his face dry.

By the time he reaches me, he's half-smiling.

'This isn't so bad, actually,' he says.

He flips onto his back. I do the same, enjoying the sensation of cold water reaching untouched places, spreading across my scalp. Weightless, I open my arms, forming a 'T' shape. I stare up at the clouds. Floating here, it feels as though there is no separation between us and the sea.

105

25 June

Mia calls at the station early in the morning. I head down to where she's waiting at the entrance, suitcase beside her.

'How was the hostel last night?'

'Fine.'

'Are you going back to London?'

'Yep.'

'I've spoken to the superintendent. We're charging you with threatening behaviour towards the Moffats, Stuart Marsh and Georgia Reid. Is that understood?'

She nods.

'If the Procurator Fiscal decides to prosecute, then you may have to come back here and go to court, all right? Don't make me come and find you.'

She nods again. But she doesn't move. She's waiting for something.

'What is it?'

'There's something I should have told you. When I was looking into your daughter… I saw something.'

'What?'

'He posts about her. Online.'

'I know that.'

'No, you don't. He asks what other men would do to her.'

Her gaze stops me cold.

'What's that supposed to mean?'

She looks past me at the doors to the station. 'I think I should tell one of your colleagues,' she says.

I'm getting annoyed now. 'Tell me.'

'He posts pictures of her on these forums. On the dark web.'

I blink rapidly. What she's saying doesn't compute. Why would he do that?

I search her face for any sign of cruel delight. But she's completely serious.

'Is this a trick?' I ask.

She shakes her head. 'I never made anything up. I've only ever said what I've found.'

Anger rises within me. 'Why are you doing this? Can you not help yourself?'

'I'm only saying what I saw.'

And I've spent enough time with her now to know she's telling the truth. She has that same haunting look that was in her eyes that night on the mountain.

Then the full horror of it dawns on me.

'Was – was she hurt? In the pictures you saw?'

'I think she's alive. But she isn't safe with him.'

Which isn't an answer to what I asked. My breath is coming out in short, sharp gasps.

'Why didn't you tell me this earlier?'

'I'm sorry. I wanted to say on the mountain. But I thought now would be better.' She reaches into her pocket and pulls out a USB stick. 'I put everything on here.'

She hands it over. It feels like the tiny device is emitting its own pulse, running right through me.

'Can you tell Kirsty I'm sorry? I know she probably doesn't want to hear it. But I really am. I'm sorry.'

106

Max looks at the contents of the USB stick in the tech room while I wait outside. I'm drenched in sweat and can't stop shaking.

Eventually the door opens and Max steps out.

'What is it? What's on it?' I ask.

His face is white.

'I want to see,' I say.

'I'm telling you right now,' he says. 'You don't want to see that. There's no need.'

I grab his shirt. 'You need to tell me what you saw. I have to know if she's all right.'

And he tells me and the world around me disappears.

'Connor was right. I let her go and then I did nothing. I did nothing.'

'Now you can do something. He can't hide from this. It's him. He's fucked.' He grips my arms. 'You're going to see her again, Ruth.'

107

30 June

THE UNIT DRIVES ME to the edge of a forest. It feels like an underworld; the trees are so dense that barely any sunlight gets through. The officers and I weave between trunks crusted with lichen, picking our way over a carpet of thick, damp moss.

It reminds me of the wood from my dreams. With her running up ahead.

Except this time I've finally caught up with her.

The cabin sits in a small clearing up ahead. I follow the armed officers as they approach cautiously. We gather around the door, me pressing my body against the wooden wall. It shudders as they swing the enforcer into the door. On the third try the door shakes open. They pour inside. Even though I hear shouting, I stay where I am. I keep thinking about that day running into Kirsty's house, the nightmare that came for her, and wondering is it my turn, is that same nightmare waiting for me here?

Minutes later they re-emerge except this time Reece is locked between them, thrashing in their grip, his straw-coloured hair flying around his eyes. I'm not sure he sees me. And right now I don't care.

It's my turn now. I take a deep breath and enter the cabin.

For the first time in years, our eyes meet.

108

1 October

My calves ache as I climb up the mountain. At this time of year, purple heather and russet-coloured grass cover the landscape. The ridge gradually steepens, exposed to the wind which roars in my ears. On one side of me are rolling fields and the glassy bay – on the other, the Devil's Hand, each of its five peaks free of cloud cover.

My fitness has improved since the end of the case. I make more time for walking now.

But these days, I usually have someone with me.

I stop to catch my breath and look back at Kirsty, hood up to protect her hair from the wind.

'Don't wait for me,' she calls. 'Your pity only makes it worse!'

'We're almost there,' I reply.

Vanessa follows close behind, out of breath, leaning on her walking poles. I wait until they reach me. Then we continue up together. The mountain seems to run on endlessly; just when I think we've reached the peak, it continues rolling into the distance. But eventually the cairn appears at the top of the ridge. I take in deep lungfuls of air as I force myself up the final stretch. Together, we flop towards the pile of stones, using every last scrap of energy to reach out and touch the one at the top.

Relief floods my body. We cheer and embrace, euphoric with the rush of endorphins and the beautiful view stretching out beneath us. Vanessa takes a series of unfocused selfies. I think back to the case. I never imagined we would be here, us three, four months later, finishing the walk that Lily never started. As we drink from our bottles, Vanessa looks around proudly.

'If you told her I would climb something like this,' she says, 'she wouldn't have believed you.'

'Nice of you to join us,' says a voice.

I look round to where Connor stands looking out over the hills, backpack planted on the ground by his feet, a layer of sweat on his face. His hand rests on Molly's shoulder.

She looks round at me and smiles.

109

Mia

IT IS A COLD day in October. The fallen leaves collect in a slippery rug on the pavement. A teenager on a bicycle hurtles past as I walk into the cul-de-sac with my shoulders pinched in, hands in my pockets, fingers still numb from the earlier rainfall.

I should have been able to remember where it was. But I couldn't. I had to comb through my emails to find the house number. It appears to me now on one of the doors of the houses – number 38. The curtains are closed. There is no one home.

As I look at the familiar house I feel a pit opening up in the bottom of my stomach. The flowers in the window box are still here, glistening with raindrops. I force myself up to the front door, ducking under the porch, and peel off my cold, damp rucksack. Unzipping it, I pull out the letter. I try not to think about how I've worded my apology. I rewrote the letter three times and every time it felt too much. I push the envelope through the bristles of the letterbox and listen to the sound of it gently hitting the floor.

By the time I've left, I can feel a few tentative drops of rain falling onto my scalp. I pull my hood up and think *I hope Jackie replies to me.* She hasn't responded to my text. I haven't received a message from Jackie Pieterson since they found Lily's killer.

I hope she replies. But I'll give it two weeks. After that, I won't contact her. I'll leave her alone.

ACKNOWLEDGEMENTS

Thank you to my wonderful agent Kate Nash for championing me and my books. This all started because you picked up the manuscript for *The Blame* when I was an unpublished writer. Thank you also to the fantastic team at Bedford Square – particularly Jamie Hodder-Williams, Polly Halsey and Victoria Chapman – for getting *Sleuth* out into the world, and thanks to Donna Hillyer for editing the book.

Thank you to my family and friends. Thank you to Mum, for reading everything I write and for your extremely helpful feedback. Thank you to Rosie, for being so supportive. And thank you to Eloïse, for writing with me in cafés around London. I'm so lucky to have friends like you.

Finally, thank you to Sam, for introducing me to Galloway, the beautiful place that inspired *Sleuth*. Your support means the world to me.

ABOUT THE AUTHOR

Charlotte Langley works as a reporter at the *Telegraph* and is a fresh, breakout voice in gripping psychological police dramas. Her first book *The Blame* has been adapted into an ITV series.